Zazoo

Other Graphia Titles

COMFORT
by Carolee Dean

3 NBS OF JULIAN DREW
by James M. Deem

48 SHADES OF BROWN
by Nick Earls

OWL IN LOVE
by Patrice Kindl

DUNK
by David Lubar

Check out www.graphiabooks.com

Zazoo

by

RICHARD MOSHER

GRAPHIA
AN IMPRINT OF HOUGHTON MIFFLIN COMPANY
Boston

 Published in the United States by Graphia, an imprint of Houghton Mifflin Company, Boston, Massachusetts. Originally published in hardcover in the United States by Clarion Books, an imprint of Houghton Mifflin Company, New York, in 2001.

www.houghtonmifflinbooks.com

The text was set in 12-point Bembo.

Library of Congress Cataloging-in-Publication Data

Mosher, Richard.
Zazoo / Richard Mosher.
p. cm.
Summary: Amid old secrets revealed and rifts healed, a thirteen-year-old Vietnamese orphan raised in rural France by her aging "Grand-Pierre" learns about life, death, and love.
(HC) ISBN 0-618-13534-0
(PB) ISBN 0-618-43904-8
[1. Secrets—Fiction. 2. Love—Fiction. 3. Vietnamese—France—Fiction. 4. Grandfathers—Fiction. 5. Orphans—Fiction. 6. France—Fiction.] I. Title.

PZ7.M8485 Zaz 2001
[Fic]—dc21

2001028291

HAD 10 9 8 7 6 5 4 3 2

For my mother, Alice Wynne Mosher

1. Soon

The boy on the bike came and went. And he was like the gray cat in one way: when he was gone, I remembered everything about him, yet I couldn't be sure, absolutely sure, he had been there at all.

It was a wispy October dawn, with scraps of mist waiting to be burnt off the canal once the sun cleared the far hills. A school day but still early. I was out in my flat-bottomed boat, one oar dragging and one up, dripping just off the surface. The blade's wooden tip patiently *plip-plip-plopped* as I watched the willows shift along the canal. There was only the chorus of autumn birds, calling *wake up—wake up—wake up,* and the faraway bark of a dog. Insects were asleep or gone for the season. Our corner of France lay dozing except for the treeline chatter, *wake up—wake up—wake up—*

Then came a faint whirring of tires around the towpath bend, the spinning of an old bicycle, and there he appeared among the far sycamores, scanning the canal as he came. Before he could spot me, I shook off my sandals and sweater and slipped over the stern to sink into the green of the canal, taking in one last deep breath as I went.

One was enough. I knew the power of my lungs, knew I could swim in one breath beneath the lily pads to the far side where the willow shadows would hide me. Many times I had made such underwater escapes, but they had always been practice for a future adventure I trusted would someday arrive. So now, when I saw the unknown bicycle boy in the distance, in and down I went in one smooth motion, eyes wide, the water cool above me.

Breaking the surface at the far side was what concerned me, not getting there in one breath. I came up delicately, to make as few ripples as possible. Through the veil of reeds I watched the bike boy approach, binoculars swinging from his neck. Stopping his bicycle, he peered down at my boat as it drifted toward him.

"Sandals," he muttered. "But where are the feet?"

I cupped one hand over my mouth to throw my voice. "The feet," I moaned, "are under the water."

"Ah." He nodded. But he didn't look at the water; he gazed high into the willows, as if expecting my ghostly voice to moan down from their branches.

"The water," I reminded him, "is below."

"Ah," he said again. "Below." And kept staring into the willow tops.

I liked the calm way he let the dawn rustle around him. Also I liked that his bicycle wasn't new and shiny, with a million gears; it was a three-speed with rusty fenders, like mine in the shed behind our mill. Taking a fresh breath, I sank into the reeds and glided back beneath the lily pads. Between the boy and my boat I made a half-spinning dive toward the bottom, lifting my feet above the surface before stroking down into the depths. When I came up, just behind the boat, the boy could see only my hair and my face and my fingers curled over the stern. But I could see all of him as he smiled peacefully across.

"You," he said, in a slow accent of the south, "have a lovely boat."

"Thank you." I folded my arms across the stern. "My grandfather made it for me. I helped, but he made it. We soaked the pieces of wood in tubs of hot water, then curved them into this shape. You like the color?" Sailors passing through our canal lock frequently commented on the rich rosy purple of my little boat.

"Lovely," the boy said again. A willow strand blew like an uncombed hair across his face. Instead of brushing it aside, he leaned with the tiny leaves, as if making room for them. "So slender for such a small boat."

"We designed it ourselves. To have the look, Grand-Pierre said, of a boat I saw in a picture when I was little, after he brought me here from Vietnam."

"Vee-yet-*nahm,*" the boy repeated, as if tasting the word. His eyes gazed intently at mine.

"I'm French, of course. *French.*" Hearing how nervous I sounded, I tried softening my voice. "Born in Vietnam, but this is where I've lived since he brought me here. I was just two, so this valley's the only place I know. And the only language I speak—"

"—is French." The boy nodded. "But your boat . . ."

"We call it my punt."

"Punt?" He tilted his head. "Punt?" Like one of those tree-line birds who endlessly repeat their sounds in the dawn. "Punt? That's not a French word."

"No, and not Vietnamese." I shivered from dangling in the water so long. My sweater lay on the floorboards before me; I longed for its warmth but was shy of pulling myself up where the bike boy could see me. At least for the moment I wanted nothing to change. "Punt is an English word. Grand-Pierre says that one day—when I was six or seven—I saw a picture of a punt in an English story and admired it so much that he said, 'Would you like a punt of your own, Zazoo? We should make you one.'"

"Zazoo." A smile crinkled the corners of his eyes. "Zah-*zoo*."

"My name, yes. He made it up while we were on our way here from Vietnam. Seems to fit, somehow. A girl like me who looks so different on the outside—I mean, who looks so Vietnamese—"

"Yet on the inside is as French as anyone else?"

"Something like that." Could it really be so simple for him to understand? No one else understood except Grand-Pierre, who understood everything.

"Zah-*zoo*," said the boy again. "So then you made this beautiful . . . *punt?*"

"Except it isn't really a punt, since I row it with oars. In England, punts don't have oars; they're pushed along with poles."

"Then your boat isn't an English push-punt, but more of a Frenchified row-punt." The boy stood there so relaxed, one leg at each side of his bike, his straw hair arranged in no particular way, his sleepy smile showing teeth that weren't quite straight. Was he fifteen? Undoubtedly older than *I* was, not yet fourteen. "Your plum row-punt," he said slowly. So *calm*, he was—

so different from the boys at school, all knee-pumping and toe-tapping. "But aren't you cold out there in the wet?"

"Frozen." I hauled myself up, twisting onto the stern seat in what might have been one fluid motion if I hadn't been shivering.

The boy backed his bike around to face where he had come from. "Sun's up," he announced. "Time to go."

"So soon?" popped out before I knew it. I pulled the baggy sweater on over my soaked shirt.

"So soon, yes. I must."

"Like Cinderella, except you're not a girl and it's not midnight. You have to go to school?"

"Not today." He turned to peer back at me. "Before I go, please tell me one thing. This village of yours. I know it has a bakery." On the clip rack above his rear tire, two thin loaves of bread, the kind called baguettes, were clamped in place. "A bakery that opens early—I was there already. But does your village also have a pharmacy?"

"I've given you a headache. All my talk about punts."

"No, I don't need pills, just this tiniest bit of information. *Is* there a pharmacy?"

"Yes, with a green cross in front."

"Like every pharmacy." The boy nodded. "And . . . do many pharmacists work there?"

"Only one—a man named Monsieur Klein. He has a mustache." I wished I had brought a towel along to dry my legs, but they looked kind of slinky, all summer-brown and wet. And my shorts were a lucky touch—soaked as they were, so baggy and green, they were just the kind of tangled sea skirt a canal girl *would* wear.

"Klein," the boy repeated. "Klein the Pharmacist. Perfect. Then what I need to know—" He stopped himself. "First, tell me this. Can I trust you, Zazoo? I mean, to keep a secret?"

"You can trust me." I was glad to promise, since he was kind enough to remember my name and to know I was French inside. "I won't tell a soul in the whole village. Not my best friend, not my grandfather."

"And not Monsieur Klein?" His smile was so gentle it almost made me sad.

"Certainly not." I couldn't imagine why anyone should keep secrets from our village pharmacist. "But why should I not tell *him?*"

"Because this secret is about him."

"It is?" His question—still not asked—grew more mysterious when I considered that many children of our village made fun of Monsieur Klein for being boring. "Well, then, ask your question. I'll see if I can answer it."

"First you must promise not to tell him a teenage boy was snooping around your canal."

"I'll promise if you'll tell me your name, and where in the south you pedaled your bike from, and why you have binoculars looped around your neck."

"For bird watching—always best with binoculars. And I'm not from Marseille, if that's what you're thinking. Northerners always guess I come from Marseille—but I'm not. I'm from the mountains between Marseille and here." He didn't say which mountains, and I didn't ask. I was too busy staring at his freckles, which I decided must be, next to blondness, the surest sign of beauty in the world. "My name, since you let me know yours, is Marius. And my question is this: Your Monsieur Klein, the mustached pharmacist—is he married?"

"What an odd thing to ask. You won't say *why* you need to know?"

"Sorry, I can't."

A silence fell—but not the tormenting kind of silence that paralyzed boys at my school. With this boy, such a long pause didn't ruin our talk but seemed to sweeten it.

"So." He smiled. "You won't tell me."

"Of course I'll tell you . . . Marius." I repeated his name the same slow way he had repeated *punt* and *Vietnam*. "No, our Monsieur Klein is not married." How disappointing; I'd hoped his question would involve something more romantic than an aging pharmacist. "And Monsieur Klein is too old to *get* married. Not as old as my grandfather, but—gray hair, you know? *Old.*"

"Your grandfather is how old, exactly? Your Grand-Pierre?"

"Let's see." I took my time. "He was sixty-seven when he found me in Vietnam, eleven years ago. I'm thirteen now, and was two then. That makes him—"

"Seventy-eight, yes? But are you truly just thirteen?" Marius squinted across from the towpath. "You seem at least fifteen to me. I mean, here you are, out by yourself on the canal—"

"Not always by myself. Sometimes with Grand-Pierre. In

hot weather we stick a giant umbrella through that hole in the front seat and float along the river in the umbrella's circle of shade, making up poems as we go."

Marius scuffed one foot in the towpath gravel, then scanned the treetops as if searching for a new variety of bird. "I'd love to hear one of your poems, Zazoo."

"Even though you won't explain your curiosity about Monsieur Klein?"

"Even though." He examined the high branches.

"A poem." I sighed, as if this were a huge request. "Well, maybe just one. Since you've been kind enough not to ask why Grand-Pierre, old as he was, brought me here from Vietnam. That's the first thing everybody asks, but you didn't."

"And when they ask," he said, smiling into the branches, "do you tell them?"

"Never."

"Good." His eyes came back to mine. "You're here—that's what matters."

"I'm here because my parents died." My voice sounded rougher than I'd have preferred, but the words couldn't be stopped; they rushed out of me. "You say you'd like a poem? Then I'll give you one that tells exactly how they died. And Grand-Pierre didn't write this one; I did. Just last month, out here in my boat." To steady myself for reciting, I peered down at my feet on the floorboards.

"They saw what they thought was a lily,
they turned to be sure it was there—

and when they drew closer, in order to see,
a flash sent them high
  in the soft summer air.
Without time to look back
  at their baby in black,
they flew high through the soft summer air,
  summer air—
and they died in the soft summer air."

For some time Marius said nothing. When he did speak, his voice was low and his eyes no longer smiled. "How sad, Zazoo. And yet, what a graceful poem. By a girl in a graceful punt." He studied a willow branch rising and falling in the breeze between his towpath and my boat. "You've written other poems about your parents?"

"Maybe. Or maybe I don't need parents. Grand-Pierre is my family now—we've written heaps of poems. When I was younger, he did most of the writing. Now I write them alone."

"You don't want help anymore?" Marius crinkled his eyes in his sad, wonderful smile. "At thirteen, you're too proud to accept help?"

"At seventy-eight, *he* can't—well, he can't remember enough to—to—" I clenched my lip in my teeth to stop it from quivering. "He can't remember the words he used to know. Sometimes he doesn't even recognize the poems we wrote together."

"Oh," said Marius. "Sorry." He paused long enough for a bird to call out from the sycamores beyond the lock, and for another, near the triple-arched bridge, to call back. When he finally did speak, his voice was very soft. "I'd like to hear more of your poems, Zazoo."

"When you come back, then." He might be as old as seventeen, I saw with alarm. Why did he bother speaking to me at all? "You *will* come back?"

"Yes, I'll come back. And soon, since I know your Monsieur Klein isn't married. But wait—was he *ever* married?"

"I don't think so, but I'm not sure. This is important?"

"Well, it might be. But Zazoo!" He startled me again with his delicious use of my name. "It's almost seven-thirty—I have to go!"

"Or you'll turn into a pharmacist?" What, I wondered, could possibly interest such a dream of a boy in an old man who sold pills? "Good-bye then, Marius. Enjoy your bread."

"We will." Before I could ask who *we* might be, he turned his dusty bike around. "See you soon, Poet Zazoo!" With a wave, he stepped onto the top pedal and his tires bit into the towpath grit.

"See you," I said. "Soon."

I sat at my oars, shoulders drooping, and watched until he was around the willow bend, past the boat basin, and gone. Nothing remained to prove he had been there at all.

"Soon," I whispered to the lily pads.

The mist had burnt off the canal. Gazing at my oar blades sunk deep in the water, I thought of things I might have said—such as the fact that I was called not only Zazoo but Zazoo the

Gill Girl. *Soon?* I had my doubts. To fend them off, I recited some of the poem Grand-Pierre had made up when I was three years old and I first told him of seeing my gray cat.

> "There once was a cat
> down by the canal
> who never seemed able to roam . . ."

I scissored the plum punt around and pulled in heavy strokes toward the boat basin, the lock, the mill. Home.

2. The Mill of a Thousand Years

The mill where we lived was an old place with many stories told about it, which was one of the reasons I loved it.

First, its name. Or, I should say, *names;* the place was so old, it had been called many things. Long before Grand-Pierre brought me from Vietnam, it was called the Mill of Milan. The man who built it, centuries before, was so sad to be far from his home in Milan, an Italian city four hundred kilometers away, that he saved and saved until he could afford orange tiles to cover its roof and make it look Italian.

Long after he died, the place was still called the Mill of Milan, *le Moulin de Milan,* a bit of a tongue twister and a word trick as well, since from the sound of it, this name meant not just the Mill of Milan but also the Mill of a Thousand Years—*le Moulin de Mille Ans*—even though it wasn't a thousand years old, not nearly.

So we lived in a stone mill with a river on one side and a canal on the other. Some boaters called our canal the Water Forgotten by Time, since it sat in such a peaceful part of France, a part with more speckly stone walls and weeping willows than any other.

Grand-Pierre's name, likewise, meant many things, some having to do with the place where we lived, others with the man he had been.

His given name, Pierre, was simply a name, the same as Peter for the English or American travelers who floated past our mill. But the part everyone put at the start of his name—the "Grand" part—meant *big.* Which was funny, since Grand-Pierre himself was such a tiny man. Yet some people of our village told me his bravery had once been very tall. They said that this man, now no larger than I, had once been the tallest hero in our valley.

Another thing about his name was that he lived in a part of France known for its stones. Everything was made of stone: the bakery, the arched bridges, the mill where Grand-Pierre and I lived. Since the villagers were surrounded by so many stones—in so many sizes, in so many shades of gray—they had many words for them. And the most common word for stone happened to be the same as his name: Pierre.

And there was more to his name, since these two words together—Grand-Pierre—sounded very much like *grand-père,* or grandfather. But even though he had this kindly sounding nickname, some villagers—some of the same ones who told me he'd been a hero—referred to him as if they were almost scared of him. And though I was the one who knew him best, I didn't know anything about his war. If I asked him about it, he hardly said a word.

To me, of course, the name Grand-Pierre truly did mean grandfather, because he was the only family I had—although he and I were not, strictly speaking, related. I might have been born in Vietnam, but as far as my heart was concerned, I came only from him.

3. Beauty Advice

One afternoon years ago, our pharmacist took a walk along the river and spotted me splashing among the lily pads. I couldn't have been more than eight, but I was swimming alone. Monsieur Klein watched for a few seconds before observing, with great admiration, that I swam *beneath* the lily pads rather than *between* them. Then he wished me a good afternoon and continued on his way toward the village.

Ever since that day, he inquired about my swimming as no one else ever did. Almost every time I went to his shop for Grand-Pierre's thyroid pills—which I had been sent to fetch as far back as I could remember—Monsieur Klein mentioned it. So when I stopped in at his pharmacy three days after meeting Marius the bird watcher, I wasn't surprised by his greeting.

"Good afternoon, Mademoiselle Zazoo, our beautiful swimmer." And he half-bowed, this man who could be formal in a way that bordered on fussiness.

"Hello, Monsieur Klein." In our valley you did not enter a shop, any shop, without greeting the shopkeeper by name, lest you be thought a foreigner or a Parisian or a person of no upbringing. "Nice weather we're having."

"A lovely day for swimming up the canal to Lock Forty-four and back." His eyes twinkled behind their glasses. "Is that not so?"

"Yes, Monsieur, although twelve kilometers would make a long round trip."

"Even for you, our canal explorer?"

"Even for me. It *is* October—the canal will freeze soon." How could I steer us to the odd question Marius wanted answered?

Monsieur Klein straightened his blue-dotted bow tie. "Last year, I seem to recall, you swam once or twice in the month of November."

"You have an amazing memory." I gazed at a shelf loaded with beauty aids. "*And* you have so many creams. So many fine lotions."

"Yes." He sighed. "Millions of lotions for the women of France."

"And millions more for removing the first ones?" A poster showing off a flawless blond woman mocked me from across the aisle. *She* certainly didn't have Vietnamese eyes or cheekbones, not to mention a teensy Vietnamese nose. Her nose was perfectly long, perfectly elegant. "Will I look like that woman, Monsieur Klein, if I use her lotion?"

"Identical." He peered at me over the rims of his spectacles. "But it might take weeks, even months—and you'd have to apply the lotion just so. Every morning, every evening, and six or ten times in between."

"You're an expert on . . . beauty, Monsieur Klein?" *Here* was a way I might slip in my question.

"As a pharmacist, I'm supposed to know everything about beauty." He glanced behind me as if to be sure no one eavesdropped from the next aisle, even though we were alone in the store. "Of course, you don't need lotions, Zazoo, and never will, so long as you swim among the reeds and rushes. But please don't tell the others. Not the women, not even the girls your own age."

"I'll keep quiet, Monsieur, if you'll tell me one thing."

"Yes?" He tapped his fingertips softly on the glass countertop.

"Why, Monsieur Klein, if you are such an expert on beauty, and appreciate women so much"—I paused—"why are you yourself not married?"

His eyes darted to a nearby stack of bee-sting remedies.

"I'm sorry, Monsieur. I shouldn't have asked."

"Nonsense." He flashed me a tight smile. "It's nothing."

I wondered which of the girls in my school had been the first to say Monsieur Klein was boring. "*Did* you marry, Monsieur? Ever?"

"No, Zazoo." His hands rubbed themselves as if they had suddenly grown cold. "And marriage might have been nice. Yes. As you say, I do appreciate . . . women."

Just because he always wore a white jacket and was polite, I wondered for the first time, did that make him boring? "Weren't you ever in love with a woman, Monsieur Klein? A *special* woman?"

"No, I was never in what you would call—" He saw my look. "Well, yes. Once. Such a long time ago, it hardly seems real now."

"Ah," I said, as people of my village often say to fill awkward silences.

Monsieur Klein inspected his ringless fingers. "And yet, when I ask myself to be entirely honest, I must admit that nothing, in all the years since, has seemed quite as real as that time I . . . fell in love. Does this make sense, Zazoo, or is it the blithering of an old fool?"

"You're not *that* old." I felt terrible to have hurt him so. "Not *nearly* as old as Grand-Pierre."

"No, sixty-two isn't seventy-eight. Different numbers, different . . . men." He gave the word *men* a twist I might have puzzled over if I hadn't been more concerned with a distant bird watcher.

"Monsieur Klein, is love always so sad?"

"I really can't say, Zazoo. You'll have to ask someone with more experience. Some boater, perhaps, cruising your canal."

With his cheery bow tie, he didn't look dull or snobbish at all. His eyes showed nothing but pain.

"Oh, I'm *sorry,* Monsieur. I had no idea my question would be so unkind."

His shrug broke my heart. "Not at all. You're young, you

want to know things, so you ask. The world would be much simpler if we were all so direct."

"I wonder." And I wondered again why Marius had to know whether Monsieur Klein had ever been married.

"Your grandfather has enough thyroid pills? He won't need any for a while?"

"No, Grand-Pierre is fine. At least, his pill situation is fine."

Monsieur Klein nodded gently. "But in other ways he isn't so fine?"

"His memory." It was my turn to shrug. "His memory comes and goes."

"Yes, this happens to us all. Some things—from as long ago as the war, and perhaps best forgotten—we remember with great clarity, while yesterday is a blur. But I suppose you've never had this happen."

"Not with yesterday." *Three* yesterdays, it had been—and still I saw each look, heard each word, as if at that very moment Marius were riding his bike down the towpath away from me.

"Was there anything else you needed, Zazoo? Anything at all?"

"No, Monsieur." I turned to go. "I was just on my way home from school and stopped in to ask about lotions. I'm sorry if I said the wrong thing."

"Don't be silly. Please stop any time. My beauty advice is free, although truly you don't need it and never will."

"Thank you," I said, blushing. "Good evening, Monsieur Klein." I edged toward the door.

"Good evening, Zazoo."

His smile was so sad, I felt like a brute. How could people call him a finicky old snob, as if he had no heart? His doorbell tinkled overhead; I walked home in the gathering darkness.

4. The Terror of the Doudounes

Two days later—five days after Marius had promised to be back *soon*—my friend Juliette LeMiel stayed overnight with me. It was one of those last warm evenings of autumn; I opened the windows of my tower room so we could taste the soft breeze.

Juliette brushed out my hair in a hundred slow strokes, then let me brush hers. Our hair was so different, hers wavy blond and warm as sunlight, mine straight, gleaming black as crow feathers. She claimed I had the most beautiful hair in our school, but I happened to know *she* did.

When Juliette stayed at the mill, I never went out on the water early in the morning; it wasn't the sort of treat she liked. She preferred lying in bed chattering until the sun was well up. We usually started by discussing our teachers, then moved on to boys—but we came around, always, to her problems at home. Juliette had two older brothers named Jacques and Jules; we lumped them together, calling them the Jay-Jay as if they made up a single nasty nuisance like a yappy, ankle-nipping dog.

Part of the trouble was that Juliette, unlike me, was starting to have breasts, which made a fascinating home entertainment for her brothers. Her new little breasts—or *doudounes,* as boys in our valley call them—delighted the Jay-Jay. She told me how they competed to see who could embarrass her more, thrusting their chests before them, puffing out their shirts like top-heavy overgrown girls.

"Ho," I said to the ceiling. "Ho-ho. Makes me almost glad to be flat." From my bed I stared out the tower window onto the morning towpath. The weather would soon turn cold. Not a single barge had passed through the lock in days—and not a single bicycle, pedaled by a crinkle-eyed bird watcher, had appeared. Each day before school I went out on the water, wearing my most sensitive-looking scarves and reciting poems under my breath. But no boy with binoculars rode past.

"You won't be flat forever," said Juliette, blankets pulled to her chin. Her eyes were still closed.

"I wonder sometimes."

Which was when Grand-Pierre called up the spiral staircase: "Enough dawdling, you two! Third call for oatmeal! Breakfast like they eat in Ireland!"

"Ireland." Juliette rubbed her eyes. "Always *Ireland* he goes on about. Do they eat in the middle of the night *there,* too?"

"Actually," I said, "this is a lit—"

"I know, a little *late* for you and the old rock to have your—your—"

"Our oatmeal. We're odd, yes." Juliette had always loved Grand-Pierre, but couldn't quite understand the oatmeal. "He's old and eats hot cereal, and I'm a Gill Girl with no sign of *doudounes.*"

And Marius? I longed to tell Juliette about him, but knew I couldn't. First, I had said I wouldn't talk about him, not to her, not to anyone. Second, I was scared of mentioning him even to myself. How could any bird watcher with such a sweet smile be interested in me? No doubt he had said "soon" as a politeness before riding off with the baguettes he was about to share with some girl even blonder than Juliette. I listened to the river lapping over the dam where a millstone had once turned to grind the village wheat. The sound of falling water usually soothed me, but now it seemed to say that every twig bobbing away on its surface, just like that boy, was floating away forever.

"Why," Juliette asked Grand-Pierre for the hundredth time, "don't you eat bread in the morning like everyone else?"

"Bread and jam." Grand-Pierre polished his bald crown with one hand. "Jam and bread."

"They're good enough for *my* family."

"Certainly, I remember those breakfasts. Bread and jam, jam and bread—it was all I ate as a boy before racing off to school."

"And sometimes," said Juliette, smiling, "perhaps a croissant?"

"Never a croissant in my family. Mine was a *French* family, not a tribe of Parisians. We ate *bread* for breakfast—and not today's bread fresh from the bakery, but yesterday's stale scraps."

Juliette swallowed her last bite of oatmeal—which, she had told me in private, she actually enjoyed. "Well, then." She glanced out at the canal. "I suppose there won't be any boats today?"

"Season's over," said Grand-Pierre. It was the right answer, but I could see, from the dimness in his eye, that his mental battery was running low. "One last boat to go through." There was a long pause. "He hasn't arrived yet."

"He?" asked Juliette. "Isn't a boat always named for a girl?"

Grand-Pierre sucked at the corner of his mouth, producing a popping sound he had made ever since he stopped smoking his pipe. But he didn't reply.

"By *he,*" I said, "Grand-Pierre means the Englishman who is the captain of this particular boat."

"Always the same boat?" she asked Grand-Pierre. "The same one's always last?"

He said nothing. As talkative as he had been a few moments before, now his mind seemed to have gone on strike like postal workers or railroad employees. Everything refused to work but his lip corners, popping around their invisible pipe.

"Yes," I answered for him. "The same boat. We call the captain the Doubtful Duke, right, Grand-Pierre?"

His head nodded forward, a big stone indeed.

"Every spring," I went on, full of false cheer, "his yacht is the first one through our lock, when he and his silent wife chug north to England to eat cabbage. And every fall they're the last through going south, headed for the gambling tables of Monte Carlo."

Juliette and I washed the breakfast bowls and cups; Grand-Pierre sat at the table and held his newspaper before him. In former times he would have read it from front to back; now he stared through its pages and out beyond the terrace.

When the sun was high above the trees, Juliette helped me

wheel my little boat around from the canal to the river. Once we had it in the water, and I had stuck the yellow umbrella through the hole in its front seat, she rowed us up-current past the triple-arched bridge to the stake we had pounded into the bank beneath the lindens. We played the mooring rope out as far as it would go, then bobbed in the umbrella's shade among the rippling jewels of sunlight.

In my row-punt, as someone had called it. Someone whose bicycle had not reappeared for six entire days.

5. *Altitude and Gravity*

During our lunch of cheese and bread and fruit salad, Grand-Pierre asked Juliette about her grandfather, who was dead, and her grandmother, who was alive.

"Oh," said Juliette, "Grand-mère is dull as dust. Can't we talk about something else? Even though I've lived here all my life, no one but you ever teaches me about your canal. It's so wet and romantic." *Romantique*—Juliette LeMiel's word of the week.

"If you wash dishes, I'll try to remember."

"But there's nothing to wash! We used one plate each!"

"And there's not much to remember."

We brewed tea and took our cups to his stone bench facing the lock. In happier days his custom after lunch had been to sit on the terrace and read; now most often he sat, book in hand, and slept. But always, however blustery the weather, he needed to spend part of each day on his blue stone bench. Its stones, from the nearby river, were a mild soft gray, but under the sky they seemed blue.

"Tell us about the canal," Juliette repeated as we sipped tea. "If you're not too drowsy—"

"Not drowsy." Grand-Pierre nestled between us on the bench. "Not drowsy a bit." He stirred a spoon in a teacup that no longer held any tea. "The canal. Well. Before this mill was built, there *was* no canal."

"Only the river?" Juliette leaned into his shoulder to nudge him along.

"Only the river, without even a name." He consulted his empty cup, as if it might offer the missing name. "A nameless river, winding through the woods. Then a family or two—settlers, you know. Eight, nine hundred years ago."

"Before the Italian who yearned for an orange roof?"

"Before the homesick Italian." Grand-Pierre gazed up the canal toward Italy, a country I had heard about but had never visited. He looked very wise, gazing into the distance—and then his chin rocked forward and he was asleep. Like that.

"Well." Juliette sighed. "I did try."

"Yes. These days he sleeps a lot. But I can tell you his history of the valley—I've heard it often enough."

"And it never bored you?" At school, Juliette was not an enthusiastic student of history.

"Never. He makes it more real than old Gigot ever could." Our history teacher who was, according to Juliette, the dullest teacher in the entire world. "At least, he *used* to make it real." I contemplated Grand-Pierre's hands clasped across his stomach. "He says that understanding the canal—you know, with its rising and descending locks—means understanding altitude and gravity, and how they get along. Altitude and gravity, which seem to be enemies but aren't really, if you help them cooperate. Oh, but it's complicated."

"Tell me anyway." Juliette didn't have that slack-bored slump she fell into during Gigot's lectures. Sitting taller than the old man who rumbled between us, she looked upright and perky. "So. Altitude and gravity. Water flows downhill . . ."

"If there's just one dam, then yes, the water can only go down. But with two dams close together—or water gates, which are dams that open in the middle—you can fill the tub between them to the higher or lower level. Just by using gravity. What we want is to lift a boat to a higher level, arranging it so gravity and altitude do the lifting for us. Like here." I pointed at the half-filled lock in front of us. "We can float a boat *up* from one level to the next."

Juliette raised her hand as if it were an up-floating boat. "And once locks were invented, your canal was in business?"

I nodded.

"And your mill?" asked Juliette through Grand-Pierre's snoring. "Your *Moulin de Milan,* with its orange roof? Did it come before the canal or after?"

"Oh, this mill sat here on the riverbank for centuries before they added the canal. Now it sits between what Grand-Pierre calls our twin ribbons of water."

Juliette bent toward me above the snoozing old man. "With a grandfather who talks like that, Zazoo, how could you *not* write poems? *Twin ribbons of water.*"

"The old lockkeeper," I said cheerily, as if his falling asleep in the middle of a sentence were of no concern to me. "The old napping poet."

"He *is* old, isn't he." Hearing how she had spoken, Juliette raised a hand to her mouth.

"He's always been old. When he brought me back from Vietnam, he was sixty-seven—"

"But Zazoo, now he's *old* old. What are you going to do?"

Grand-Pierre spluttered between us. I untucked one of his hands from the other and wondered how it was possible for fingers so ancient to be so lovely. "I have no idea. Maybe I'll buy a lottery ticket. Maybe I'll sit here and cry."

I *did* have an idea of what I would do, but I couldn't tell her. I would sit in my boat and wait for my gray cat, invisible to everyone but me, who had been such a comfort in my earliest years and who would, I knew, return to comfort me again. This wasn't something I could explain to Juliette LeMiel or anyone except Grand-Pierre. Foggy though the old man might be, he knew what I meant when I described my gray cat—which he always called, for some reason, my *sad* gray cat.

But now there was someone else who might understand: Marius the bird-watching bicyclist. The smile tugging at the corners of his eyes hinted that he, like Grand-Pierre, would understand the idea of my sympathetic gray cat. *If* he and his bicycle ever returned.

6. The Doubtful Duke

Grand-Pierre sighed in his sleep; behind us the river curled over the dam. Birds called in the towpath weeds, then waited, then called again. From far down the canal I heard the blaring of a familiar klaxon. And again, nearer.

"Grand-Pierre!" I jostled my knee against his. "Do you hear *that?*"

He forced his eyes open. "Don't hear a thing." He winked at Juliette. The clamor was too loud not to hear.

"It's the Duke, Grand-Pierre! This is October—I hear the Doubtful Duke!" The klaxon's donkey-like braying ripped around the canal curve. "It's back to work for us—our last customer of the year."

"Idiot," muttered Grand-Pierre. "Boater bullhorn idiot." So the nap had done him some good: he knew exactly where he was and who was spoiling his sleep.

The screeching blasted the leaves back from the willows and brought a flicker of a smile to his face as the yacht, its upturned snout pushing the water aside, rounded the bend toward us. Painted English white and blue and red, it was a hooting flag of a vessel. And there on the bow stood the Doubtful Duke himself, in white sailor's trousers and a navy blue shirt, all but flapping the Union Jack.

Grand-Pierre didn't budge from his seat, didn't rise to give the nobleman his usual salute. Still, his lips were moving.

"What, Grand-Pierre?" I bent closer.

"Rule, Britannia. The fool has arrived. Is she still naked?"

"Of course she is." Grand-Pierre meant the carved nude woman who jutted from the bow of the vessel while, above her, the Duke pranced, honking away on his bullhorn. Arms at her sides, the statue drove steadily toward us: the same young woman as always, her hair flaming scarlet, her blue breasts tipped with white nipples, her blue legs tapering into the water. As the boat slowed for the lock, she settled her nakedness deeper in the canal.

"What a knockout!" whispered Juliette. "Do you see her *doudounes?*"

"I see them. Good thing the Jay-Jay aren't here—they'd faint dead away."

"Overdose of testosterone?" Juliette's pet biology word. We chuckled, glad to have her brothers far from us. I trotted to the down-canal gate, which stood half open, as we always left it between customers. After cranking it the rest of the way open, I joined Grand-Pierre, still seated, as he watched the figurehead's breasts guide the boat into the lock.

The Duke had ceased blatting on his horn and had taken the wheel from his silent wife. Now he cried out in abominable French, "I am, I hope, the last to go south?"

"Yes," I replied, when Grand-Pierre didn't. "Your proud record is still—"

"Intact?" he trumpeted. "*There's* a bit of luck. And how is our old warrior? Our Big Stone, our Rolling Boulder? No longer spinning the paddles?"

Grand-Pierre said nothing.

"Today," I replied, "it's my turn to bring you through."

"Lovely," shouted the Duke. "That will be lovely."

I reminded myself that even if the Duke was what we called a canal crow, the loudest bird in the valley, he was a good sailor. A big part of the lockkeeper's job, Grand-Pierre always said, was to sense which oafs, steering through the lock, were most likely to damage their own boats or the boats of others. If you could guess what brainless move a boater was likely to make *before* he made it, you might save him from ramming his pleasure craft and humiliating himself in front of his family.

The Doubtful Duke, for all his racket, did know when to cut down the speed of his yacht. Now it coasted into the nearly empty "tub" of the lock. The Duchess looped the middle of her line up around the stubby iron bollard on the lock's rim, then tied one end near the bow, then carried the other end to the stern. When Juliette and I cranked open the sluice paddles of the upper gate, and water began filling the tub, the Duchess held her line snug, keeping the yacht close to the side and safe from rough banging.

Up and up thundered the water—and up and up, above the churning rumble, piped the Duke's voice. "So! Taking a break from gate-keeping, old chap?"

Grand-Pierre gazed above and beyond the bobbing boat. His eyes looked bright enough; I figured he was simply determined not to take part in any nonsense.

"And the girl is right? We are the last southbound craft, are we not?"

Not a word from Grand-Pierre. And no word from the Duchess—but this was no surprise. She had never spoken, not once, in all her years of being the first woman each spring, and the last each fall, to cruise past us. Still, she did have a perfect nose—a slim, aristocratic nose—which guided her through the world with as much style as a nude figurehead ever guided any yacht.

"Teaching the child to do our work, are we?" Now the Duke's rising voice came from nearly our level. "The charming water sprite? *Zay*-zee, wasn't it?"

"Zah-*zoo!*" I bellowed, wondering how the Duchess might sound if she ever answered the old fool.

"Zah-*zoo,* of course, silly me and my faltering bean! Zazoo it was and Zazoo it remains. Staying busy, are we, at old Gate Forty-three? Sufficient commerce?"

"Sufficient stupidity," sighed Grand-Pierre without moving his lips.

"Lovely." The Duke couldn't hear a thing over his own commotion.

Although he mangled my name, something about the Duke made me smile; I was always sorry, when he left, to hear his voice trail away among the sycamores. But he had never given us any sort of tip, the way most boaters did—a franc or two, sometimes a hunk of cheese or a loaf of bread.

So what he said next stunned me. "It's time we gave the Boulder a little something, dearie, to thank him for so many years of service. Lash us fast—we'll just tie up right here in the box. There's no other craft coming."

His wife hopped ashore as lightly as someone half her age, then looped their painter—their front rope—around a bollard. The Doubtful Duke, one hand on the wheel, tossed her another line; soon she had the yacht secured fore and aft.

Her husband stepped cautiously across to the stone terrace. In one hand he held a dark round bottle. "You're a brandy drinker, am I right, old boy?"

From his perch on the blue bench, Grand-Pierre made no response.

"Well, *be* a boulder. But I happen to remember the autumn, years ago, when we survived the worst of ice storms on this very canal. You remember *that*, Old Stone?"

Grand-Pierre nodded just noticeably.

"Ferocious wind." The Doubtful Duke turned to Juliette. "Blistering cold. We were headed south for the winter but had suffered a late start—funerals to attend, I'd say, funerals or weddings. We were further north than we should have been. The sleet and hail that caught us here nearly drove us to our *own* funeral. That gives you some conception of the cold. Hands so numb from the storm, we could scarcely make fast. The deck a glaze of ice, the lines like pipes, impossible to knot—"

"And Grand-Pierre took care of you?" asked Juliette.

"Indeed." The Duke puffed and blew like a sea lion. "Wearing no more than a slicker—not so much as cotton gloves—he helped tie us down, then ushered us into his mill and poured hot brandies to thaw the ice in our veins."

"Speaking of chilly," said Grand-Pierre abruptly, "it's cold. I'm going in."

"Inside?" The Duke was shocked. "At this hour? Three in the afternoon?"

Grand-Pierre pulled himself to his feet and headed toward the mill.

"Our Boulder," the Duke muttered to me, his voice lower. "Our Boulder has changed."

I didn't wish to be reminded. He had changed. Yes, I knew.

"And in such a short time," the old spout went on. "Let's see. How long ago was it, dearie, that we passed through on our way north?"

Was he addressing his wife? But why bother, if she never answered? Perhaps he called *himself* dearie?

"Late April, I believe—no ice storms *then.* Correct—six months ago. Such a change in the old gent. Makes one *think,* doesn't it? Gives one *pause?*"

"Gives one pause all right." I followed Grand-Pierre to the door.

"Oh, don't listen to my blather—just the prattle of an old jackass." The Duke held the round bottle in one paw and his wife's elegant hand in the other. At the door he huffed past me, caught up with Grand-Pierre, and led him inside as if the place were his own home. Then, when I feared he was going to mock Grand-Pierre for feeling cold, he added, "I should say, it *is* a bit brisk—freezing my bones if not my jaw, ay? Haw haw!" And he held the door open.

Juliette and I followed inside; I looked on in wonder. The

Duke seated Grand-Pierre at the head of the kitchen table, then bustled to the sink. He filled the kettle, lit the gas, found wine glasses, poured two generous helpings of his Norman brandy into them, and handed one to "our fierce old stone." Through all the babble I watched Grand-Pierre, expecting him to go stony indeed; but to my surprise the flood of attention made him puff up like a little boy.

"Your *pipe!*" shouted the Duke. "You've lost your pipe, have you, Old Rock? Shall I find you another?"

"The girl," said Grand-Pierre sheepishly. "Zazoo. She made me."

"*Made* you? The *snip?*" The Duke bounded to the woodstove, clanked its fire door open, and threw a half dozen sticks of kindling inside.

"Bad for me, she said."

"And it *was,*" I put in. "I had always loved that pipe, the smell of its smoke, but last spring it started making him cough, so I told him to stop. It would kill him, and I didn't want anything to kill him."

"Right." Grand-Pierre nodded. "Just what she said. Loved me."

"It's what I said then, and I say it now." I didn't care if I sounded as bossy as old Gigot. "So there'll be no more talk about pipes, if you don't mind—you can sit and drink your brandy and be considerate."

"Well, then!" chortled the Duke, as if he loved to be scolded. "Let's have that sip to take off the chill. Just a smidgen, mind you—a dribble to lubricate the engine, a wee *smidge.*" He reached behind him for another glass. "And one for you, dearie, as well?" He poured out a smidge for his silent companion. I watched to see if a smile or frown crossed her brow. She held the glass beneath her cultured nose and swished it from side to side, but she didn't drink.

Grand-Pierre took a tiny sip. The Doubtful Duke's glass had emptied itself, but not for long. A new smidge replaced the old one.

"*Do* have a smackerel, old dear." His voice was almost sweet. "You're so sad today—and little wonder."

She brought the glass to her mouth and wet her lips with the brandy.

Sad? How on earth, I wondered, could he tell? "Why are you sad, Madame la Duchesse?"

She stared into her glass.

"We had," the Duke began, "a bit of a loss today."

At the word *loss,* his wife took a sip and her chin trembled slightly.

"Such a lovely young cat," said the Duke. "Came and went."

Grand-Pierre—who hadn't, I thought, been following any of this—nodded as if he already knew. "The sad *gray* cat?"

"Not gray," corrected the Duchess, speaking for the first time, in our presence, ever. Her voice was low and deep and refined. "Not gray at all. Our kitty was as white as the whitest sand, the whitest—"

"Snow?" Grand-Pierre glanced at me. "Then it wasn't your sad gray cat, Zazoo."

"Madame," Juliette broke in softly, "you lost your white kitty where?"

"Not far from here. At the stone pier just below Lock Forty-seven."

"And," inquired Grand-Pierre, "how far had she come with you?" His clouds seemed to have parted.

"A few kilometers along the towpath, Monsieur. But at Lock Forty-six, she—she—"

"Departed," said the Duke, ever so gently. "Vanished. We had hoped she would join us on board, but she chose not to."

By now the Duchess, I saw with alarm, was beginning to sob.

"It's all right, old darling." The Duke took her hand. "It's all right."

Grand-Pierre ran a finger around the rim of his brandy glass. I wondered if we had lost him. Then he whispered, "Tell them our poem, Zazoo. About *your* cat."

"If you'll help. After all, you made it up." I peered at him to see if his eyes were alert. " 'There once was a cat . . .' "

" 'Down,' " he murmured, " 'by the canal.' But *you* say it. Refresh my—"

"Your doubtful memory? All right, Old Boulder." I inhaled, as if preparing for a long underwater swim.

"There once was a cat
down by the canal
who never seemed able to roam.
He considered a swim
but hated the wet—

he thought of a cruise
but couldn't quite settle
for drifting away
from his cozy dry home—
    from his gray-château,
    bridge-below,
    cozy dry home."

The Duchess snuffled into her brandy glass, a sight that tore at my heart but also came as a relief; for years I had wondered if she had any feelings at all.

"So . . . dignified," she sniffed at last. "We yearned for her never to leave us."

"But Madame," I explained, as kindly as Grand-Pierre had once explained such things to me. "That's the way of such cats. Gray or white, if a cat lives by the canal, it sees the world float past and can't help being . . . sad, and restless, and, as you say, dignified. Too dignified to swim, for example—"

"I should say *not.* Swim? Not *this* cat."

Grand-Pierre slowly swirled his brandy glass. " 'Who never seemed—' "

" '—able to roam.' " I beamed across at him. Which was when I saw him make our private spooning signal, a signal we had shared ever since I could remember: our sign that it was time to fix some oatmeal. No one else noticed, or if they did, they had no idea what he meant, spooning with one hand like a child.

But I knew. I climbed our pantry ladder, returned with one

of our many tins of oatmeal, and laid the gold-lettered container in the lap of the Duchess. "Grand-Pierre thought you should have this, Madame, to help ease your loss. From Ireland—the very best oatmeal, so you can have a proper breakfast on your way south."

She knelt on the stone floor and took me in both arms. "Dearest girl," she whispered, and didn't have to say more. "*Dearest* girl!"

"It was Grand-Pierre's idea. He acts gruff sometimes, but he likes you more than you might guess. And the white kitten—"

"Yes, I know. There will be another. But how soon, child?"

That made me wince. I didn't care for the word *soon*.

Juliette untied the stern line and held it as our visitors stepped onto their yacht; the Duke was actually quiet as his wife steered them out into the canal.

"We'll be back!" he shouted above the thrumming of their engine. Which was, for once, all he shouted. The Duchess waved twice, shyly; they disappeared into the curving curtain of sycamores.

7. Out on the Water

We sat with Grand-Pierre on the stone bench until the water stopped sloshing in the lock and every ripple from the yacht was gone.

"They'll make it," he told the water. "Every year . . ." His voice faded as he remembered, or failed to remember, other years.

I remembered other years, and the banter he had shared with sailors drifting past. It struck me that he seemed more comfortable with foreigners who came and went on the water than with people from his own village. I leaned toward the lock, thinking hard. *What* people of his own village? When had any friend or neighbor come to visit Grand-Pierre? I couldn't recall. Were his visitors only on boats that floated through our lock and then floated away?

Juliette interrupted with thoughts of her own. "It doesn't make sense! That white kitten making your Duchess so miserable? How can she feel broken up over a kitten she never had?"

"She had her," I said.

"But she *told* us—"

"I know, the kitten didn't get on their boat, it only walked the towpath beside them, the way kittens do. But the Duchess *had* that kitten, just the same. In her mind."

"Oh, please. Do I look like such an idiot?"

"A few kilometers, she said. That's a long way to go, puttering beside a kitty who's growing more and more at home in your mind."

"Then tell me about *your* cat." Juliette glared at the canal, which looked as sleepy as Grand-Pierre. "This gray cat you go on about—this *sad* gray cat. What's the *story* with this cat? Is he really real?"

"I've seen him, Juliette."

"Fine. You've seen him. But were you seeing him for *real,* or just in your mind?"

"But Juliette, what's the difference?"

"The difference is between what's real and what's floating around that canal of your gill-girl head!"

"Good one. I love it when you get upset—it improves your zingers."

"I'm not upset, I'm just irritated by your sloppy thinking."

This wasn't Juliette LeMiel talking, as we both knew; it was our Natural Science teacher, Monsieur Croque, known to his students as Monsieur *Croque Monsieur,* which also means a melted-cheese-and-ham sandwich. Monsieur Croque Monsieur often accused Juliette of sloppy thinking.

"There are many cats . . . in this valley." Grand-Pierre's eyes remained closed. "Sad cats. Searching."

We waited.

"Searching," asked Juliette, "for what?"

"Oh . . ." Grand-Pierre popped his lips around the long-absent pipe. "Searching."

"This special gray cat of Zazoo's—have you seen it, Grand-Pierre?"

"If *she* has," he said, his face tipped up toward the rustling leaves, "it's there."

"You two! A pair of sloppy thinkers!"

Grand-Pierre smiled without opening his eyes.

Juliette stamped across the terrace to the up-canal gate, which we had left open behind the departing Duke. Furiously she cranked the near side of the gate shut.

"Good girl." Grand-Pierre nodded. "Learning our lock routine."

"Guess I'll go home." Juliette could be as moody as anyone.

"That sounds smart," I said. "The Jay-Jay have probably been missing their *doudoune* entertainment. Some amusement for their moronic twin brain—"

"Oh, right." She tapped one foot. "Guess I won't go home."

"Why don't we take a little cruise? Might straighten out my sloppy thinking."

"Not likely." Juliette tried not to smile. "Out on the river, then?"

We strapped my boat onto the "punt-mobile" Grand-Pierre had built years before with parts from an old baby carriage. After rolling the wobbly boat-on-wheels into the river, we floated the punt free and climbed aboard.

Juliette, full of nervous energy, wanted to row. I was happy to let her. It was such wondrous work, rowing—pushing with your legs while pulling with your arms, your back unwinding like a muscular spring, your legs coiling to push again, over and over and over.

We tied our painter to the stake under the lindens, planted the yellow umbrella in the front seat, and then sat back, half-asleep on the river, as the current moved past. I watched and waited but couldn't tell Juliette why.

No cats, gray or otherwise. No boys on black bikes.

And why, I wondered for the thousandth time, had Marius made such a huge impression on me? Was it just that so little happened in my sleepy village? No. A great deal happened. Every moment, the trees bent toward one another and whispered about all the things that were happening. Then was it that the boys of my village—and most of the girls—were so dull? No, not that either.

Marius on his rusty bike had possessed some quality that had nothing to do with freckles or windblown hair. Was it his manner, so direct and unguarded? The look in his eye? I wasn't even sure what color his eyes *were*.

"Are you all right?" Juliette peered closer. "Still worried about Grand-Pierre?"

"I'm always worried about him."

"He is different now," said Juliette. "Isn't he."

"Yes." I closed my eyes to feel the sun on their lids, and to avoid meeting her look. "He's different. Tell me—do you recall ever seeing him in the village?"

She seemed unwilling to answer. "Who?"

"Grand-Pierre, of course."

"No," she said at last. "I've never seen him anyplace but here. My mother asks the same thing. She wonders where he spends all his time."

Eyes still closed, I waved in the direction of the mill. "That's easy. He spends his time on the terrace, or walking the towpath out toward the Gnarly Oak Grove. Or inside, you know, reading, knitting . . ."

"So he spends all his time at home." A long silence. "He never goes anywhere?" Juliette's amazed tone was enough; I didn't need to open my eyes to see her face.

"Nowhere else. No."

Finally she spoke. "He used to walk into the village. That's what my mother says. After the war, even much later, when he brought you here. He'd buy things, talk to people. But ever since you grew old enough to do his shopping for him, no one sees Grand-Pierre anymore."

"I see him, Juliette. And so do you, when you come visit."

"Yes."

Even with my eyes closed, I could tell she feared hurting my feelings.

"He's sweet to me," she whispered. "But why doesn't he go into the village?"

"I don't know." My voice came out more grouchy than I'd have liked. "Maybe you should ask him." I opened my eyes and flashed what was meant to be a radiant smile. "Oh, it's such a golden day, it makes me feel like swimming."

"It *does?*" The idea of swimming always made Juliette queasy—even swimming in an indoor pool free of weeds and tadpoles. "Isn't it kind of *cold* for that now? I mean, the middle of October—"

"Not at all." I was certain Marius would not have thought the day too cold—for swimming or bird watching or anything else. Thoughtfully, slowly, he would have repeated "Swimming" while nodding his head. As I imagined him saying such a thing, the world suddenly appeared much wider and brighter. The sun slanted onto us; I could see how it looked from under the surface, its rays drilling bits of dust that hung in the water. "In cool weather, you know, the canal stays warmer than the air. Plenty of times I've gone swimming in November."

"You *have?*"

"Many times." No, I couldn't tell her about Marius—the only one, apart from Grand-Pierre, who would have understood my need to swim in October or November or any other time. "But don't worry, I won't swim today. We'll stay in our cozy dry punt." Like the verse about my gray cat, in his cozy dry home.

"Ah, Zazoo." Juliette stretched luxuriously. "Isn't this blissful? The sun, the birdies, no Jay-Jay in sight?"

"It is, yes." The current nuzzled our boat, the papery linden leaves rustled—and most magic of all, sunlight reflected up under the arches of the ancient stone bridge in overlapping flashes that looked like so many sunshiny minnows.

"The bridge!" whispered Juliette. "Every time, I think I know how it will look—but then, when I see it again, it's new. Every time."

"Yes." I could feel her relax as she stared at the swirls of reflected light darting up under the bridge. The sun made me so careless I was tempted to rave about freckles, say the name Marius, and parade his virtues before her. But Juliette spoke first.

"Tell me again," she asked, "about your cat. Your sad gray cat. I'll try to understand."

"Well, then." Closing my eyes, I could feel the breeze caressing our umbrella. "The first time I saw him, I was three years old."

"You were living here with Grand-Pierre?"

"Yes, but I hadn't been here long. A year at the most."

"Then you still spoke Vietnamese."

"No, by then all I spoke was French. But a three-year-old can say quite a bit—and the first serious thing Grand-Pierre remembers me saying was that I'd had a visit from a gray cat."

"You saw him—where?" Juliette wasn't mocking me now; the bridge's spell had calmed her. "Near the water?"

"I was on Grand-Pierre's bench beside the lock, sitting alone, reading a book."

"Liar! You couldn't read when you were three!"

"I could pretend. I used to sit on that bench with a book because I saw Grand-Pierre reading there, and whatever he did, *I* did. When he swam, I swam. He even made up a poem about it:

> "She swam like no one I had known,
> this little girl of mine,
> as if into a fish she'd grown,
> all silver-finned and fine. . . ."

"My grandparents," said Juliette, before I could get into the sad part of it, the beautiful part, "never wrote poems for *me.* So. When the cat appeared, you were pretending to read."

"Yes." In a way, I was just as glad not to share the most tender part of the poem, since she was only half listening. "I sat there with that book in my lap, chattering away to no one—when, from the corner of my eye, I saw this shape moving across the terrace, and I turned and saw a gorgeous gray cat padding toward me."

"Did he let you pet him?"

"It's funny, but I'm not sure I had *seen* a cat before. Maybe I didn't know you were supposed to pet them."

"But weren't there cats in Vietnam?"

"That's just it, Juliette—by the time I was three I couldn't remember Vietnam. And I still can't. But I do remember that this cat was very *dignified,* as the Duchess would say. He knew his business in the world."

"Which was what?" Juliette smiled with her eyes closed, her face tilted toward the sun.

"His business was to move gracefully. And, well, to keep searching. He climbed onto the far end of the bench, silently, and sat as near as you're sitting now. We watched the canal together. Seems like two minutes ago. We sat and watched and—I don't know how to say this—we shared our sadness."

Juliette's eyes opened wide, as if she were three herself. "But what were *you* sad about? Being adopted?"

"Why should I have been sad about that, when Grand-Pierre was so good to me?"

"I'm sorry, Zazoo. Everyone knows there's nothing wrong with being adopted."

I winced. "Everyone except the Jay-Jay."

"Oh, I should never have told you about that." Juliette had taught me the word *orpheline*, for a girl orphan, after learning it from her demon brothers.

"I don't know exactly why I was sad that day with the cat. But I was."

"Maybe you were thinking of your poor dead parents, exploded by the hidden bomb." This was a moment Juliette loved to revisit.

"No, I don't think so. I had Grand-Pierre."

"But still." Juliette adored any story coated with tragedy. "It was sad, what happened to your parents—"

"I wasn't even there, Juliette. Anyway, who really understands sadness? But here's the strangest part—you know, about that sadness I felt, when I was three, sitting with the gray cat? It had a *sweetness* to it."

In a less peaceful mood, Juliette would have mocked such a notion; now she nodded toward the bridge's flickering golden squiggles.

"The cat sat with me, and I told him the story I'd been reading aloud to the canal—and then he went away. But here's the main thing."

Juliette waited; the river waited with her.

"Once I had seen him . . . once he'd sat with me on the bench?"

"Yes?"

"I never felt alone again. I mean, of course I've been alone. Often. But once that gray cat appeared, he could always be with me, in my mind, when I needed him."

When Juliette didn't snort with disbelief, I wondered if the bridge and its flickering gold minnows had soothed her into accepting the idea of my gray cat. "And so," she asked lazily, "have you seen him since?"

"Not so nearby, but yes, twice more. One morning a few

years ago I was out walking and saw him on the towpath, sitting straight up, chin tucked into his chest—like one of those Egyptian cats, you know, in pictures?"

"Hmm." Juliette swung her blond hair toward the mill. "What I *do* know is, I'm hungry. Shall we go make Grand-Pierre some toast?"

So she didn't ask me about the most recent time, and I didn't tell her. When Juliette LeMiel was hungry, gray cats and everything else had to wait.

We pulled the boat upstream, loosened its line from the stake, and let the current carry us back to the Mill of a Thousand Years. And what I couldn't share with Juliette, as we floated downstream, was something Grand-Pierre had described years before—the faint faraway voice of a two-year-old girl, dressed in black pajamas, asking over and over, in Vietnamese: *Mama go boom?*

8. Time Under Water

One week passed, then another: a time of cold October rain and rain and more rain. The last leaves clung desperately to their branches until finally, soaked by cold showers, they were dragged to the ground and turned to mush. I slogged through them and knew they would be tough for any bicyclist to pedal through.

On many such rainy afternoons, Grand-Pierre and I went out walking under our gray and black umbrellas, as we had every autumn I could remember. But this autumn was so *slow.* There was no sign that the boy from the south would ever be back. The echo of his word *soon* was a mockery as it gave way to *later*—one week, then two—until *later* seemed more like *never.*

Grand-Pierre's feet, like time itself, moved ever more slowly. They had stepped along briskly just a year earlier; now they shuffled through the soggy leaves. He seemed to be winding down, as our kitchen clock did when we had forgotten to rewind it. But who could rewind *him?* And if he couldn't be rewound, what would I do?

"Tell me—" I had asked during past walks, during previous autumns that had moved less slowly. "Does it rain very much in Vietnam?"

"Oh, yes," he had replied in those days when words still came easily. "Vietnam has rain like nowhere else, especially during the season called *la mousson.* Hot steamy rain of a sort we don't have in France. Nothing like these cool showers along our canal. I didn't care for *la mousson,* Zazoo, and I doubt you would, either—you who have never enjoyed humidity. *La mousson* wouldn't suit you at all."

So now, weeks after Marius had come and gone, walking the same path but more slowly, I asked again. "Tell me, Grand-Pierre. Does it rain much in Vietnam?"

"Yes," he said. And that was all. Nothing about the rainy season. We continued along the towpath in the fading light.

"The twilight," I said, "is so beautiful."

"Yes," he said again. And no more.

At moments like that, it was good my invisible gray cat

walked nearby, helping me feel less alone. The last time I'd actually seen him had been during the spring, just after sunset; he had sat as still as an owl on the high limb of an oak. Now I tried convincing myself that it wouldn't be long before I saw him again.

After endless days of rain came a spell of sunshine and gold breezes. The nights were cool but the days shirtsleeve-warm, even naked-warm in my vine-shielded pool no one else knew existed. One late afternoon I slipped from my clothes and stroked into the sun-slanted depths, proud of my strong lungs, my muscled arms and deep-seeing eyes.

Clouds rolled in; thunder boomed. I swam deeper and gazed up to watch marbles form as drops came whap-slapping through the branches and hit the roof of my private world—marbles in heaven, exploding above me as I clutched deep-anchored weeds to keep myself from floating up to them. I held my eyes open and watched and waited.

9. In Most Ways

Grand-Pierre ran out of thyroid pills the morning of our first skimpy snowfall, a gusty day in early November. It had been three weeks and two days since Marius biked into our village to learn if our pharmacist had ever been married.

I handed Grand-Pierre his last pill; he sloshed it down with coffee.

"It's time to refill your prescription," I said. "Care to come with me? A nice walk to the village," I added, as if wandering through the village were something he still did regularly. "Then you can stroll back home while I go on to school."

"You get my pills," he said sharply. "By yourself."

"I usually do, yes, but I thought you might like an outing. If you don't want to walk back alone, I can come back with you, then take the towpath to school. No terrible detour, really, on such a fine day—"

"I," he stated, "don't *go* to the pharmacy."

"But why, on such a lovely day, with scraps of snow drifting down—"

"I don't *go,*" he repeated, "to the pharmacy." And he set his cup on the table with such a knock it sent a geyser of coffee into the air. "Now look what you made me do."

"A spill." After a perfectly peaceful breakfast he was, in that instant, more upset than I'd seen him in weeks. "A spill is all, Grand-Pierre. Here, I'll wipe it away."

"Wasted the last of it."

"Oh, there's more in the pot. And see, the table's dry again." Keeping my voice calm was not always easy. "Okay, I'll go to the pharmacy by myself."

"Yes you *will.* I won't."

"No," I crooned. "Not ever. And not into the village? Ever?"

"Not ever." He glared out at the gates of the up-canal lock, one closed and the other open. "Enough for a lifetime. Never again."

I nodded as if this made sense. "All right, then. Never again."

* * *

I didn't stop at the pharmacy until after school, but this didn't mean I had forgotten Grand-Pierre's outburst. Through one class and another, I spent my day staring at the ragged flakes and brooding about his behavior. Which was why, as soon as I entered the pharmacy, before Monsieur Klein could mention swimming or beauty lotions, I blurted, "Please tell me one thing, Monsieur. I can't remember—has my grandfather ever refilled his prescription? I mean, has he ever done it himself?"

"No, Zazoo." Monsieur Klein studied the poster of a brunette whose eyes could never have come from Vietnam. "It's only these last five or six years that he's needed thyroid pills. And he's always sent you to collect them."

"But before I came to live with him—did he ever—"

"As far as I know," said Monsieur Klein, his eyes fixed on the creamy-cheeked brunette, "before this thyroid trouble, he was never ill in his life." Why couldn't he look at me directly, as he normally did? "A very strong man, your Grand-Pierre. In most ways."

"I see." But I didn't see. *In most ways?* Old men don't talk the way teenage girls do, gabbing around and around our secrets until the truth squirts out. Old men shut things up and hammer the lid down. All I saw was Monsieur Klein smiling tightly, and Grand-Pierre whacking his cup so hard its coffee shot into the air.

"A delightful day for a dip, no?" His eyes slid painfully to meet mine.

"If you say so, Monsieur." I squinted across the counter at him. He wasn't nearly as old as Grand-Pierre, but old enough to be stubborn. "Lovely weather for a snow-swim."

"A few white scraps, Mademoiselle Zazoo. A few feathers." He glanced into the street. "I knew you'd be coming for his pills, and I have them ready. Green pills to keep old Grand-Pierre alive."

"Emeralds." Taking the plastic bottle, I examined its contents. "Would he have died without these?"

"Most likely, although one can never be sure." Monsieur Klein's eyes widened and he gave me his first cheery look since I had arrived. "But Zazoo, I forgot the best part of my day! Such interesting correspondence came in the mail!"

"You got a letter?"

"Yes, the postman brought me something—but it's for *you!* Addressed for some reason not to your grandfather's box at the post office but to 'The Pharmacy of Monsieur Klein.' Do you often ask friends to contact you here?"

"Never. A . . . letter?" Three weeks and two days. I felt dizzy with hope.

"Actually, a postcard." He handed it across the counter. "Which, since it features the Eiffel Tower, was most likely sent from Paris."

"Ah." I was a French girl, but I'd never received a postcard from Paris. Along with the Eiffel Tower, the card's painting also featured a yellow cat with the face of a man, as well as an airborne figure floating under a tiny parachute.

"Whoever sent this card," said Monsieur Klein, "has a wonderful knowledge of art. Do you know this painter, a Russian who moved to Paris, the dream-weaver Marc Chagall?"

"No, Monsieur."

"One of the best." Monsieur Klein looked almost dreamy himself.

"I see what you mean. Such colors! And this man in the corner, with two faces, one pointing one way, one the other—"

"Yes. Hypnotic. And is there a message?" Monsieur Klein leaned across the counter, eyes gleaming behind his spectacles.

I turned the card over. "One line. 'Dear Zazoo, I've been wondering: What do you do when it gets too cold for swimming and punting?'"

"Swimming and . . . punting?" Monsieur Klein peered up at his ceiling lights. "What, please explain, is *punting?*"

"The practice," I lectured, grinning down at my card, "of navigating a small boat called a punt. Such as may be found in England—"

"Along the banks of the River Thames? Yes, now I see. Punting, with a pole. And no signature? No return address?"

"It's signed 'The Boy with Binoculars.' With an address, yes—of another pharmacy! Some street number in Paris!"

Monsieur Klein seemed to bounce gently on his toes. "A pharmacy. Your binocular boy has an obsession with toothbrushes?"

"No doubt." My knees felt so wobbly, if there had been a chair nearby, I'd have collapsed onto it.

"No indication why he wrote to you here?"

"Not a word, Monsieur. Quite the riddle." Holding my card in both hands, I watched Monsieur Klein beam at me.

"Indeed. This binocular boy—I suppose you met him by the canal."

"Last month, yes." My voice came out strangely wheezy. "At dawn. I was in my boat, and he came riding along on his bike. We talked for a while, then he pedaled away. I never saw him again."

"You will," said Monsieur Klein.

"Seems unlikely. This funny return address—"

"You'll see him, Zazoo. He was thinking about you. Wondering what you do when the canal freezes over. Maybe he was looking at the river in Paris—the River Seine—and it made him think of you."

"The River Seine," I repeated drowsily. "The River Seine. But he told me he came from *southern* France."

"That's *good!* More mysterious. I'm glad he sent his message here. It makes me feel part of your—what shall I call it?—your adventure? But what was he looking for in our valley? A beautiful rowboat girl? Or should I say, a beautiful *punt* girl?"

"He was looking for birds, Monsieur Klein. It was so early in the morning, the mist hadn't burnt off the canal. He had binoculars around his neck."

"And did he say which species he hoped to find?"

"No." *He was looking for birds, Monsieur—but also for information. Information about you.* I tried picturing Monsieur Klein, with his neatly trimmed mustache, as a young man in love. In our village? Or perhaps far away, beside the River Seine? "It's a pity you don't sell postcards here."

"No, for that you must try the tobacco shop. They sell, I believe, photos of your stone-arched bridge." His eyes narrowed. "But wait—I might have something of my own, here in the drawer. Your friend likes birds, you say?"

"Yes, he likes birds." *My friend.*

"Let me just look. Yes, here's a card he might appreciate. A large card, giving plenty of space for your message. The picture's very old, a shot of a heron. A purple heron, I'd guess, though the photo's in black and white. Please, take it."

"And I owe you how much?"

"Don't be silly, Zazoo. I'm happy to be part, as I say, of your—"

"Adventure?" I started toward the door; Grand-Pierre would grow fretful if I didn't have our supper ready soon. But the thought of him and his flying coffee stopped me. "Monsieur Klein . . ."

"Yes, Zazoo."

He looked so very kind, and so delighted with my intrigue, that I couldn't bring myself to ask why Grand-Pierre never came to fill his own prescription. "I'll be back for more pills, Monsieur. Next month."

"Stop any time, Zazoo. Any time. Good evening."

"Good evening, Monsieur." The doorbell tinkled as I stepped into the cool night, holding the pills and cards. The day's few scraps of snow were gone from the street, leaving no trace that they had ever fallen. But Marius had not melted away. The proof lay in my hand, smiling up at me.

10. Paris Through My Window

In my tower room, with candles lit, I gazed through my window reflection to the dark trees, the black canal, the clouds tumbling under a quarter moon. In the shadows of the forest I knew my gray cat sat purring. Thinking of the poem I had started reciting to Juliette some weeks earlier, I wrote on the back of the heron card, using my favorite pen with its spidery black ink, producing the tiniest writing possible.

> *Dear Boy with Spyglasses—Since you ask what I do when the canal freezes over, I'll send this poem Grand-Pierre wrote years ago—a poem I've never shared, except the first few lines, with anyone but him. It answers your question. Please write again, from your pharmacy to mine—we can trust M. Klein to deliver anything you send. And in answer to your question, he is not, and never has been, married. Here's my grandfather's poem.*
>
> *She swam like no one I had known,*
> *this little girl of mine,*
> *as if into a fish she'd grown—*

all silver-finned and fine.
But when the surface glazed with ice
that sealed away her paradise
she couldn't bear my sage advice
on nature's sweet design,
and wept—like no one I had known—
this little girl of mine.

But then she slept in air so clear
that she could hardly help but hear
the sound of someone coasting near
along the bright divide.
When she awoke, two slender skates
sharp-edged for carving figure eights
lay winking in the sunlight by her side—
two glinting blades on midnight boots,
longing to be tried.

Even writing smaller than I ever had in my life, and even though it was, as Monsieur Klein had said, an oversized ancient postcard, I couldn't squeeze the final verse—my favorite—onto the message side. But in the heron's picture, above and beyond the proud head, I found a space just large and pale enough for me to float the last ten teensy-tiny lines.

And now she flies, on nights so cold
the dry canal ice sounds too old
to creak and crack and barely hold

her blades from slipping through—
this under- and yes, over-water,
liveliest, by far, granddaughter
ever to have worn a skating shoe:
this loveliest,
no longer little
girl I call Zazoo.

The next morning, walking the river path on my way to school, I was stopped by the spindly shape of the purple heron himself. I'd seen him before but always at a distance, upriver from the dam. Always before he had stood quite still, balanced on one leg as he surveyed the water. But now he took a stride forward—then a pause—then delicately lifted his four-pointed rear foot as his long neck bobbed up for a higher river view.

In the soft morning air I stood admiring his progress. He couldn't have missed me there in the weeds, book bag slung from one shoulder, heron card in one hand. I left him and made my way to the post office.

11. Brittle Weather

Sunday, after Saturday's half-day session, was the only day of the week we had no school. I slept as late as I ever did, until the sun cleared the far treetops.

"Oatmeal!" Grand-Pierre called up the spiral stairs. "First call, Zazoo!"

Downstairs, from the smell drifting up to me, I could tell he had the fire going and the kitchen cozy, much cozier than my tower room. My little round room had so many windows facing in all directions that it was chilly all winter—nice for a bird watcher but not great for heat.

"Bird watcher," I murmured, pulling the covers tighter. "Bird watcher." Beyond the east windows I could feel the river flowing, as I felt the canal, to the west, shifting and chilling and bracing itself to freeze. It was a sense I had, one I seemed to have been born with. I didn't know anyone else who had it except Grand-Pierre. Even when we were inside, we knew exactly what the water was doing.

"Second call—"

"—for oatmeal!" I threw on the robe he had knitted me two years before. Knitting was what Grand-Pierre did in the winter; it was the only good thing, he said, he had learned to do during the Awful Time, his name for the war. "Here I come, old man—third call." I skipped down the stairs in my slippers and reached out my face for our morning double-cheek kiss.

The oatmeal steamed in our bowls. Grand-Pierre had been up since dawn; the kitchen was filled with smells of woodsmoke and coffee dripping and bacon sizzling.

"Winter." He turned a strip of bacon. "Makes me feel like a boy."

It was fine to see him so chipper. But then I tasted my oatmeal and dread filled my stomach. I tasted another spoonful—again, terribly salty. Grand-Pierre had made the oatmeal wrong after making it right for so many years. I waited while he poured our juice.

"Well, *eat,* Zazoo, eat. Where's your appetite?"

I picked at my oatmeal. Finally, he took a bite.

"Oh," he said. *"Oh."* And glowered into his bowl. "I see."

Silence. We stared at his bowl.

"Ugh. What a mess I've made." He rose and spooned our bowls back into the saucepan and carried it to the bathroom. The toilet flushed and flushed. He returned with the empty pan, set it on the counter, sat down, and shot a look at the bacon.

"I can make more oatmeal, Grand-Pierre."

"Don't bother." His mouth sucked furiously at its absent pipe. "Couldn't eat now if I tried. What a mess."

"Then I'll make some toast. And you fixed coffee as well? You're spoiling us!"

"Spoiling something. Coffee's probably too strong."

"It's perfect. And the bacon's wonderful." I cut two slabs of bread, laid them out to toast on the woodstove, watched to be sure they didn't burn—and, from the corner of my eye, watched Grand-Pierre. He glared at his uneaten bacon.

"A walk by the canal," I announced. "A walk would be just the thing."

"Not going—too cold out. Ruined it."

But when I brought him his coat, he put it on.

* * *

Arm in arm, we made our way along the towpath under the willows. Birds chittered; distant dogs howled; I waited for the water to have its effect. Water was good for Grand-Pierre, always. It soothed him. We walked and walked and finally, by the unbending of his elbow in mine, I felt him start to relax.

I didn't ask the main question troubling me, of why he avoided Monsieur Klein's pharmacy. And I didn't share my news about Marius. Boots crunching the gravel, we made our way north to the Gnarly Oak Grove, and then slowly back, to sit on his blue stone bench facing the lock.

"How is it possible," I asked, "that you and I get along so well? Juliette and her parents wrangle all the time. You told me once that you didn't get along with *your* parents—"

"Didn't." His head tilted away from me. "Didn't get along with *people.*"

"Any people?"

"Not most. Not my parents." The words jumped from him in short bursts. "Odd people. They could row across the river but couldn't sit still to watch it."

"Then they were nothing like you."

"No." He peered north along the canal. "Fern shadows, ripples on the water—so much they didn't see. Small things, some might say." He shook his head. "But there were big things, too."

"Big things like . . . the war?"

Grand-Pierre so seldom spoke of the Awful Time that I hesitated to ask. The Second World War, which grandfathers of our valley had fought in, or not fought in, half a century earlier. We children learned not to ask too many questions about a war that brought such shame and anger into the faces of old men we loved.

"Well," he said at last. It came out more a groan than a word.

"Well *what?*" I felt less patient than usual. "They didn't see the war coming?"

"Not until it was draped over us like a bloody blanket. No. Odd people, my parents. I just couldn't fit in with them." His voice dropped. "Or with the others. Teachers, priests—most of this *village* I couldn't fit in with. And when the Awful Time came over us, I wanted to be free of my family ties."

"But Grand-Pierre, I don't want to be free of *you*. Am I not your family now?"

"Of course, Zazeezoo." But calling me by my baby name didn't help him smile. "This is so different from what I knew with those people. My world now—it starts and ends with you."

I thought he would say no more, and was quite content to have heard this much.

He cleared his throat. "You changed me to something better than I was."

"Better now, you mean, than who you were during the war?"

"Much *much* better." He stared far beyond the forest.

"But you were a hero! People say you were the biggest—"

"People are confused." He studied his weathered hands. "This word *hero*, Zazoo. What does it mean?"

"Someone who—who risks his life for others?"

"A fine thought. But is that what people do in a war? In a truly Awful Time?" His fierce look stunned me. It was good to hear him speaking so clearly, but hard to see the despair in his eyes.

"In a war," I finally answered, "people kill each other."

"Yes, and get so confused they don't think straight. And cover up the awfulness of what they do with awful ideas."

"Such as—?"

"Such as the idea," said Grand-Pierre, "that a man who kills well is a hero." He continued to examine his hands.

I felt the blood rushing into my face. I didn't know what I was hearing, but knew I didn't want to hear more, yet had to keep asking. "If someone good risks his own life," I said, "and kills bad people who are going to kill his friends, his family—"

"Bad people?" Grand-Pierre looked up from his hands. "Good people?" His smile was terrible to see.

"But if you kill soldiers—in a *war,* I mean—it's all right."

"I was told the same thing, Zazoo. In school. And at home. They taught us well."

"But they were wrong?"

"They weren't right," he said slowly, "to confuse a good hunter with a hero. Listen to me. At school what they *don't* teach is that war, more than anything, is an excuse to let our worst side out. Our very worst side."

We sat on the blue stone bench facing the lock. He didn't move, didn't pop his lips on the stem of his invisible pipe.

"What," I whispered, unable to stop myself, "did your worst side do during the war?"

For the longest time he was silent. "Those *hero* people." The effort of saying so much seemed to have clouded his mind. "Heroes *save* lives."

I leaned my shoulder against him and waited. But then,

miraculously, we were both saved. His head sagged; his lips parted; he slept.

The water in the lock told me nothing about the gentle old man I had always known. The river, licking over the dam behind us, told me nothing.

After supper he sat at the kitchen table, whetstone in his left hand, sharpening the paring knife. The clock on the wall ticked and tocked; outside, the wind whooshed in the linden tree above the empty blue bench.

RRRR RRRR RRRRR rasped the blade. He'd been sharpening the knife a long time; I wondered how sharp it had to be. Perhaps he would forget to stop and would sharpen it down to nothing. *RRRRR RRRR RRRRR*—

Up the canal an owl hooted, went silent, then hooted again.

"Our owl," I said, hoping to lure Grand-Pierre into conversation. "He sounds so dreamy tonight."

No response. But when the owl hooted again, Grand-Pierre lifted his head from his sharpening.

"Dreamy," I repeated. "And what do you think such an owl dreams *of?*"

"Of his girl owl," replied Grand-Pierre without hesitation. As if he had said nothing of interest, he bent back to his knife. *RRRR RRRRRR RRRRR*—

I felt my eyes narrowing. "And I suppose this owl *loved* his girl owl?"

"Loved her." Grand-Pierre laid the whetstone on the table. "Yes, he did."

I let the fire crackle, then crackle again, before asking. "And how long ago did the owl love her?"

"When he was young." Grand-Pierre gazed at the ceiling. "A young foolish owl who danced the latest dance."

"The owl *danced?*"

"Naturally. He was young, he had a favorite dance."

"Which was what?" I asked breathlessly.

"The tango, Zazoo. The owl tango, you might say. From Argentina."

I hoped not to upset him, but needed to know. "And this was before the war?"

Still gazing above me, he tested the knife edge with his thumb.

"Did this owl dance the tango *before* the Awful Time?"

"Anything any good," whispered Grand-Pierre, "came before the Awful Time. Except you." He looked around our kitchen as if he'd never seen it before. "You wash a lovely stack of dishes, Zazoo."

"A wise old owl taught me how."

"Maybe not so wise." His chair creaked beneath him.

"I wish he would teach *me* to dance the owl tango."

"Couldn't manage if he tried. With feet that aim for the wrong boots, hands that dump salt in the oatmeal—"

"Then I wish he'd tell me about the owl girl he loved. The color of her feathers, let's say."

Grand-Pierre took some more time testing the knife blade against his thumb. "Brown. Deep dark brown."

"And did she dance gracefully with this owl?"

He set the knife on the table. "You'll have to ask elsewhere. I can't recall about the . . . dancing."

"Is it too awful to recall?"

"Yes, Zazoo. Cowardly of me. But yes. You'll have to ask elsewhere."

"You said that already." I felt merciless but couldn't help myself.

"Ask," he said, "at the house of the green cross."

I felt my mouth drop open. "Monsieur Klein's pharmacy?"

"His pharmacy. Yes. Monsieur Klein's pharmacy." Grand-Pierre shuffled across the kitchen to the cupboard and put our paring knife away.

12. *Orphans Behind the Green Cross*

Sometimes you go looking for one thing and find another. I wanted to ask Monsieur Klein about Grand-Pierre's young owl who loved to dance, and instead learned more about orphans than I had ever known. I, who had been one myself.

This knowledge came by way of Madame Meunier, my biology teacher's wife and the most tireless gossip in our village. When I entered the pharmacy, she stood at the counter, face pink from the pressure of all the tidbits straining to burst free of her. She greeted me, took in a huge breath, and paused, not knowing whether to continue her report. I drifted to the back of the store to give her some air.

"So!" Her voice was low but carried everywhere. "Those boys are such devils, Monsieur, I can't tell you." She told him anyway. "The worst boys ever, Jacques and Jules LeMiel. They drive their poor mother crazy. And their sister, Juliette? They torment the poor thing." Her voice dropped to a hiss. "I'm sure it's because she's adopted that they treat her so."

As Monsieur Klein said something in a soft tone, I stared into the little mirror on the dark glasses rack. Juliette *adopted?* I'd never heard such a thing. Surely, if the Jay-Jay tortured *me* for being adopted, they would be even nastier to *her?* Being nasty to Juliette was their main joy in life. So either they didn't know she *was* adopted or, more likely, she wasn't adopted. Madame Meunier was renowned for her stretchers. But if Juliette LeMiel *was* adopted, it meant we both were! No wonder we were best friends—we were members of a secret society! The thought made me so dizzy I unhooked the darkest pair of glasses from the rack and stepped toward the counter.

"Boys will be boys," said Monsieur Klein. "Jacques and Jules haven't grown up yet—"

"I should say not!" sputtered Madame Meunier. When she saw me approach, her mouth flapped shut and she stirred in her bag for some francs. Over the rims of the dark glasses I watched Monsieur Klein, and watched my reflection in the window behind him, and wondered which of us looked more embarrassed.

Madame Meunier clicked her purse shut, grabbed her bag of pills, and left without a word to me, tossing Monsieur Klein a quick thank-you-see-you-soon.

"Thank you, Madame," said Monsieur Klein softly as her figure receded down the sidewalk. Then he shrugged, as shopkeepers do when they have nothing more to say.

I set the dark glasses onto the counter and frowned down at them.

"And for Mademoiselle Zazoo, who swims like a trout?" He tried smiling. "You're not serious about that ugly piece of plastic, I hope?"

"No." I sighed so deeply I alarmed myself. "Some other day, Monsieur."

"Perhaps you're hoping for mail? I'm sorry to say there isn't anything new—"

"So *what* if Juliette's adopted," I snapped. "It would be a surprise—I mean, she never told me—but it's not such a big thing. I'm adopted myself."

"I realize that, Zazoo. Madame Meunier was only saying—"

"Madame Meunier," I declared, "was only saying she's so crammed with gossip it can't help but leak out."

He fussed with the sleeve of his white jacket. "Well, perhaps. Indirectly, she may have been saying that. Yes." He smiled weakly at his cuff.

"Grand-Pierre says I'm *lucky* to have been born in Vietnam, and to look different from everyone else in this valley."

"And why would that be? Because the rest of us are so ugly?"

"He says that since I look different, gossips don't need to say I was adopted; my eyes show it. No whispers are necessary."

Monsieur Klein said nothing to this.

"My 'slanted eyes,' as the nastier gossips like to say."

Monsieur Klein winced as if I'd slapped myself, then fiddled some more with his cuff. "And have you been swimming lately, Zazoo?"

"Not today, no. Not in my winter coat." Finally, I remembered why I'd come calling. "Monsieur Klein, I have a question for you." I rocked the dark glasses, like a tiny toy boat, on the counter between us.

"Yes?" He crossed his arms.

"Did you work in this pharmacy during the war?"

"No, Zazoo." On hearing the word *war,* his face softened like the faces of so many old men—from sadness or fear, I couldn't tell which. "During the war I was too young to have a pill maker's degree. I was just twelve when we were invaded—even younger than you are now."

"But during the war you lived in this village?"

"During the early part of the war. Yes." He nodded down at the dark glasses. "For the rest of it, I went away."

"Grand-Pierre won't call it the war. He calls it the Awful Time."

"And he's right to do so. Has he told you what happened during the Awful Time?"

"Well, he started to, last night after supper. But when I asked a few questions, his only answer was that he used to *dance.*"

Monsieur Klein kept gazing at the dark glasses. "That's true." He paused, as if to be sure of what he said. "They danced and we all watched. They had a rare grace when they danced."

"The tango?"

"Yes, it was the tango they loved best."

"You said *they?*"

"They. Your Grand-Pierre and . . . So. He didn't tell you."

"No. He couldn't. You see, it started with an old game we used to play when I was little, about an owl that lives near the canal. But last night our game went in a different direction. He made it seem like during the Awful Time he was an owl himself, who danced the owl tango."

"The owl tango." Monsieur Klein's lips clamped together. "So. He can't say it."

"Something seems too terrible for him to tell me. Too awful. He said it might be weak of him, but he couldn't answer my questions, I'd have to ask 'elsewhere.' At the house of the green cross."

"I see." Monsieur Klein removed his glasses and rubbed his eyes. I had never seen him without his glasses, had never noticed how tired his eyes looked without them. "So he wants you to hear my version. He thinks that I, perhaps, am somehow less weak than he is?"

"He said it was cowardly of him, but he couldn't tell me more."

"A curious man, your Grand-Pierre." Monsieur Klein surveyed his display shelves of beauty aids, pain pills, foot products. "It's too bright in here."

"But this is a pharmacy, Monsieur Klein. It *should* be bright." I wanted to cheer his tired eyes. "And it smells so wonderfully clean!"

"Yes, I run a clean shop." He slid his glasses onto his nose, but now that I'd seen them off, I wouldn't forget how he looked without them. "Come, Zazoo."

"But—" I watched as he wrote a few words on a square of paper and taped it to the glass front door. Monsieur Klein, as far as I knew, had never closed his store in the daytime—except during lunch, like all the other shopkeepers of the village. "Where are we going?"

"Into the past, Zazoo, where things are not so neat and bright. Come."

He took my hand and led me through a small wooden door I had never noticed, half hidden by a display case of vitamins. As we stepped back into what he called the past, the clean smell of medicines fell away behind us, replaced by a cozier fragrance of fresh baking.

Monsieur Klein ushered me through a dim middle room, its walls lined with small paintings, into a kitchen that looked out on a backyard garden. He turned a light on above the small table, pulled back a chair for me, then filled the kettle and puffed the gas jet blue beneath it. He seemed in no hurry, even with his pharmacy unattended. On a pink plate he laid a circular pattern of star- and triangle-shaped cookies of a sort I'd never eaten.

"Gingerbread, Zazoo. Have as many as you please."

"I've never seen these at the bakery."

"The baker doesn't make them. I do. My mother taught me. And she taught my sister, Isabelle."

"I didn't know you had a sister, Monsieur Klein."

"That's because I don't, anymore. She's—well, she's gone.

And yet she's still here whenever I bake gingerbread. Memory, Zazoo. A most peculiar companion."

"Grand-Pierre says it's one of life's major riddles, memory. Your sister was named Isabelle?"

"Yes." He tapped the teapot with his fingertips. "And Isabelle was the one who danced the tango with Pierre." When the kettle began to sing, he poured the pot full and folded a cloth around it, as tenderly as if it were a baby. "Pierre sees many more riddles in life, now that he's old, than he did as a young tango dancer. Our tea will be ready in five minutes, Zazoo."

"Good. I have lots of time, lots of time."

"So have I." Monsieur Klein sounded almost sad to have so much time.

"But your shop, Monsieur. All your customers—"

"They have time, too, sweet girl. My note says for them to wait at the bakery."

"Isabelle," I repeated, reminding myself of slow-speaking Marius. "She had brown hair?"

"Dark, dark brown."

"And she danced the tango."

"It was their favorite, yes. Ah, Pierre. There was a time, you know, when his classmates didn't call him Grand-Pierre. Back when they were all very small children and didn't know who would grow up to be tall."

"But when he danced with Isabelle, he was already Grand-Pierre?"

"Certainly. By then he was in his late twenties and had long since stopped growing. Everyone else was much taller.

Yet Pierre was larger, in some quiet way, than they could ever be. And they knew it."

"Was Isabelle tall? Your sister?"

"A shade taller than Pierre. And rounder, of course. Softer." He poured tea into my cup, then passed me the sugar. "Isabelle." He held his cup in both hands, as if for warmth. "Isabelle was as different from Pierre as anyone could be. For one thing, she wasn't quiet—no one could have mistaken *her* for a stone."

"She laughed a lot?" I thought of Sylvie Tarvan with her constant silly laughter.

"Yes, she laughed. But not the way some of these girls do." Monsieur Klein seemed to be guessing my thoughts. "She laughed often, Isabelle—with a sort of twinkle that made you feel good to hear it." He set his cup onto its saucer. "Like an angel, she laughed. But that may be something I decided later."

"How else was she different from Grand-Pierre?"

"Oh, many ways. She made stars differently."

"Stars?" I peered across the table at him. "You mean stars on paper?"

"On paper, yes. And on other things."

"Stars on cookies?" I held up a gingerbread star I was ready to bite into.

"Cookies and . . . other things," whispered Monsieur Klein. "How many points does that star of yours have, Zazoo?"

"Five?" I guessed, and counted. "Yes. Five."

"Five points. Just cookie dough, baked in an oven. Gingerbread, like in *Hansel and Gretel*. But look at the star I'm making now." Taking two triangular cookies, he laid one on top of the other to make a new star. "Six points, this one has."

"Yes," I said. "Pretty."

"For some people this star with six points is, in fact, the prettiest shape on earth. And for others, as difficult as this is to explain—for others, a six-pointed star is so ugly they can't stand to look at it. Tell me again, what does Grand-Pierre call the war?"

"The Awful Time." My cookie tasted wonderful, yet stuck to the roof of my mouth. I stared at the other cookies and smelled their spicy scent.

Monsieur Klein took his star apart, laid its triangles side by side, and regarded them for a long moment before popping one into his mouth. He sipped some tea. "During the Awful Time in this valley, some of us were forced to wear stars on our chests. Yellow stars, with six points."

The doorbell to the pharmacy jingled faintly, jingled again, and went silent. When it jingled yet again, the sound seemed to come from a great distance. Monsieur Klein, gazing at the cookies on his pink plate, gave no sign of hearing.

"Then—you and your family were Jewish?"

"Yes," he said quietly. "And to us the six-sided star was a symbol of something sweet and good. We called it the Star of David, or the Shield of David. It was the sign we put on our graves in the cemetery."

"Because you were Jewish?"

"Yes." The second triangle disappeared into his mouth.

I picked a new one from the plate, set another onto it, and studied the design.

Monsieur Klein watched me. "Is your tea cold, Zazoo?"

"Doesn't matter."

"Please. Let me warm it for you." Gently he unwrapped the teapot and lifted it toward my cup.

"Did they kill her? Your sister Isabelle, who danced the tango?"

Monsieur Klein set the teapot down.

"*Did* they?"

He gazed blankly around the kitchen as if he couldn't recall how he had come to be there. His voice, when he finally spoke, was very faint. "Pierre told us we should leave the valley. He had the best nose of anyone for . . . blood. And he knew. As soon as they made my family wear those yellow stars, Pierre smelled death and told us we had to leave."

"He wasn't leaving himself?"

"He wore no Star of David," said Monsieur Klein, his voice louder. "We were the only Jewish family in this village, Zazoo—we alone wore yellow stars. His star was the safe kind, the kind with five points. As safe as gingerbread."

"The Christian star," I whispered, "that hung over the cradle where Jesus was born?"

"Something like that."

"Grand-Pierre doesn't go to church," I went on, rather than ask the question I dreaded having answered. "And neither

I, since he doesn't. But everyone knows about the Christian ar hanging over Bethlehem."

Monsieur Klein didn't lift his face from studying the triangular cookies on their sparkling pink plate.

"They *killed* her?" I blurted.

He pulled his eyes up to meet mine. "They killed her. Yes."

The clock ticked and tocked on the wall beside us, ticked and tocked again. "But, Monsieur Klein, why *didn't* you leave?"

Glancing around the kitchen, he shrugged. "Because this was home. We were French people, Zazoo, we knew only this place. True, there were rumors of terrible things happening, but we didn't know what to believe. This was France, birthplace of Rousseau and Victor Hugo, who wrote that we should believe in human goodness. We told ourselves that whatever happened in Poland or Germany couldn't, surely *couldn't* happen in our valley."

"But where did Grand-Pierre want you to go? To England?"

"Only to the Cévennes Mountains, southwest of here. A few hours by train, although we couldn't have gone anywhere by train with yellow stars on our coats. But Pierre said he knew the way and would guide us—we could walk at night and hide in the daytime. He was a skillful hunter and knew the country well, and had, as I say, a delicate nose for danger. Yet this was our home. We couldn't leave."

"If you had left, who would have helped you in the Cévennes Mountains?"

"Some farmers, Pierre said, whom he

They would hide us until the Awful Time end

like him—"

"Grand-Pierre, you didn't like?" Monsieur Klein

it so casually. I had never heard anyone, ever, claim not to

Grand-Pierre. "But why not?"

"He seemed so *old* for my only sister to love. Remember, I was just eleven when war broke out. Pierre was in his late twenties, but was already bald, and looked like such a tiny old man—except when he danced. When *they* danced. And they did love to tango, those two, any chance they got. As if they knew there was little time left."

My tea was cold, but I didn't ask for more. "And where did they dance?"

"At the village cinema. In those days, the seats weren't bolted to the floor as they are now. There were benches. On Saturdays, after the movie, we carried the benches out, then went back inside and danced."

"Even you, Monsieur Klein? When you were twelve?" I wanted to help him smile.

"Even me." His voice dropped. "With Isabelle. *I* loved her, too."

"Of *course* you did."

"A most patient teacher, she was. I remember her teaching me to waltz. But mostly she danced with Pierre. And they did move wonderfully. Old Bonnier played the accordion, and the grocer Pepin played gypsy-style violin. They're all dead now, of course. Have been for years."

His face was too sad to watch; I stared at my cup of cold tea.

"All dead." Monsieur Klein rose from his chair. "But I should get back to my shop. Those fine ladies and gentlemen are waiting at the bakery, eager to buy more allergy pills, headache pills—"

"No," I said, surprising myself. "You have to tell me how they killed her. And, and—*why*."

Standing behind his wooden chair, Monsieur Klein grasped the rim of its back in both hands. "The why, Zazoo, would be impossible for any man to explain—any man with a heart. Impossible. They hated her. They hated, for some reason, all four of us. They thought we wanted only to mumble Hebrew prayers and take their money, or so they said. Hah! In our family we scarcely knew any prayers—and our language was French! But that didn't matter, they hated us anyway. As for the *how,* Zazoo, they didn't do it nicely—as if there could be a nice way of killing such a sweet-natured girl."

"I've heard terrible things before, Monsieur Klein. In school they've taught us all about the war. The most awful things—"

"They've taught you"—he smiled strangely—"*all* about the war?"

"Well, yes. I mean, the concentration camps in Germany—"

"That's fine." His tone was calm. "But have they taught you about the barbarities right here in this valley? Between Frenchman and Frenchman?"

I didn't know what to say. Some very bad things had been described at school, but I didn't recall hearing "barbarities" blamed on anyone except German Nazis.

"At school," he went on softly, "I suppose they mentioned some few French citizens who spied for the Germans?"

"Yes, Monsieur—"

"And I suppose these French turncoats were called *collaborationists,* a polite word for traitors?" He gripped the chair so hard his knuckles stretched tight.

"Yes, Monsieur Klein, we were told about collabor—"

"But Zazoo," he said without raising his voice, "were you told how *many* such spies and Jew haters there were, during the war, even in our peaceful valley? Even in our peaceful *village?*"

"No, Monsieur. I don't think they taught us that part."

"They couldn't, Zazoo. It strikes too close. Even now, such a long time after the war." His hand trembled on the chair back. "Even family members can't talk about it. An Awful Time indeed." The breath came raggedly from Monsieur Klein, as if something inside him were torn. "You ask me how she was killed, my sister, Isabelle." He stared out the kitchen window at the bare branches. "You need to know, really, how she was killed?"

Clutching my cold arms, I nodded.

"Well, then. How can I describe such a thing? How can I—" He struck the top of his chair once, and then again. "There is no way of saying it. No decent way." He forced his eyes back to mine. "They hanged her, Zazoo. With a rope. From a lamppost."

He said it so simply, my mouth sagged open. I held my cold arms over my stomach.

"They hanged her in a public place—I won't tell you where. It's somewhere you know and like, and to tell you would only ruin the place for you, as it has for me. But they strung a rope over a lamppost that has since been removed—I helped remove it myself, after the war. They tied the rope around her neck"—his voice wavered but he forced it to go on—"and yanked her up off the ground and left her there, gasping, until she suffocated. With a yellow Star of David stitched to her coat. *That* was how they killed her, on a day as cold as today." His shoulders slumped in their white jacket. "And once they knew what length of rope to cut, they hanged my mother as well. And then my father."

The air sucked itself from my chest. I could only stare at him. He leaned closer, and placed his trembling hand on mine, and didn't cry. I didn't cry either; I couldn't. My insides had turned to dust.

"Your whole family?"

Monsieur Klein tried to smile. "So your friend Juliette," he whispered, "is not the only orphan this village can gossip about. And neither were you, Zazoo, when you joined us. The Awful Time made me an orphan, too."

"You were eleven?"

"I turned twelve the month the Germans invaded France. But when Isabelle was killed—and our parents—I was thirteen, not quite fourteen. Your age, no?"

"Yes, Monsieur." Birds, I noticed, were singing outside the kitchen window. It didn't seem possible for any bird to be singing anywhere.

"Pierre got to me in time, or I'd have been hanged with the others. I was playing soccer when my parents and sister were killed. Playing soccer. Alone." His voice sounded dead. "Pierre was more clever than the Germans. As soon as he realized what they were doing, he crept away from his hiding place across the canal from your mill, then raced to find me on my way home from the soccer field. You see, the Germans hadn't allowed me to attend school, but they didn't stop me from practicing soccer if I did it alone, not with Christian boys. I was two minutes from this house when Pierre called to me from the woods by the Plowman's Spring—you know the place, above the footbridge? He said the Gestapo had taken Isabelle and our parents. I hope they've taught you this word *Gestapo* at school."

"Yes, Monsieur. The German secret police?"

"Correct. The Gestapo—who had made us sew yellow stars on our coats, and then complimented our tailoring." Monsieur Klein's voice fell into a steady drone. "Pierre guided me from the valley. It was broad daylight, and we were lucky not to be seen. But it wasn't just luck. He was clever at blending into the fields. He found some blankets he had hidden, and a bit of food. Then we headed south. Night after night after night. Daytimes we lay in hedgerows and hoped no dog would find us. At night we walked—for eighteen nights, southwest to the Cévennes Mountains. All I remember was my lack of socks, even after he gave me another pair. Such cold toes. But my family was gone—I didn't care if I lost my toes or anything else." His chair, when he leaned onto it, creaked so loudly it made him flinch. "But Zazoo, I should go back to my pill poppers; they think they need me. So now you've been to the house of the green cross, as Pierre recommended."

"Was he a—coward, Monsieur Klein?"

"Oh, most people wouldn't say so. They'd say Pierre was an inspiration to our underground army, the Resistance. A great . . . inspiration."

"But I mean was he a coward *yesterday,* Monsieur Klein, for sending me here? He said—"

"That's hard to judge, Zazoo. Maybe he couldn't tell you about it but thought somehow I could. And now I have. A shameful time, it was—with all sorts of Frenchmen accusing each other of being cowards. Who can say?" He paused, as if listening to the birds outside. "But yes, it was cowardly of him to send you here. Although quite natural. We're all cowards, one time or another."

"He sent me," I whispered, "to learn about his owl girl, Isabelle."

"Well, yes."

"Your sister."

For a long moment Monsieur Klein didn't speak. When he did, his tone seemed as much puzzled as angry. "And all because of Pierre's vanity. His terrible pride."

"You mean because he danced well?"

"Not his dancing, Zazoo. You say he referred to himself as an owl—" Monsieur Klein grimaced as if the word gave his mouth a bad taste.

"But that was just a game. Did he say something wrong?"

"The owl tango," said Monsieur Klein with a sour twist. "Fine. But he didn't tell you what else this owl did? Besides dance?"

"I don't think so. No."

"This owl," said Monsieur Klein, "was not a cuddly puffball hooting in the night. Ask your Grand-Pierre about his eyes, Zazoo. His *owl* eyes. I suppose it's nice for you to know about the dancing. The dancing was beautiful. But ask Pierre about his *eyes* as well. And don't let him say he can't remember."

Even in the warm kitchen, I was overcome with shivering.

"His eyes and his hand, Zazoo, his steady hand. He can't expect me to tell you everything. Ask."

Monsieur Klein stepped around his chair, took my arm, and led me through the inner room with its scent of freshly cut wood. So many paintings lined the walls, each in its own wooden frame; I wanted to stop and inspect them. I couldn't bear to leave him alone in that house. But when Monsieur Klein asked if I would be kind enough to tell the people at the bakery that he was open again, they could come and buy their pills, I said of course I would, and left him standing at his front door beside the electric green cross.

13. The Dark Valley

Flakes of snow brushed ghostly around me as I walked home. They clung to the top sides of branches and fluttered against my lashes and failed to do their usual job of helping me feel cozy in the world. No, they whispered, the world was in mourning, and not only for Monsieur Klein's sister and parents. For my parents as well.

Mama go boom? asked a little girl deep in the back of my mind.

I didn't think of my dead parents very often. But learning of Monsieur Klein's loss, and feeling hollow for him, made me feel hollow for myself. I didn't remember my parents—why should I? My home was this French village with its canal, its river, its sad snowy ghosts.

And even though I knew Grand-Pierre would worry when I didn't arrive for supper, I needed to be out in my boat. Ice patches had spread, day by day, along the canal, but the river was still free of all but a shoreline skimming here and there. I needed to feel the river flowing around me.

It was good I had on a thick coat or I couldn't have let myself try it, however sad I felt. But my boots were strong, the mittens Grand-Pierre had knitted for me were layered and warm. I slid the bow of my punt down the bank, through the rushes and thin-crunching ice, then pushed off and stepped aboard in the smooth dry motion Grand-Pierre had taught me.

Up the river I rowed, by the light of the shrouded moon and the dim, distant streetlamps. Stroke after stroke, bending my back, glad to be pulling, pulling, bending my legs and pulling again with my mittened hands until I was warm top to toe except in some darker place I supposed must be my heart.

Since a rower sits facing the stern, it was good I knew the river's shallows and angles, the twists where its current was tricky. The moon was so wrapped in snowy clouds that I saw only vague shapes, and steered from old habit. Rowing was fine in the dark, in the falling snow. My boat didn't whisper hero or coward, Gestapo or Vietnam. It didn't whisper at all, only groaned with the pull of its oars.

I left the triple-arched bridge in my wake, then the Long Bridge, then the Pebble Shallows—kilometer after upstream kilometer, all the way to the Haunted Hill Dam. Then, glad to have worn myself out, I let the current take me, with only the creak of my steadying oars, back downstream toward home.

Papa go boom? asked the same baby voice, wistful and faint in the darkness.

Had my father or mother, I wondered, ever drifted like this down some moonlit river in Vietnam? And why had I never wondered such a thing before? The snow glided around me like frozen tears.

Watching dark silhouettes slip past, I wondered who lived where in the world and how the dead had died. When the wind chilled me, I bent again to my oars. The clouds parted, the snowfall stopped, and the half moon peeked out. I wished I could look up from the current and see my gray cat padding along the riverbank. But he felt very far away.

14. *The Mill of a Thousand Names*

I glared down at Grand-Pierre in his kitchen chair. "No, I *don't* feel like eating. Not warmed-up stew, not beets or potatoes. If you had seen Monsieur Klein's pain—"

"I have seen."

I stared into the old man's eyes and wondered how clear his head might be.

"I should have told you myself," he said.

"Yes, you should have. Why send me to that poor man?" I felt too worn out to cry. "That man, who lost everything. Parents, sister—"

"We've all had losses." Grand-Pierre's voice sounded dead. He didn't pop his lips at the corner of his mouth; he just sat in his chair looking old. "I should have told you. *Meant* to. But a year went by, then another. I waited for the right time. But the time was never right for you to hear about such . . . awful things."

"But Grand-Pierre, *you* didn't do awful things!" Unable to stay angry when he looked so beaten, I sank to the floor and held his hand against my cheek. I had to ask but was terrified of what I might learn. "You *couldn't* have done awful things. You were the hero of our valley. My teachers say you inspired the Resistance with your—"

"Hero," he broke in. "I told you, that's just a word for idiots. I was stupid like all the rest—my only excuse was, I went out of my mind. When the Germans killed her, it all got jumbled in my head. Things were awful and I made them worse, not better. Yes, I did awful things. If that's what Félix tells you, he's right."

"His name is *Félix?*" I had heard the first name of almost every adult in our village, but never that Monsieur Klein was called Félix. Perhaps it was a sign of how stiff and proper the villagers took him to be that no one, even adults, called him by his given name.

"Yes, Zazoo. His name is Félix." Grand-Pierre sighed a deep, groaning sigh. "Maybe you should call him Uncle Félix, as a sort of kindness to him and me both."

"But he isn't—I mean, he wouldn't have been— Did you ever *marry* her? His sister Isabelle?"

"There wasn't time. And her parents were against it. Félix was against it, too."

"I know." I nuzzled Grand-Pierre's hand with my cheek. "He says he didn't like you, that you and his sister danced too beautifully together, it made him jealous."

"Félix said this?"

"In different words, but yes, he did. Do you think he'd *like* it if I called him Uncle Félix?" It was easier to discuss Monsieur Klein than to hear what awful things Grand-Pierre might have done.

"He's a lonely man." Grand-Pierre paused, as if to untangle his thoughts. "I'm sure he'd love for you to call him your uncle. A fine man. A man of fine breeding."

"Fine Jewish breeding."

"And," said Grand-Pierre sharply, "is something wrong with that?"

"Of course not—except that the Germans killed her because of it. Had *they* seen you dance the owl tango with her?" I held my face against the soft weave of his old jacket. It was more tolerable to hear such things if I didn't have to look into his eyes. "Were they jealous of you and your brown-haired owl girl?"

"Perhaps." He shrugged against my cheek. "Yes, perhaps they were. I can still feel how it was to dance with her. My owl girl, as you say."

"Monsieur Klein," I whispered, "said you weren't like an owl in your dancing only. He said I should ask about your eyes." I twisted around to look up at him.

"My eyes?" Grand-Pierre squinted behind his glasses.

"Something about your owl eyes, he said. And the steadiness of your hand."

"Ah." Grand-Pierre sagged in his chair. "The steadiness of my shooting. I see what he means."

"Your *shooting? Shooting* a *gun?*" Never, not once, had I heard Grand-Pierre mention guns.

"Yes. My shooting." He let out a long deep breath. "Félix has a point. It's time I told you about my . . . marksmanship." Suddenly he was breathing as hard as if he had climbed a high hill. "But first, Zazoo, please promise not to hate me."

"Grand-Pierre!" It was a shock to feel him needing comfort from me; he had always been *my* comfort. My rock.

Shaking free of me, he crossed the kitchen and fed sticks to the woodstove, then sat down beside it, as if to face me from a safer distance. "I wear glasses now."

"You always have."

"Not always. Not when I was your age and had eyes like—well, eyes like an owl. I saw things no one else knew about, they were so far away."

"And your hands?"

"My hands were . . . steady. Yes. As Félix says." He held them out, palms down; they quivered and jumped and wouldn't hold still. He watched them as he might have watched two misbehaving children. "My hands, when I was young, were as steady as—well, as steady as stone. And my brain wasn't so bad, either. It had a special sense that told me exactly how far a breeze would push a bullet to one side or the other."

"A bullet?" I had never heard him discuss such things.

"In the air, a bullet fired from a rifle." He spoke flatly, as if reading from an instruction book. "Marksmanship is not just a question of holding the rifle steady and sighting down the barrel, Zazoo. There's a mental part no stone can perform. A part that senses how far to the left or right the wind will drift a bullet, and how far gravity will sink a bullet, before it hits the target."

"What target?" I asked, my stomach heavy as iron. *Please,* I added silently, *don't tell me you shot people.*

His eyes darted away from mine. "I didn't shoot the German lieutenant."

"German—lieutenant?" *Please. Soldiers, maybe, but not normal people.* "You've never told me anything about a lieutenant."

"All I did was enter shooting contests. Between our village

and other villages. And when I won them, I puffed myself up. Pride was my sin. Pride. But that was enough to get the lieutenant upset."

"What German lieutenant?"

"Oh, he was part of the occupying army. An excellent shot himself—and just as puffed up as I was. He didn't want any little Frenchman shooting better than he did. When he heard about me, he organized a special contest to settle the question. This was in 1942, halfway through the war. The Germans had a garrison here—near your school—but the village was peaceful. No one had been killed here, on either side." He frowned at me from where he sat beside the woodstove. "I was thirty. The lieutenant was younger. Tall and strong, with enormous hands. I must have looked like an old man beside him. Bald already, but still free of glasses. Eyes as sharp as anybody's. Sharp eyes, sharp brain. But too much pride."

"What sort of . . . targets?" Outside, the wind howled along the canal; I imagined some last few oak leaves clinging to their limbs. "Paper targets?"

"Bottles. The lieutenant said his greatest joy came from blasting bottles to bits. So we took turns on the same rifle—a Swiss repeater he owned—exploding one bottle after another. On a dark, gusty day like today, the wind sweeping left to right. We started at easy range—two hundred meters—then shot from farther and farther, using smaller bottles, until no one could see them except the lieutenant, who had sharp eyes—and I, of course. I saw them. If only I had let him win—"

"Isabelle would be alive today?"

"Possibly." The wind rattled a loose pane in the window. "And others. Did Félix mention their father and mother?"

"Yes. He said they were—hanged, too."

Smiling frightfully, Grand-Pierre rapped his knuckles against the oven door. "Her parents were wonderful people."

"But they didn't want you to marry her."

"That doesn't mean they weren't wonderful people. So jolly and kind."

"Jolly? Monsieur Klein's parents?" A fresh gust rattled the loose window.

"Yes, Zazoo. I should have let the lieutenant win. Should have gone off to the hills and knitted socks."

"Just because you broke more bottles, he killed Isabelle and her parents?"

Grand-Pierre's shoulders twitched. "Losing the contest turned the lieutenant meaner, even to his own men. His pride was so hurt he punished everyone around him—made his platoon march up and down the village, made the Klein family wear yellow stars—*and* he announced that Isabelle could no longer dance. I should have let him win."

"But surely there was no harm in dancing—"

"He posted a rule that prohibited Jews from dancing in public. Later, he banned his troops from dancing with any French girls, Jewish or not."

"Then his men must not have liked him."

"Hated him. So did the local people. He mistreated everyone. Made fun of the priest, the Mayor—and me, naturally."

"Just for breaking more bottles with bullets?" Shaking my head, I rose from the floor and settled into a chair facing Grand-Pierre.

"Yes, and for dancing with Isabelle. He ordered me to post a sign out here on the terrace." Grand-Pierre nodded toward the lock. "On this sign I was to declare, in huge letters, that I would never dance with a Jew again."

"And," I whispered, "did you put up such a sign?"

"Perhaps I should have." Grand-Pierre listened to the trembling pane of glass. "After all, it would have been only words. But my pride was as great as his, so I had to disobey him. At the spot where he wanted his sign, I left him a river stone. A round blue river stone instead of a pledge not to dance with Jews."

"Which must have made him angry."

"Furious. He sent men to arrest me, but by then I had gone into hiding—south of here, in the hills. I asked Isabelle and her parents to join me—and Félix, who was still a boy. But they wouldn't leave."

"He told me. You were going to lead them to the Cévennes Mountains."

"Their only sin was to be Jewish. They said they would stay." Grand-Pierre gripped his knees to stop their shaking.

"But didn't Isabelle want to join you? In the hills?"

"Her parents wouldn't let her. And then it happened."

I waited. Outside, the wind tore through the miserable treetops.

"Someone," said Grand-Pierre, "perhaps a villager, perhaps one of his own soldiers, shot the lieutenant. Shot him dead. Two weeks after I left."

"But it wasn't you, Grand-Pierre?"

Eyes closed, he shook his head. "I was far away. Far away."

"Then who *did* shoot him?"

"No one knows. A doctor who examined the body said the bullet came from a German army rifle. The German colonel who commanded our valley claimed I must have stolen an army rifle and used it. There was even a rumor that a German soldier, disgusted by the lieutenant's behavior, had shot him. Lots of rumors. No one knew then, no one knows today, who killed the lieutenant. But the colonel was certain I had done it. If I gave myself up, he announced, no one else would be hurt."

"But you hadn't done it!"

"No." Grand-Pierre smiled a ghastly half-smile.

I didn't want to hear more but had to ask. "Then—you didn't turn yourself in?"

He pried his hands free of his knees. "Later, I *wished* I had, but who could have guessed that the colonel would—would—"

"No one could have guessed, Grand-Pierre."

"And who could have guessed where." His face shuddered; his shoulders yanked upward as if they had been given an electric shock. At last, his trembling went still and he frowned down at his feet, so tiny in their worn slippers.

"Did he hang them near here?" My heart felt sick.

"*Near* here?" Grand-Pierre gazed at the window but

couldn't see outside any better than I could; all either of us saw was our own pathetic faces staring back at us. "Very near, Zazoo. They were hanged—very near. Exactly where I'd left the river stone. My message for the lieutenant."

"On our *terrace?*"

Grand-Pierre hunched forward, head over his knees, arms clamping his ribs.

"Were there lampposts," I whispered, "on our terrace? In front of our mill?"

"Just one. But one was enough. So. Félix mentioned the lamppost."

"He didn't say where it was, just that it was in a place I loved, and he didn't want to make me hate it. He said he removed it after the war."

"That's right. And I helped him." The stove roared as the wind whooshed down our chimney. "He despised me—wouldn't so much as look at me—but he let me help take down the lamppost."

"Why should he despise you? You saved his life!"

Grand-Pierre let out a hollow, coughing laugh. "That's one way of seeing things. But Félix believed I had killed his family—by beating the lieutenant at shooting bottles, and then by not giving myself up to be executed."

"Ah." I felt as if I had swallowed wave after wave of poisonous smoke; I wanted to throw the windows open but couldn't budge from my chair. "Did you stay in the Cévennes Mountains with Monsieur Klein?"

"He told me to leave, and I couldn't blame him. In a way,

I had to agree that my pride had killed Isabelle and the others, even if I hadn't shot the lieutenant. But by then I was so bitter I didn't care. About myself, about anything. So I came back here and lived in the hills, and for more than two years—the rest of the war—I preyed on the Germans in our valley. Like an owl, truly. A wounded, careless owl."

"And that's why people call you a hero? Because you were good at being—an owl?"

"I suppose so. Mindless, stupid revenge."

"Oh, Grand-Pierre! So the owl flew down from the hills and killed—mice? Mice in uniforms?"

His voice was so soft I could scarcely hear it. "First, I waited for a soldier who carried the type of rifle I needed. Then I waited for the colonel to leave his garrison—that timbered building across from your school. Cloudy day. Almost no wind. I needed one bullet to drop him and another to finish him."

"The *owl* did."

"No, Zazoo." Grand-Pierre's face beside the woodstove was gray with fatigue. "Let's be clear on this. I was not an owl, and the colonel was not a mouse. We were men, both of us. Ridiculous men."

"He killed Isabelle and her parents." I couldn't stay across the kitchen from Grand-Pierre. He looked so forlorn, I had to cross the tiled floor and throw my arms around his frail shoulders. "He *killed* them!"

"Yes. And then I killed him. But that didn't make me a hero. Do you understand? Only a fool, Zazoo. Only a fool."

I sobbed down the front of his jacket. He crooned to me,

my sad old man and the only hero I had, in the kitchen of my only home, the Mill of a Thousand Years, the Mill of a Thousand Tears.

15. London Bridge

Weeks went by. When the ice closed across the canal, Monsieur Trottoir, our school principal, thundered his annual tale of woe about the boy who went skating too soon and ended up a statistic, drowning a horrible death as he clutched for the twig ends of willow branches. Some sarcastic girls snickered it wasn't a tragedy if only boys drowned—old Trottoir never warned *girls* not to die from taking risks.

No one but me skated much anyway. I mean really *skated,* up and down the canal, as Grand-Pierre had taught me to do. Some winters a few of my classmates skated dainty swirls beneath the Long Bridge, in the heart of the village, but they never went far enough to learn the muscular *glide* of it.

The frosty towpath mocked me, reminding me of Marius and suggesting I would never hear from him again. The Pharmacy Mail Service seemed to have broken down. I wondered if my poem had reached him, and wondered if I would ever have more than my one friend, Juliette—and when I thought of her, I wondered when the right moment would come to ask if she truly was adopted, as Madame Blowhard Meunier had claimed.

Then a new terror arrived, faint at first but soon worse—

an ache in my chest so strange I couldn't speak of it to anyone. It didn't make me cough, like the women in those Russian movies who spit up blood and move to Switzerland but die anyway, far from their goony lovers. Still, it hurt. But I was too worried about Grand-Pierre, who had grown silent since our talk, to burden him with any problems of my own.

It seemed small-minded to ask a doctor about this ache in my chest. Lately, *everything* seemed small-minded. Even the image of reckless boys drowning in the canal seemed mild compared to my new constant companion, a brown-haired girl dangling from a lamppost. Hadn't the drowning boy died of his own stupidity? Isabelle Klein was entirely different. Why had she died?

I sat by my tower window and looked down at our terrace, wondering where the lamppost had stood. I asked the darkness how anyone could pin a yellow star on some eighteen-year-old girl and choke her to death for—what? For being too pretty? For dancing too well? There was no reason to kill such a girl. And to force her parents to watch, and then hang them, too? From my window I stared down at the frozen corpses dangling together, turning in the wind.

So it made me feel selfish and small to worry about the ache in my chest or to admit that I yearned for more news from Marius in Paris. But what could I do? How could I tell part of my mind not to wish for happiness? How could I tell it to blot happiness out and let in only misery? In school, in my room, wherever I went, all I felt was confusion. I told myself I should feel grateful not to be drowning in the canal and not to be choking from a rough-twisting rope, and yet—as shameful as it felt—I couldn't help stopping in at the pharmacy to see if there might be another postcard from Paris.

It was hard to traipse through Monsieur Klein's door as if the world were the same as it had been a few days earlier. It was hard trying to greet him without staring at his eyes behind their silver frames and seeing the eyes of a thirteen-year-old boy, my age exactly, a sad lonely orphan of war.

"Hello, Zazoo," he said, not a boy but a gray-haired pharmacist. "You look so sad today."

"I'm sad every day, Monsieur. Nothing's the same."

Bending slightly at the waist, he peered closer at me, and it wasn't too bad until he tried smiling, which was so very sad it made me burst into tears.

"No, Zazoo. You're right. Nothing can possibly be the same once you've looked into hell." He made his hands busy adjusting his bow tie, then his glasses. "But we must try just the same. The weather is fine?"

"Weather," I repeated, as if it were a foreign word.

"The air is clear, the breeze is fresh?"

"I suppose so, Monsieur Klein. Yes." I tried a smile of my own. "You're a brave man."

"Ah?" He shrugged. "I don't know—we live one day and then we live the next. Sometimes it doesn't seem possible, but we do."

"To work here in this store, in this same village where it happened—how can you bear it? Living in the same house where you lived with them—"

"It's my home. We take the bitter with the sweet." His eyes softened. "Speaking of which, I have some sweet for you, Zazoo. No letter, I'm afraid—"

"That's all right, Monsieur." I couldn't admit that although the world was so bleak I didn't deserve a letter, I wanted one anyway.

"No letter," he repeated, smiling. "Just another postcard. Yes, from Paris." He drew the card from beneath his cash drawer and handed it across the counter—a gorgeous little painting, a city-and-river scene of wide green water spanned by a many-arched bridge. All done in red and gold, with an orange-red sky in the background. "For the second time, your friend shows admirable taste. This picture by André Derain dates from 1905 or 1906. An amazing work." He gazed across the counter. "Can't speak?"

"I can speak, Monsieur. It's just that I walked in here so filled with pain—your sister, Grand-Pierre, the war—and then you hand me this beautiful card and I'm flooded with—with—"

"With joy, perhaps?"

"With joy, Monsieur Klein. Yes. But also such sadness. Sadness and joy all at once. How can it be possible?"

"As I said, Zazoo, a cliché but nonetheless true: we must accept the bitter with the sweet." He rocked back on his heels. "Perhaps your young bird watcher sends you a message along with this painting of the London Bridge?"

"I'm too excited to read, Monsieur. Too happy, and, at the same time, too sad. It's hard to explain."

"Certainly. And perhaps you'd rather not read it here?"

"Maybe not, no. Maybe along the canal—"

"Where you met him. Yes, that sounds like the place."

I felt like hugging Monsieur Klein, but couldn't manage it. I felt like saying Grand-Pierre had suggested I call him Uncle Félix, but was too shy for that as well. All I could do was thank him, and thank him again, and make my way out the jingling door into the street.

When I reached the towpath and found a good place beneath the sycamores, I was pleased to see how tiny Marius had made his words, fitting as many as possible into his small rectangle of space.

Dear Zazoo, A thought that strikes me when I walk beside the River Seine here in Paris—or study this painting of a river in London—is that the same water flowing beneath those bridges flows beneath your stone bridge, too. And this thought of water leads to thoughts of swimming, and to thoughts of who swims most gracefully and why. It seems the loveliest swimmers <u>splash</u> less by elegantly pointing their feet when they disappear into the water. Remember when you swam under the canal that morning, rising just enough for me to catch a glimpse of your feet, then pulling them down out of sight? You pointed your toes so perfectly they made no splash at all. Did someone teach you, or—as I suspect—did you learn from watching the fish? As for me, there's something I must tell you. When I was seven, an illness kept me home all year. I was cared for by my grandmother, who was better at *dealing with a sick boy than my parents were. But more on this later. Out of room.*

Your friend, Marius

Wonder of wonders.

What else could I think of, all through my school day? What else could I read, over and over, pretending it was a binomial equation or a biology chart? What else could I write in my notebook but my careful reply?

But I needed a suitable card on which to copy out my message. I didn't go to the tobacco shop, with its postcard photos of tourists holding strings of fish. I went back to Monsieur Klein's pharmacy.

He wasn't surprised. "Mademoiselle Zazoo—I've been expecting you. You've grown more curious about modern art, perhaps?"

"All sorts of art, Monsieur. I loved your photo of the purple heron, as I'm sure our bird watcher did—but do you have any cards in that drawer of yours that include, you know—"

"Reproductions of dazzling paintings?"

"Exactly, Monsieur. *Dazzling,* like that dreamy painting he sent me, with the white Eiffel Tower in its orange-brown sky."

Monsieur Klein chuckled with pleasure. "Yes, I thought another Chagall might appeal to you. Just last night, I rummaged among my dusty postcard masterpieces—to set up, shall we say, a tiny art gallery here under my cash drawer. And in my search I came across two Chagalls, both gems. One is perhaps too gloomy for your purpose, more appropriate for me to keep. Here it is—*The Cemetery Gates,* which Chagall painted during the First World War. I thought it might interest you, since we were discussing the Star of David you see here at the center of the gate—above this writing in Hebrew—"

"A lovely painting." I worked hard to keep my voice cheery, but couldn't look at the Star of David without thinking of his family. "These folded chunks of blue in the sky—they look like a storm coming. But it's such a *sad* painting, Monsieur! Does everything Jewish have to be sad?"

"Then take a look at this one, Zazoo. Slightly less sad. A man playing the violin—"

"On a roof ! Is he in the sky, too, like the Eiffel Tower on my wall? Oh, I like this one, Monsieur, may I send it to Marius? It's sure to make him smile."

"With my blessing, take it. I'll explore my archive for others. You're a good influence, Zazoo, you remind me to think of pleasant things."

"Marius is the good influence." I felt myself smiling. "He, after all, sent us his shimmering Eiffel Tower."

"Then please thank him for me, too, when you write." Seeing me dig in my pocket for money, Monsieur Klein held up his hand. "Not a franc. Sending the boy my gratitude is payment enough. When you said he was a bird watcher, I *knew* he must be all right. Encourage him to visit my pharmacy whenever he chooses—we can discuss birds, and floating fiddlers, and the miracles of modern art."

"I'll tell him, Monsieur. If I have room on the card."

Marius—As you can guess, your saying that my feet don't splash has made me walk the school halls with my nose very high. But more seriously, your card arrived at a time of great sadness to me. (Things I've learned about the war, and my grandfather, and Monsieur Klein and his family.) You've done more than you could ever have guessed to help me feel better. Thank you. Monsieur Klein, by the way, praises your choice of art and invites you to visit his pharmacy. He helped me pick out this painting by your same Russian magician Marc Chagall. I'd love to meet your grandmother. She must be very kind—I'd like to know what she looks like, how her voice sounds, how she laughs. Does she have a name? Stay warm in Paris— *Zazoo*

The postcard, with its half-sad, half-happy rooftop fiddler, slid into the postbox to make its way to Paris. Walking the towpath back to the mill, I saw the kindly eyes of Marius, who had been ill as a child but now rode his dusty bicycle and watched for birds and called himself my friend. His face was as real as my gray cat, who silently walked the path behind me, just out of sight but close now, close, ready to reappear.

16. The Empty Cup

The first Saturday night of that cold December, Juliette stayed with us at the mill. On Sunday morning, when I heard Grand-Pierre lighting the stove in the kitchen—a sound I had trained myself to listen for even in my sleep—I crept from bed, taking care not to awaken Juliette.

From the way Grand-Pierre sat inspecting the coffee pot, I guessed it wouldn't be one of our better mornings.

"Not starting with tea today?" I asked softly. "Having coffee with our oatmeal?"

"Why—yes." He blinked at me. "Coffee."

"Here, let me help with the filter." He had, in fact, forgotten the filter, and was set to pour boiling water onto the coffee in the bare funnel, producing the same grainy mess he had made two days earlier. "So many things to remember."

"It's these newfangled gadgets," he said.

"I know, Grand-Pierre." For years, the Old Stone had been making coffee with those same filters. "Now let's measure out our oatmeal."

"Done it."

"Good. And you put in the salt? Just a bit?"

"Not yet, no."

I watched him concentrate on shaking salt from the shaker. These days, any simple task could be a challenge. Yet he didn't get *everything* wrong, only the unexpected salt or vinegar. But what he never forgot, when he did make a mess of something, was to be furious with himself for doing it, and with me for seeing him do it.

After the second call to oatmeal, Juliette tottered downstairs trailing my blue blanket. In recent months, with her new *doudounes* and her rosy complexion, she had bloomed. There was no other word for it. Even Grand-Pierre didn't fail to notice.

"Ah!" he exclaimed. "Our Princess of the Mist."

"Oh, please." She stood shivering beside the stove.

"What you need—" Grand-Pierre began.

"Is some oatmeal. Yes, undoubtedly."

Breakfast went fine until Grand-Pierre's second cup of coffee, which he calmly poured not into his cup but into his piece of toast. I knew what his brain had decided. It had seen the piece of toast—on its green saucer on the table—as a cup, and into this cup it told Grand-Pierre's hand to pour a cupful of coffee. Only when the toast soaked through, and the saucer overflowed and the puddle spread across the table, did Grand-Pierre set the pot carefully down and clench his jaw and glare at me. I tried smiling.

"It's only coffee," whispered Juliette. "Doesn't matter a bit."

Grand-Pierre sucked at the corner of his mouth and was preparing, I could tell, to fume. But even in his confused state, he seemed to realize there was no one for him to fume *at,* except possibly the cup that had turned into a piece of toast.

"A sponge." I fled to the bathroom before he could blow up at me because he expected me to blow up at *him*. When I returned with the sponge, he had moved outside, arctic air or not, to sit on his blue bench and pop his lips.

"Maybe," I told Juliette, "you could talk him into coming back where it's warm. Sulky as he is, he won't listen to me."

She made him another piece of toast, took it out to him, and ate it herself when he waved it away. But she stayed and talked and coaxed him inside.

"Imagine, Zazoo," she said brightly, following him through the door. "I never thought to ask Grand-Pierre where he picked up his oatmeal habit. Have you heard about the general in England?"

Only two or three dozen times. Until the past awful week, it had been the only tale he'd ever told me about his war. Now I saw why: it made a nice story, free of yellow stars and German soldiers being shot and bodies swinging from a lamppost. But I was glad to hear about oatmeal again if it meant his mood had improved. He stood at the stove pouring coffee—this time into his cup—and describing the bald American general.

"Why did they send *me* to England, you ask? Why not some other member of the Resistance? Because they thought I spoke English! There was a year left in the war. I'd spent months hiding in the caves near Clamecy, tucked above the chalk cliffs with nothing to do but peek down at the river and feel homesick for our canal."

"Nothing to read?" asked Juliette. "No books?"

"Only one. In a field outside Bonnard I'd found something called *How to Learn English in Ten Days.* All through the war I carried it with me, and I did learn a few English phrases. But my friends in the Resistance saw me leafing through it so often—more like ten months, they said, or ten years—they came to assume I spoke English. So when the Allies were preparing to invade France, I was sent to England to advise the big general—in my supposedly fluent English—how to fight a war in France."

Juliette nodded. "And was he eating oatmeal?"

"As a matter of fact, when they showed me into his room, he *was*. Oatmeal from Ireland, he said. The best thing English life had to offer, better than whisky or beer—when he invaded France, he planned to take a trunkful along. Finally, I asked, in my slow English, 'And what is oatmeal, please? Feed for horses?' The bald American thought this hilarious. Said he liked me because I didn't talk much—and because I had no more hair on my head than *he* did."

Juliette rewarded this line with a smile, as I always had. "So you told the general how to fight Germans? How to fight like a—stone?"

"A stone?" Losing his way, Grand-Pierre peered at the tabletop.

"How to fight," I reminded him. "In France."

"How to fight. Of course. Well, I had never led a gigantic army like his—or an army of any size, or even a squadron. I knew a few men in the Resistance but had always fought alone. So there wasn't much I could advise the general except to stay in the undergrowth—for hours, days, even weeks—and let the enemy come to him. He listened patiently and suggested I eat more oatmeal."

Juliette LeMiel, history scholar, nodded gravely. "And, when he reached France, this general took your advice?"

"Oh—" Grand-Pierre shot me a glance, as if wondering what I thought of hearing his oatmeal business again, now that I knew about the colonel lying in his pool of blood. He didn't seem to enjoy saying the word *oatmeal* quite as much as he once had. "Oh, I doubt I was the general's main influence. But he was friendly enough. When I asked for a machine gun to take back, he gave me two. When I asked for some cigarettes, he gave me five cartons."

"You smoked cigarettes?" Juliette asked her questions as lightly as I had always asked mine, before I'd learned that every funny twist had a darker twist beneath it. "I only remember your pipe, back before Zazoo made you stop."

"The cigarettes were for other Resistance fighters, waiting in Normandy. So I took some along. All dropped by parachute, like I was, shoved out the door of a plane."

"And you brought oatmeal, too?" Juliette smiled just as I had smiled in the past.

"No. There was no room for anything but grenades, guns, and tobacco—mostly lost in the drop. Even most of the men were lost—you know, the men who jumped from the plane."

Here was something new. Previous versions had made it sound as if cigarettes and machine guns drifted gaily down from the sky. I leaned toward him. "What do you mean, Grand-Pierre?" I gave him a look to let him know I understood everything was different now, the world was darker, he didn't have to be embarrassed if his story wasn't the same for Juliette as it had always been for me. "Their parachutes didn't open?"

"Our chutes opened, but we weren't dropped in the right place. Bad weather, bad luck. Of the fourteen men who jumped from that plane, five survived the night. And of those five, three were killed within a week. A bloodbath. An awful time. Believe me, there was no oatmeal in France in those days. At least, no oatmeal from Ireland."

Juliette looked back and forth between Grand-Pierre and me. Her new interest in history didn't seem to include its darker twists. "The story isn't over?"

"No." Grand-Pierre studied his boots standing empty beside the front door. "Not quite over." He seemed to have lost interest in finishing his tale.

"And so a funny thing happened," I continued. "Years later, after the bald general's invasion had driven the Germans away, and Frenchmen were busy rebuilding France—"

"Years later," Grand-Pierre interrupted, "when Frenchmen were still deciding which survivors should be shot and which should be kissed, a funny thing happened. Five years after the war, right here outside our mill."

"On Grand-Pierre's birthday." I tried smiling as I had always smiled at this point. "This is the best part. That morning—"

He was no longer smiling himself. "That morning an American Army jeep screeched to a stop over there beside the lock."

Where the lamppost used to stand, I added silently, *from which Grand-Pierre's true love had been hanged.*

"And," Juliette guessed, "the bald general jumped out?"

"No, a young soldier. In English slow enough for me to understand, he said he had a gift for me, for my birthday, from the general."

"A machine gun?" Juliette was the only one smiling. I wondered if history always worked this way, with its listeners hearing just the parts they chose to hear.

"No, not a machine gun. The soldier was a strong young man, but it took him some effort to unload a crate that had been ordered in New York and shipped from Dublin, Ireland." Grand-Pierre was back in the rhythm of his story, but he didn't look at me as he spoke, only at Juliette. "Inside the crate there was no letter, no birthday greeting, just a dozen big cans filled with the finest Irish oatmeal. 'Do you read English?' asked the soldier. 'The directions for cooking it are in English.' 'I can read it,' I said, 'and I can make it. And tell your general I can eat it, too.' 'All right, then.' The soldier climbed into his jeep. 'Just let us know when you need more.'"

"And you did?" Juliette beamed at him. "When you ate up everything in the twelve cans, did you—"

"There was no need to let them know. Every year on my birthday, even after the general was president of America for eight years, and then lived another eight years, and then died—still, every year on my birthday, the crate arrives."

"By jeep? With a soldier driving?"

"These days it comes by delivery truck. But still a dozen cans, from Ireland, the best oatmeal in the world. Another box came last spring. Right, Zazoo?"

"Yes, Grand-Pierre." Eventually, I would have to ask if the owl had killed other mice after killing the German colonel mouse. I would *have* to. And I'd have to stop using animal names for soldiers who had been people. But I couldn't do it yet. "Yes, a box comes every spring." I nodded to let him know it was all right to pretend things were the same as they had been. "And we eat it every morning."

"With cream," he added too cheerfully. "Good French cream. What a sparkling day! Shall we go skating, girls?"

"You old fool," I said with a real smile. "They warn us in school about boys like you. The ice isn't thick enough yet. Anyway, Juliette doesn't have skates."

"And yours have started to pinch?"

"You remember!" Some things his brain held onto without effort. "Yes, my old skates are too small. Or I'm too big. When you bought me this pair, they were so roomy I had to wear three pairs of your thickest socks."

"We could still walk along the canal," said Juliette.

"That's the spirit." Grand-Pierre reached for his boots. "We'll hike down the canal and check out conditions."

Which we did. And it wasn't bad at all, it was quite good, except for the way it reminded me that Grand-Pierre no longer walked as fast or as far as he had once walked, and wasn't the same man I had once thought I knew. And yet the day did sparkle. We walked north of the second stone bridge and slowly back again, and then it was time for bread and soup and Grand-Pierre's nap.

* * *

Juliette and I climbed the spiral steps to my room. Maybe now, I hoped, I could put sadness away for a while. And maybe now I could ask about her past, and talk about mine. I knew I would feel lucky if it turned out we both were adopted and had that to share, as well as the way we brushed each other's hair and laughed about boys.

Juliette settled onto the chair in front of my mirror. "When Grand-Pierre went to England to meet the general," she asked, "was that when he learned about punts on the River Thames?"

"Must have been. I don't think he ever went back." I stood over Juliette to brush out her rich blond hair.

Closing her eyes, she hung her head to the side. "And did he pole a punt beneath the willows, with a picnic basket and a book of poems—and did a girl in a long skirt lean back in the cushions and wink at him, all warm and drowsy? Did he learn to say 'kiss' in English?"

"I never asked, you naughty thing. But he might tell *you*."

"Mister Moldy," said Juliette, smiling at her nickname for our English teacher, "says the best way to learn English is to 'experience' it. For learning the verb 'to row,' you should go rowing under the lindens, reciting its conjugation with each stroke."

"And for the verb 'to kiss'?"

"You should kiss Mister Moldy!" Juliette collapsed with laughter, then straightened up so I could brush the other side of her hair. "Kiss and conjugate!"

"There, there." I mimicked our biology teacher. "A passing crisis, Mademoiselle. An overabundance of hormones."

"Poor old Meunier." Juliette closed her eyes as I went on brushing. "What would *he* say about kissing?"

"Not much." I hadn't seen her so relaxed in ages. "But his wife would say something, the old busybody."

"I don't see how my mother stands her. Spreading slander about everyone—"

"Yes," I murmured, soothed by the glide of the brush through her hair. "No secret is safe with Madame Meunier. Even secrets about you."

Opening her eyes, Juliette squinted at me in the mirror. "What did she say, Zazoo?"

"I was in the pharmacy a few weeks ago, minding my own business. She thought only Monsieur Klein was close enough to hear, but anyone within fifty meters could have caught every—"

"What—did—she—say."

I delivered the news as gently as possible, hoping it would please Juliette as much as it pleased me. "She told Monsieur Klein you were adopted."

Juliette's face in the mirror went deadly pale; her mouth hung open; her lips worked themselves in a circle that made me think of a fish struggling to breathe. "I am *not!* How dare you *say* such a thing!"

"There's nothing wrong with being adopted, Juliette. You've told me yourself—"

"But that's *you!*" When I tried brushing her hair again, Juliette twisted away from me. "Don't touch me—you can't be my friend and spread such lies. How could you *repeat* such garbage? That's what slander *is.*"

"I repeated it," I said faintly, "because I hoped it was true."

"You *what?* You hoped I was *adopted?*" Juliette LeMiel, my sweetest, best friend, shrank back from me as if I were a vampire.

"That way, you see, we could share being adopted. We'd have it in common. It would be our own thing no one else understood."

"You," said Juliette, "are weird."

"I'm sorry you find it so important. Then I guess I hope it isn't true—I mean, if being adopted is such a calamity to you."

"Shut *up,* Zazoo." She glared at me in the mirror. "I'm asking my parents. And if you've made this up—"

"Yes?"

"I'll never speak to you again."

"Great." The room was so quiet I heard my own blood thundering through my brain. "And if it's true?"

"Can't be. For *you* it isn't so bad. You're lucky old Grand-Pierre took pity and saved you from where nobody wanted you, where all they eat is rice."

I tried telling myself such insults couldn't be Juliette talking, they must have come from her moron brothers. But at that moment I hardly cared if she *did* speak to me again.

She stamped home to have a talk with her parents, leaving me alone with the old man who had adopted me.

17. The Word That Wasn't

Two days after the crisis in my tower room, I asked Juliette between classes if she had spoken to her parents. She looked away and didn't speak.

"So." The sight of her misery made me feel like crying. "Then it's true. You're adopted, like me."

"Not like you," she whispered, and added something I could barely hear.

"*What* did you say?"

"Nothing." Juliette's lower lip trembled. "Just something my brother said."

"The brilliant Jacques or the brilliant Jules?"

"Jacques. He called you *une petite niaque.*"

Niaque was the foulest way possible of saying Vietnamese. In my entire life I had heard it just once, during a terrible movie about the French war in Indochina. Hearing it now from an actual person, I was so stunned that for a moment I couldn't speak, could only feel the roots of my hair burning. "Juliette, did you just say what I think you did? Did you just call me—"

"I called you nothing." Her voice seemed to come from far away. "I just let you know what Jacques calls you."

"Oh, then it's harmless. Not hateful at all, if you're just repeating what the noble Jacques says."

Her face was sickly gray; the knuckles of her fingers, clamped around her books, were splotched gruesome yellow. I couldn't help wondering why Asians were called yellow when so-called whites had yellow knuckles and pinkish-yellowish skin.

There was nothing more to say. As we stood glaring at each other, our Great Thundering Silence began. Working hard to keep my knees from buckling, I turned and walked away.

18. Cold, Cold Canal

Grand-Pierre gazed from the towpath out onto the canal.

"Is the ice thick enough now, Grand-Pierre?"

"Doubtful. Need to be *on* it to know for sure. Need to hear its—well, its—"

"Its voice?"

"Yes, Zazoo. Its voice."

"To hear if the ice feels comfortable?"

"A good way of putting it." He forgot he was the one who had put it that way first. "Comfortable. Just so."

But if he had forgotten many things, I hadn't: such as the countless hours that he, an old man, had spent teaching a tiny girl how to skate. For I hadn't learned by magic, all at once and all by myself, as he made it sound in his poems.

He'd been endlessly patient when I was four and he taught me to judge the thickness of ice by the way it felt, by the cracking groan it made as I skated across it. A cracking sound,

Grand-Pierre said, didn't mean the ice was about to break open and swallow me—just that it was alive and was rearranging itself to be more comfortable.

By the time I was six, he no longer held my hand when we skated. He moved off to the side a few meters, then a few meters more, but didn't stop reciting his rhymes or describing the life that went on below the ice even in the coldest months. We discussed turtles burrowed deep in the canal mud, snoozing the winter away, and fish goggling up through the ice to admire the linden branches all free of summer leaves.

While pointing out such marvels, Grand-Pierre stroked steadily nearby, his strides swinging down the canal, down the valley, down the years from one winter to the next. Seven, eight, nine. By ten, when I was as strong and fast on my skates as he was on his, he let me go onto the canal alone, at any hour of the day or night, because he had watched me, he said. He had studied my ways and knew I was strong and fast but also wise—much wiser than he had been as a boy of that age, skating the same canal. He tied a silver whistle to the zipper of my parka and told me to blow and blow on it if I ever fell through, but he said he knew I wouldn't, since, if I went through and drowned, I'd have to give up skating in the winter and swimming the rest of the time.

Even when I was eleven and twelve, I loved to have him along late at night, with the moon out, its reflection wavery on the ice. We might not say a word for the longest time, for as long as it took us to pass under the road bridge to the north, our blades carving *scrape, screep, scrape.* By this time, he was a slower skater and couldn't keep up with my cruising pace, but I preferred slowing down and skating with him to anything else I knew.

"Should we try?" I asked him now. "Should we put on our skates and go out on the ice to see if it sounds comfortable?"

"Time hasn't come. Not quite." He took my elbow to steady himself, as he did often now during our walks. "A few more days, from the look of the cracks. Then it should be safe."

Safe, I repeated silently. Safe was not how the world felt to me. Other years I had waited before venturing onto the canal by myself, but this year I couldn't wait for the ice to be safe.

So that night, once I'd seen Grand-Pierre off to bed, I slipped out to the blue stone bench, pulled on my tiny skates, laced them as tightly as I could without losing my toes, and hoisted myself from the lip of the lock down onto the ice.

It creaked. It moaned. It matched my mood perfectly. "So *young,*" I heard old Gigot telling my history class after the funeral. "So full of potential, was Zazoo, to perish alone in a cold, cold canal."

Through the lock's half-open gate, I skated toward the village, then past the bakery—the only building still lit so late—then under the Long Bridge, also called the New Bridge, since it had been built only a hundred years before. Then southeast toward the Far Side of the World, which lay beyond the tunnel, many kilometers away, at the top of the system Grand-Pierre and I called the Lock Ladder.

An angel of death, I fancied myself, as I coasted toward the center of the canal, where the ice felt most tender. Then I swung back to the thicker side—but not too close to the bank, where sometimes an open patch of water rippled, still unfrozen, in the late-night breeze. I followed the glossy sheen of good ice, and even though I didn't care to be *safe,* I avoided soft patches that might make me the subject of Trottoir's next tale of woe. When I found a stretch that groaned solidly under my blades, I stayed for a while to circle and spin upon it.

Which was when I discovered that Grand-Pierre had not been asleep when I crept from the house. He must have heard me leaving—and, as I left, must have sensed my need to skate where the ice wasn't safe. I heard his blades, then saw his form dim in the distance, stroking stubbornly up the center of the canal. Slow he might be, and yet, in his black cap and trim leather jacket, he skated with elegant grace. On skates he didn't need anyone's elbow.

"You're looking smooth, old man."

"Zazoo." He huffed at me, his eyes dark-shadowed under the moon.

"You were *worried,* old dear."

"Not too"—he blew—"not too worried. Just that bad spot there beyond the next turn, where that little feeder"—he huffed—"feeder stream flows in. Bad spot."

"Yes, you've told me about that spot, maybe a dozen times."

"You're sure?" He blew and breathed, blew and breathed.

"But it was good of you to remind me. Are you feeling okay?"

"Never better." Already he was recovering. "No heart attack tonight."

"Then I won't go swimming tonight, either."

"Good," he said firmly. "Good."

"Let's go home. If we go down, we go down together."

"Together." He beamed. "Together. Good."

The ice made a crunching groan underfoot. We moved apart to keep from being too heavy for the young surface, and, at a leisurely pace, started for home.

"Easier," he called across. "Easier now. What do you see, little girl?"

"A black tree like a heart, a cloud like a hippo."

"Ah," he called.

Scrape—screep—scrape—

I skated away from him down the dark valley. Then, when I turned back to where he swung slowly along, I heard him talking. At first, when he murmured, "Darling, did you see the doe with her fawn in Gustave's field?" I thought Darling must be me. But he wasn't looking at me, wasn't talking to me; someone else was with us. I could feel he knew she was there, and then, when I heard him whisper *Isabelle* more softly than he'd whispered *Darling,* I knew he was with her again in his mind.

He saw I was listening, and went silent except for the scraping of his antique skates. But he didn't look flustered the way most adults do when you catch them muttering to themselves, didn't apologize or say his mind was slipping. He skated smiling down the valley, his eyes far away. It may not have troubled *him,* but it did trouble me. He didn't seem to know she was gone, gone, gone.

Back at the lock, our empty shoes sat in front of the stone bench. The sight of them waiting together had never touched me before, but now when I saw them there side by side, the trees went all smeary in the moonlight.

Watching Grand-Pierre bend over to reach his skate laces, I wanted to help but knew he had his pride, our Old Stone of the valley, shoulders worn smoother, mind rubbed smoother, with each season. When he had the left skate untied and was loosening its laces, his jacket rode up in back, revealing the bottom loop of a coil of rope he must have slung over his shoulder before putting on his jacket.

"But Grand-Pierre, you brought something with you! The mooring line for my punt?"

"Only rope I could find."

"You left in a hurry? Midnight mountain climbing?"

"Very funny, little girl."

"Mountain climbing, or planning to save someone's life? Some little gill girl out on the canal too soon?" To cover my tears, I knelt and helped with his laces. "Remember, Grand-Pierre, when you feared I might hate you? Because of the colonel and what happened afterward?"

"And you *may.*" Steam sighed from his mouth. "Of course you may."

"Well, I don't." Kneeling on the stone terrace, I hugged

him with all my strength. "Old man with a *rope* for me! Old lifesaver! All my life, that's what you've been."

On the blue stone bench, in front of our Mill of a Thousand Tears, he stroked my hair as I wept.

19. The Far Side of the Past

In my dream, it wasn't winter but bright summer—and wasn't France but Vietnam, and Juliette LeMiel came asking to be my friend. We walked alongside a river through thick-growing ferns to a place filled with drooping purple flowers, then took off our clothes and dived into the water.

Normally Juliette was an awkward swimmer, terrified of the current and mud and slimy creatures she imagined wriggling around her. But now she swam gracefully in my wake—and when we climbed out, we were, by the easy mystery of dreams, back in France. Stepping across the shallows where schools of minnows darted in the sun, she handed me a dark red towel. Then, when I finished patting my hair dry, and slid the towel over my shoulders and dried my breasts, breasts were exactly what I found—full and free and warm in the sun. We lay on our backs, the rocks glowing beneath us.

Grand-Pierre's call to breakfast awakened me. The dream had felt so real that at first, looking around my bed, I didn't know where I was. When I realized I was back in our same mill, in my same tower room, the fact of what I might not find inside my nightshirt chilled me.

I lay there trying not to cry until Grand-Pierre called up the stairs that the water was boiling, if I wanted to make our oatmeal I had better come do it or he'd do it for me. I jumped into my slippers and robe, caught a sad glimpse of my flatness in the mirror, and ran downstairs.

Sprinkling oatmeal into the saucepan, I glanced sideways at him. "I had a wondrous dream, Grand-Pierre, of Vietnam, and ferns, and swimming in a beautiful river. And at the end of the dream, I had breasts." Just like that the news came out; he was so old and unjudging, I could tell him anything.

"Oh?" He patted his jacket pocket, as if for his pipe. "Round jiggly breasts?"

"Yes, just round and jiggly enough."

"Ahhh. An incomparable part of a woman, Zazoo—and you'll be a woman soon, you'll have just the sort you'd like. Take my word for it."

"You've sent away for them?"

"Take my solemn word, you'll have the loveliest curves on the entire canal. And it's not just a matter of breasts." His fingers stopped searching for his pipe. "Hips matter, too—they're part of the curve, a major part. You'll have them, and then you'll have more of them—and then, if you're like some of these buffaloes munching along our valley, you'll worry that you have *too* much of them. But for you that shouldn't be a problem. You swim too well, not to mention the way you skate."

"And will boys like me?" It was a relief to come down to breakfast and find him in such good form.

"Too many boys! I'll have to hold them at the front gate with a pitchfork."

"You're fooling." I could feel myself smile as I stirred our oatmeal.

"Nonsense, my dear—I worry about this. And then the color in your cheeks will change, and I'll be forced to keep you captive in that tower of yours, just like, like—"

"Rapunzel."

"Like Rapunzel. Exactly. Let down your hair. They'll want to climb up your tower, those boys, and lie in your bed and go to sleep with a smile on their faces, a hand on your lovely smooth breast."

I wasn't embarrassed by such fantasy because he didn't look at me while inventing it—he stared up the canal toward the tunnel that led to the Far Side of the World. Or was he staring at the far side of the past? "Grand-Pierre, did you ever spend the night with Isabelle?"

His eyes didn't leave the canal. "More than one night."

"Sleeping with her?"

His eyes narrowed but he said nothing.

"With a big smile on your face, in the moonlight, and one hand on her breast?"

"Yes, Zazoo. And I can't tell you how comforting it felt—how it helped me to sleep the most peaceful sleep. Even with the Awful Time bearing down on us. I slept like a—well, like a—"

"Like a stone?" I whispered. "Like a peaceful stone?"

"That's right, like the stone in my name. Sleeping in the moonlight, as you say. As if we were part of your dream."

20. *Sunlight and Sailboats*

"Your friend has a good eye," said Monsieur Klein when the next postcard arrived. Its painting was a view through an open window out onto a row of sailboats. "This one is by the Fauve master Henri Matisse."

"Fauve? Wild beast?"

"That's right. Some painters were given that name after the turn of the century by a critic who didn't understand them. He hated the bold way they used color. But would you look at these pots of flowers beneath this window! In just a few brush strokes!"

This time I was too impatient to wait, and turned the card over. "Good—more about his grandmother. Listen." I read aloud:

"Dear Zazoo, My grandmother was so touched by your card, she suggested I send you this little painting, 'The Open Window,' one of her favorites by Matisse. Pardon me if you meant your card to be private, but its rooftop violinist was so astonishing I had to share it with her. I don't know why, but something about the painting—or your message—made her weep. You're right, she is kind, the kindest person I know. You'll see when you meet her. *Your friend, Marius"*

Of course it was wonderful to hear from him. Every day at school, and every night in my tower room, I admired the sunlight-and-sailboat card, and chanted the word *fauve* again and again in my head: wild beast, wild beast, wild colorful beast. And yet, as time passed and I sensed the ice growing thicker on the canal, he seemed farther and farther away.

Marius—Here is a card Monsieur Klein found for me in his cabinet. He's become my art adviser; the drawer beneath his cash register is, we joke, our village's secret art gallery. You sent me sailboats; I'm returning the favor. This cheery harbor at Collioure is by the same André Derain who did the London Bridge painting you sent me, which still gives me joy. But this autumn has not been a joyful season. Instead of turning bright, the leaves sank to the ground all limp and dull. Your cards have been my warmest light. I'm glad they arrive. But you slip deeper and deeper into the mist. Please greet your grandmother for me, whatever her name may be. I'm sorry my card made her cry.

Zazoo

21. The Dark Door

Grand-Pierre used to say that the water wasn't always deep but it was always long, by which he meant that it went everywhere if you followed it far enough. One afternoon the week after our midnight skate, we stood together on the towpath.

"Looks thick now," I said, pointing toward the canal.

"Thick enough." He nodded. "I miss that girl."

Guessing his mind had drifted back to Isabelle, I said nothing.

"That feisty girl who made fun of our oatmeal."

"Oh." I sighed. "You mean Juliette."

"Of course I do. But why do you frown?"

"Let's go skating while we still have the chance. If it snows for Christmas, the ice will be covered up and we'll have to trudge along the towpath."

"Why were you frowning, Zazoo?"

"Because Juliette isn't my friend anymore."

"Ah," said Grand-Pierre, and made popping noises at the corner of his mouth. "Not your—friend. I'll go skating if you'll explain why Juliette is mad at you."

"How are you so sure *she's* mad at *me?*"

"By the way you say it. You hide pain poorly, Zazoo."

"And I suppose you don't?"

He looked at the backs of his hands.

"You, with your years of practice at hiding pain? She's mad at me," I said, "because I foolishly told her a secret her parents had kept from her. It turns out Juliette LeMiel is adopted, just as I am."

"Ah? Her parents found her floating on a rice paddy?"

"They adopted her, yes. I heard the gossip, and was so happy to know my best friend was adopted, the same as I was, that I went and told her. But she wasn't happy to hear it. She went home and asked her parents, and her brother called me a *niaque*—"

"He *what?*"

"It's all right," I lied. "I've heard worse."

"Well, I haven't." Grand-Pierre's eyes were slits. "What's his name?"

"Genius Jacques," I said. "Or more truthfully, Imbecile Jacques."

"But Juliette isn't an imbecile. She eats oatmeal."

"Oh, I doubt she will anymore. She won't even talk to me, won't admit I exist. All because I told her she was adopted."

I took Grand-Pierre's elbow and steered him to the blue stone bench. We sat and watched the water.

"Well, then." He peered intently at the canal ice, as if hoping to see through it to the turtles sleeping below. "What does she say about *your* being adopted?"

"When she still talked to me, she claimed I was lucky to have *you,* Grand-Pierre, because my own family didn't want me."

"That's not true. Your parents were killed by a land mine." His shoulders slumped lower. "A fiendish sort of bomb—"

"You told me." Many times he had told me. But this time I needed to know more. "They loved me? They didn't throw me away?"

"They loved you. They would never have thrown you away. Never. The girl's feisty—I like her—but she's a fool."

"Then tell me all you remember. About, you know—Vietnam."

"Of course, Zazoo. All I remember."

"Do the best you can." Ever since he had let me into the dark corners of his past, I felt more curious about my own.

"We'll drink tea, Grand-Pierre, and you can tell me what you remember." Rising from the bench, I led him inside.

He tilted his face toward the kitchen ceiling. "Of all the Vietnamese, it was your grandfather I knew best. A translator during the war."

"But my mother, Grand-Pierre." I found the tin of tea, pried the lid loose, and scooped some leaves into the brewing nut. "I've been wondering about her." I'd been wondering about all sorts of parents. Why, for example, had Marius written so fondly of his grandmother but not mentioned his mother or father?

"Let's see. Your—?"

"My mother." Often now, he needed two or three reminders to guide a thought through his foggy brain. "Tell me again how she died. Tell me everything."

"Right." He polished his head with one hand. "Well. Your father was a soldier in the war with the Americans, which came after the war with us but was, in truth, the same war. The same long Awful Time."

"I thought the Awful Time was our war against Germany."

"Confusing, isn't it. But when I say the Awful Time, I don't mean a French war with anyone. I mean my own war." He stopped buffing his head to dig his knuckles at his tired eyes. "When I say the Awful Time, I mean the time since I learned to kill."

"You mean, when you didn't shoot the lieutenant but you did shoot the colonel?"

"Yes." Grand-Pierre carefully examined the ceiling. "The colonel."

"Were there—others?" I asked casually, as I crouched beside the woodstove to throw in more kindling. If I didn't stare at him, perhaps he'd tell.

"May have been." Grand-Pierre's voice was flat. "It's hard to recall . . . everything."

"Then tell me something else." Kneeling by the stove, I spent a long time tinkering with its air vent. "My mother. Did you know her name?"

"We never met, but they told me she was called Phuong, the same as *her* mother. Also they said she was tall for a Vietnamese. And swam like a silver fish."

"You're making this up."

"No, I heard it from her parents after she died. I went back to visit them, you see, and I discovered you. Should I have found you a mother, Zazoo?"

"Don't be silly. How many girls get to grow up in a tower?"

"Not many, I suppose. Not many." He held his hands out to the stove.

"My father was a soldier?" I crossed to the sink and filled the tea kettle.

"All the men his age were soldiers, if they weren't monks. Long before you were born, your father was forced to join the South Vietnamese army, which fought with the Americans against the other Vietnamese army. He lost an arm in the fighting but was still a good farmer once the war ended and you were born. He and his wife, Phuong, were walking out to their field one morning to plant rice. They saw a lily blooming near the path. A lily is a flower."

"Yes, Grand-Pierre, I know." He could say the stupidest things in the middle of saying the wisest ones. Watching closely, I hoped he wouldn't try changing the subject, wouldn't jabber about how cozy a cookstove could be.

"An unusual flower for that part of Vietnam, the flat part where the rice grows. A friend walking with them said they were curious, and so they left the path—a path they had taken to their field many times before. They stepped onto a land mine—you know, a bomb hidden in the ground. Killed them both."

"But you said the war had ended." I stood between the table and stove, the kettle heavy in my hand. "There were still bombs in the ground?"

"Hundreds of bombs. Thousands."

"Really? But *why?*"

Grand-Pierre leaned away from the stove's heat. "War is such a gigantic stupidity, we can't even remember where we plant our bombs. Young people, with a beautiful daughter at home, step into the bushes to admire a flower—and the bomb we planted years earlier blows them to bits."

"*You* planted it, Grand-Pierre? You said *we?*"

"We." He let out a ragged sigh. "I mean *we* who fought in the war—we who kept the Awful Time going. That particular land mine may have been buried by the French, by the Americans, by the North Vietnamese—bombs don't wear uniforms.

We can't know who planted the one that killed your parents. But yes. We."

"My parents died right away? They didn't suffer?" Finally I remembered to set the kettle down on the stove.

"They died in an instant. And their friend wasn't hurt at all. From the path, he watched them blown up into the air."

"So no one ever knew if it *was* a lily." I sank onto the chair across from his.

"No, Zazoo. The plant was blasted to bits along with your parents, like so many other pretty things. A sad life we make for each other. Even for flowers."

This part I *had* heard before, in a long-ago time when Grand-Pierre had been the one tending the fire and brewing the tea. And I knew the most touching part was coming. "Where was I when the bomb went off?"

"An older cousin was watching you at home. At the sound of the explosion, she said later, you looked up and asked, 'Mama go boom?'" As always at this point, Grand-Pierre nodded in wonder. "Two years old. Still nursing at your mother's breast."

"I couldn't be nursing at her breast if she was away planting rice."

"Aren't you clever. Usually she took you along so you could nurse when you pleased, but that day she left food with your cousin. If she *had* taken you—"

"I'd have gone up in the sky with her and the lily."

"And with him. Yes." Grand-Pierre tilted his face, as if listening to some distant owl. "Yes, your mother was called

Phuong," he said again, softly. "If there were a picture, I'd show you. But pictures were all lost in the fighting. People were blown apart, pictures were blown apart—"

"But we haven't been blown apart, Grand-Pierre."

"No."

"And we won't be. Your Awful Time is over."

"Yes, sweet Zazoo." He reached for my hand. "It ended when I found you."

"You came searching and you found me?"

"Well." He stroked my hand. "It was more complicated than that."

I felt myself smile. "Then you didn't come to Vietnam searching for the perfect baby?"

"I had no idea of a baby. But the first thing I saw was you. Standing at the bow of that boat. And as soon as I saw you, I knew—"

"*What* boat?"

"On the river. You build a good fire, Zazoo." He bent toward the stove as if expecting it to agree with him. "So—I never told you?"

"Not this part."

"It was why I knew you'd love living here, between a river and a canal." He nodded at the memory as I poured his cup full. "We French had built a bridge across your grandfather's river. During the fighting we destroyed it—later the Americans built and destroyed it twice more. When I came to visit, after the American war, their bridge was still gone. So when my bus reached the river, your grandfather had to pole across and pick me up. And you came with him."

"He poled his boat across?" I held the teapot between us. "He didn't row?"

"No, he had a flat little boat—"

"Like a punt!" I set the pot down so hard it was lucky not to crack. "An English punt! Like *my* English punt!"

"That's right, smart girl." He wrapped both hands around his steaming cup. "In Vietnam most boats are rowed with a single oar, the way Italians row gondolas. But your grandfather used a pole, pushing along off the bottom—"

"Why didn't you tell me this part?"

Grand-Pierre shrugged. "He handled the boat smoothly, tipping hardly at all as he poled it across the water. And you, his two-year-old granddaughter, stood on the front seat as if you were captain of the river."

"You told me it was in France. In *France,* you said, I saw a magazine picture of a flat-bottomed English boat."

"Oh?" he asked innocently. "I claimed some picture gave us the idea?"

"That's right, old trickster."

"I never mentioned seeing you in your grandfather's boat in Vietnam?"

"No, Grand-Pierre. Maybe you were afraid to share this part with me."

"Maybe so, yes. Afraid you would try rowing your little boat back to Vietnam."

"Don't be funny—you know I'd never leave you. Drink your tea and tell me about my grandfather. I mean, my *first* grandfather."

Grand-Pierre sipped from his cup. "You brew a lovely cup of tea, Zazoo. Not everyone knows how to brew such a lovely cup of—"

"My Vietnamese grandfather."

With great concentration he inspected the tabletop, as if searching for cracks. "Your grandfather was one of the most generous men I've ever known. So many mouths to feed, he and his wife had—they were glad when I offered to bring you here. Which does not mean they didn't love you. They did. Your friend was very wrong about that."

"My ex-friend. Good. Tell me more about his boat. What color was it?"

Grand-Pierre resumed polishing his head. "All I remember is that his boat's most beautiful feature was you, standing there so unafraid, a princess of the water. As soon as I saw you, I knew why I was back in Vietnam." He gazed almost shyly across the table at me. "I was there for you to save me."

"Me save *you?* From *what?*"

"From the ghosts, Zazoo. From the things I had done." His shyness was gone. "And you have."

"Is that why, when you built my boat—my punt—you made it flat and long? To be like the boat you'd seen me standing in?"

"But," he asked very slowly, "did I ever call it an English punt? Truly?"

"Yes, Grand-Pierre."

"Well, it *is* a bit like one. But mostly it reminds me of your sweet grandfather—I wanted you to have his sort of boat. My gill girl Zazoo." He squinted out at the darkening sky. "And now you really want to skate? This late in the day?"

"That's right, old man. With you."

"Well, then, if I must." He pulled himself up from his creaking chair. "Your grandfather would never have believed this part—that his floating princess would some day skate on ice, and that I would skate with her."

"You," I said, "are my grandfather now."

22. *Cozy Dry Home*

After school I saw no purple heron, no binocular boy, no gray cat. The reeds alongshore were ringed with collars of ice, as they were every winter. I wondered how thick the ice would grow, and wondered how anyone could ever have mistaken my new friend Monsieur Klein for a stuffy old man. Turning from the river, I followed the street to his door.

"Sorry, Zazoo." And he did look sorry. "No mail from Paris—no telegram, no box of chocolates. But it's scarcely a week since his last card. We must be patient."

"It's kind of you to say *we,* Monsieur." I wondered if I could ever bring myself to call him Uncle Félix. "It doesn't seem fair for me to expect a card *every* week." I tried smiling.

"Perhaps not." Monsieur Klein bent toward me in his self-mocking half bow. Stuffy, they called him! Snobbish! When actually he was the kindest man, apart from Grand-Pierre, I had ever known. "But it has been quite some time," he went on, "since you've seen this Marius. And did he not say he'd be back soon?"

"Yes, Monsieur. Nine weeks ago."

"And is nine weeks *soon?*"

I could have hugged him. "I suppose it depends how busy Marius is in Paris, how many exams he has to take—but no, Monsieur. Nine weeks is not soon."

"Of course not. An entire autumn."

"The leaves were on the trees when I saw him that morning—now they're all on the ground."

"Perhaps you should tell *him* the same thing, in those very words. Perhaps on this card." Monsieur Klein slid open his cash drawer and handed me the new postcard as if it were my diploma. "Yesterday I came across this jewel of a painting by Odilon Redon."

"They're gorgeous!" Anemone blossoms—white, pale blue, dark red. "And such a rich background! I can't tell which glows more, those browns and grays or this blue-black jug."

"Here, have a stamp to go with it. Send your admirer this bouquet."

Pen in hand, I could think of nothing to write until I recalled how Grand-Pierre had described the river in Vietnam, which, in turn, reminded me of our river. Then the message came easily.

Dear Marius—Once, during a winter so cold the river froze over, Grand-Pierre and I saw miracles through the glassy clear ice. I'll tell you about them when I see you—you said you'd be back soon, so I'll wait until then. (But what, to you, is the exact meaning of the word soon? Enough time for the leaves to fall from the trees and the canal to blanket itself in ice?) Meanwhile, here's another miracle, a poem Grand-Pierre wrote me when I was too young to write poems myself.

Zazoo

There once was a cat
down by the canal
who could never stray far from his home.
Night after night
day after day
he sat watching the world
float past on its way:
all sorts of canal boats
in all sorts of sizes
in all sorts of colors
did quite hypnotize
his restlessly wandering eyes, his eyes—
his restlessly wandering eyes.

Monsieur Klein, when I showed him the card, couldn't hide his astonishment. "*Pierre* wrote this?"

"Of course he did—this poem and dozens more, starting when I was a baby. When I grew older, we wrote them together. This verse is part of a long poem, still not finished, about a gray cat. Grand-Pierre calls him the *sad* gray cat."

"And it's about Pierre himself, I suppose? As the old cat?"

"Oh, I don't know." I wasn't sure I understood the poem, only that I loved it—and even the parts I did understand, I felt unwilling to explain. The gray cat had his dignity; he could explain what he pleased, in his own good time. "Just a gray cat I've seen along the canal. You know, when I feel . . . lonely."

Monsieur Klein handed the card back. "The Old Stone's a poet? I know about his knitting, of course—so does everyone else. But then, everyone else knows more about him than I do."

"And what," I broke in, "is that supposed to mean?"

Monsieur Klein gazed blankly at me.

I leaned across the counter toward him. "Everyone 'knows more about him' than you do? Why is that?"

"Since the war," Monsieur Klein murmured.

"Since the war *what?*"

He spoke slowly, softly, but distinctly. "I haven't seen Pierre since the war."

I nearly fell over. "Not once?"

"Not to speak to."

"Not . . . *once?*"

"Not once," whispered Monsieur Klein—this man who wore elegant bow ties, was always spotless, and had never, that I had observed, looked sheepish before.

"Not once," I repeated. The strangeness of people was beyond belief. First, Juliette LeMiel refused to speak to me. Then

I learned that our pharmacist and my own grandfather had been carrying on, for ages, a thundering silence of their own. "Exactly when," I said at last, "did you and Grand-Pierre stop speaking?"

"Exactly on a winter day in 1942. First I stopped talking to him; then our silence became a habit. Once the habit took over, it couldn't be changed."

"Couldn't be?" My brain was too completely shocked to do anything but bounce his words back at him.

"Forty-eight years." Monsieur Klein looked up and down the aisles; the only place he wouldn't look was at me. "A long time, Zazoo. Yes. So I'm a bit out of touch, and would never have guessed that your Grand-Pierre scribbled poems."

"Lots of poems." *Forty-eight years!* "But lately he can't remember the first ones he wrote, and can't put together any new ones, so I write them myself."

"Mademoiselle Zazoo, our poet of Lock Forty-three." Though his tone seemed less serious, Monsieur Klein still couldn't meet my eye. He studied the painted bouquet on the postcard, perhaps wondering, as I was, how two grown men could be such fools.

"And now," I said, "the poet of Lock Forty-three must walk to the post office and mail a card so it catches the next train." I wrote the address of the Paris pharmacy down the card's right-hand margin. "Will Marius come back, Monsieur Klein?"

"If he doesn't, he's a hopeless specimen. You're sending him such a lovely poem—"

"Thank you, Monsieur. Grand-Pierre thanks you, too—or he *would,* if you two ever spoke." I stared at him. "As for me, I'll be back next week for his pills."

"Stop in any time at all." Monsieur Klein lifted his hands and let them drop, as if to say that he didn't understand, either. "Good luck with your correspondence."

I stepped into the street and made my way toward the post office. My chest ached, as it had often lately. The world itself seemed to ache. *For forty-eight years they hadn't spoken.* But the card in my hand combined a beautiful poem one old man had written for me and a stunning bouquet another had found for me to send to Paris. Breathing plumes of frost, I trudged away from the pharmacy.

23. The Time It Takes

How long does it take a postcard to reach Paris? How long does it take a bird, when the weather turns cold, to reach its winter home? Such questions nagged at me those dark mornings when Grand-Pierre called up the stairs that I should be dressed and ready for oatmeal, while my bones urged me to burrow deeper into my bed, away from everything new I had learned.

But however long a card takes to reach Paris, three days after I sent the painted bouquet, he arrived. Not a return card but Marius himself, the very same bird watcher, wearing a long brown overcoat. He stood beside his same bicycle under the sycamores by the canal.

When I saw him, twenty meters away, I couldn't go any closer. Not from fear that he'd disappear—I could see he was real—but from fear of him seeing too much of me. That first morning in October, I had been shielded by the water, by my punt, by my distance from the shore. Now we both stood on the towpath. Marius walked his bike toward me, not stopping until he was hardly a meter away.

"I have some questions," he said lightly, as if two months hadn't passed.

"About Monsieur Klein?" Every word seemed to hang frozen in the air.

"Yes, and about your Grand-Pierre. And about you."

"I have a few questions of my own." Hugging my schoolbooks, I leaned maybe one millimeter closer. "Does it take birds a long time to fly south for the winter?"

"To migrate?" His smile was so gentle it made his words seem even slower. "Depends on the bird. Some fly to the rim of North Africa, some fly farther. Some rest along the way, some go nonstop. Your poem about the cat came yesterday."

"The . . . cat?" It wasn't just that our words were slow; each one seemed to have its own shape as it hovered between us. "Oh. The *gray* cat."

"Yes. I wondered if there was more. When I read the last line, the poem should have continued. Is there more that didn't fit on the card?"

"Lots more." I hoped he had read the poem aloud to his

grandmother. "And it's still not finished." *But what was your childhood illness? And why, when you stayed home that year, was it your grandmother who cared for you?*

"That's a relief," said Marius. In contrast to all my babbling inner voices, he had one voice and it seemed entirely calm. "He's lonely, your gray cat."

"I know. When I first told Grand-Pierre about my cat, he wrote that verse. I was three years old." Gradually my sense was coming back to me. "Do freckles fade in the winter?"

Marius smiled, showing his uneven teeth. "Mine do. You're lucky to be unspotted."

"But I *like* freckles! Perhaps our Monsieur Klein has some lotion you could use to make them stand out more. I suppose *he's* the one you came to see, since you've learned he was never married."

Marius raised his eyebrows. "I came to see you, Zazoo."

I felt myself beaming. "And my grandfather, no doubt, since he knows Monsieur Klein's past."

"I'd like to meet your grandfather. But it's *you* I came to see. You in your ice skates, since you can't swim this time of year."

"Grand-Pierre will like you. Let's go see him and drink tea."

"And maybe go skating? I could ride beside you on the towpath."

We walked toward the mill, Marius pushing his bicycle between us.

"Since your Eiffel Tower card arrived, I've thought of you as Marius from Paris. But didn't you say, back in October, that you came from the south?"

"Yes, I was born there. But my grandmother thought I should move to Paris and stay with her and study at a better school."

"Your grandmother." I didn't know how to ask.

"You want to know about my parents." As we walked, I could feel Marius studying me. "A fair question. The fact is, I don't get along so well with my parents, and neither does Mémé Simone. But we get along with each other."

"She's the grandmother who nursed you," I said, as my boot flipped a stick from the towpath. "When you were little and had some mysterious disease?"

"First I had measles, but then it turned into a confusing sort of brain fever called meningitis. Yes, she's the one—she saved my life, Mémé Simone. A born healer. Better still, she never puts pressure on me."

"But your parents do?"

"My father especially." Marius tilted his head, as if puzzled. "Wants me to be some sort of businessman. I'd prefer to pedal my bike along the towpath."

"And watch birds." Imagine, I thought—here he is, walking beside me in his tweed overcoat. I thought of clichés about being in love—a "fever of excitement" and that sort of thing—but none fit. I did *not* feel like throwing my arms around him. I felt like wheeling my own bike from the shed and riding it alongside his on the towpath. So. It was *me* he had come to see.

"Grand-Pierre didn't get along with his parents, either. Don't feel alone."

"I don't." His eyes crinkled in their wonderful smile.

"Grand-Pierre," I prattled on, "says the smartest family *skips* a generation—works better both ways." Approaching the mill, I found myself walking slower and slower. "That's just his opinion, although I happen to share it."

"Sounds wise." Marius smiled but added nothing about his parents. "In October you claimed to be thirteen. With all the time that's passed since then, you must be fourteen by now."

"Not till April, I'm afraid. And you are—"

"A middle-aged bird watcher." He paused. "Already sixteen."

"Ah." My heart sank. Two whole years between us. *More* than two. And so much sophistication; no one at my school wore such a fine baggy overcoat or seemed so quietly sure of himself. "Let's see if Grand-Pierre is awake." Before opening the door, I turned to face Marius. "Your grandmother Simone—does she sleep a lot?"

"Not so much, no. Not yet. She's quite a bit younger. Didn't you say Grand-Pierre was nearly eighty?"

"Seventy-eight last May." I dreaded turning the doorknob, because, as always when I came home from school, part of me wondered if Grand-Pierre would be all right this time. Not that I feared any nap might be his last. His old heart was tough—what I always wondered was whether his eyes would be cloudy or bright.

But when I peeked inside, he sat in his deep chair by the woodstove, needles clicking, eyes sharp. Hearing me come in, he set his coil of knitting aside. "Survived another day of prison, Zazeezoo?"

"Barely."

"And you've brought a friend home." Grand-Pierre rose and held out his hand.

"Not from school, Grand-Pierre. From Paris. Please meet Marius, the Towpath Bird Watcher."

They shook hands—an old man with his head rubbed smooth and a sandy-haired boy who was taller, thinner, almost spindly in his Parisian coat. Grand-Pierre cleared some knitting things from a chair and waved Marius into it. "Zazoo has been needing a friend—for company she has just me and the ghosts. You're most welcome here."

"Thank you, Monsieur."

"Please, not so formal—call me Grand-Pierre."

I was relieved to see Grand-Pierre so sure of his bearings. "Marius wants to go skating with us. But since he has no skates, he'll ride on the towpath."

"The young man has a horse?"

"A bicycle, Grand-Pierre, a black three-speed like mine. And no loaves of bread clipped over the back wheel, which means he'll be eating with us after we skate."

"Paris," judged Grand-Pierre, "is a long way by bicycle."

"I came mostly by train, Monsieur."

"Grand-Pierre."

"Grand-Pierre, excuse me. Two hours by train from Paris, then another hour by bike and I was here—and the timing couldn't have been better. I arrived just as Zazoo made her way home."

"From prison." Grand-Pierre nodded. "I suppose you're institutionalized, yourself? In Paris?"

"I am, yes. They have great plans for me."

"Don't listen, is my advice." Grand-Pierre bent earnestly toward him. "Adults make stupid plans for children, then stand in the way of sensible ones."

Words, I noticed, once again seemed to be moving through the air at their normal speed. I nodded at Grand-Pierre to encourage his lecture.

"The only things I should have studied in school were poetry and, ah—poetry and—"

"Foreign languages." I had heard this before.

"—and foreign languages." He thumped one hand on the table. "Right. The rest was nothing but blather. Piffle."

"Yes, Monsieu—ah, Grand-Pierre. Would you have studied boatbuilding, in school, if it had been offered?"

"A *third* thing! Precisely! Boatbuilding!"

"Still, you and Zazoo did well on your own, making her plum-colored boat."

"Oh, I only helped."

I was struck by how easygoing Grand-Pierre could be with a newcomer, considering that he wouldn't venture into his own village or visit any neighbors.

"Wood's the thing." He nodded. "Wood understands water. Right, Zazoo?"

"Right. Where are your skates? We should go while it's light out, or Marius may drive his three-speed off the towpath."

"My skates," muttered Grand-Pierre. "We're going skating?"

"As I told you, old dear, a moment ago. I'll find your skates—you just bundle up and meet us at the bench."

If I was relieved to see my grandfather accept this stranger, I was just as pleased that Marius needed nothing explained. He seemed to sense that Grand-Pierre preferred to skate in silence, with only the singing of our blades for conversation. The old man and I skated north up the middle of the canal; Marius rolled along on the towpath to our right.

Skating between Grand-Pierre and Marius, I was pleased as I hadn't been in ages. From time to time, if I couldn't believe Marius was actually with us, I glanced across to watch him wobbling along on his bike, the hem of his overcoat flapping. Gazing all around him, he seemed to take in everything—the treetops, the bushes, the ribbon of pearly ice stretched out before us. When he smiled, I smiled back, feeling even more pleased than before. So what if my chest ached? That afternoon, nothing hurt too much to keep me from being happy.

This time I didn't speed out ahead of Grand-Pierre and return to circle past him; I was happy to accompany him in the falling darkness, while Marius felt his way alongside us. The world was our double *screep, scrape, screep,* our three frosty breaths, our two whirring tires on grit. We moved homeward through the dusk.

24. The Same Eyes

At the stone bench, Marius helped Grand-Pierre off with his crumbly leather skates, then turned and saw me struggling with mine.

"But these," he said, lifting the skate I had managed to remove, "are tiny!"

"My feet are tiny."

"Not this tiny, Zazoo." Marius said my name as gently as anyone ever had. He lifted my other skate—with my foot still inside—and loosened the laces. "I thought foot binding was outlawed eons ago. Anyway, that wasn't in France."

"No." I hoped he wouldn't make the mistake of guessing that foot binding had been devised in Vietnam. The insensitive lunks at my school assumed that everything that took place anywhere in Asia must have taken place in Vietnam.

"Wasn't that in China?" asked Marius. "Foot binding?"

"I really don't know. But surely someone in Paris would." If I hadn't laced my skate so tightly, I told myself, I might have had enough sensation in my foot to feel his fingers touching it. "Aren't there Chinese women in Paris?"

"Thousands. And thousands of Vietnamese women—some ugly, some beautiful—but none as graceful as the skaters along your canal." He opened the boot of my skate delicately, as if afraid my foot might shatter. "It isn't healthy to wear these torture devices." He removed the skate and rubbed my foot. At first, I felt nothing but pins and needles, which was too bad. No boy had ever rubbed my foot before.

"That *hurts,*" I yelped.

"Good. They won't have to amputate." He slipped my right shoe onto my foot. "You skate wonderfully."

"It's a wonderful thing, skating. Almost like flying, when I let the dream of the canal float past me and don't *think* but just . . . Oh, it's hard to explain."

Marius picked up my skates. I opened the front door and led him inside.

Grand-Pierre sat by the woodstove, shoes off, massaging his left foot.

"Hot chocolate?" I asked.

"And then some supper, yes? Some of that beef stew you made."

I was glad he remembered. "Yes, stew for a winter night. And maybe a glass of wine for our guest."

"So formal." Grand-Pierre winked at Marius. "So formal when she's shy. But everyone's that way from time to time."

"Yes, Monsieu—Grand-Pierre. Yes."

Bustling in the cupboard for cocoa, I remarked over my shoulder, as if the thought had just entered my head, "But Marius, where are you staying tonight?" I saw Grand-Pierre smile and didn't care. "Surely you can't be going back to Paris?"

"Tomorrow, on the first train. Tonight I'm staying at the hotel in town, near the train station. Clean and cheap—they're saving me a room."

"Oh." I didn't have to look to know Grand-Pierre was still smiling. "But it's dark out now. And you said the ride to town takes an hour—"

"I've ridden farther. Let me help with the cocoa."

"Stay there and warm yourself. Grand-Pierre, would you mind putting some bread in the warmer?"

"*That* at least I can do." Marius took the bread, wrapped it in a cloth, and slid it into the warming compartment of the woodstove, the side away from the fire. He placed the stewpot on top, in a spot where it would warm slowly but not burn.

"We should play some music," I decided. "Perhaps the radio—?"

"Zazoo," said Grand-Pierre. "Zazeezoo." His eyes were closed; his head leaned down as he rubbed his other foot. "Isn't the fire music enough? Be calm."

Marius gazed at Grand-Pierre with such tenderness, it was all I could do to hold myself back from crossing the kitchen to touch my new friend's shoulder, his eyes, anything. I wanted the world to love my Old Stone the way I did, and I wanted no one, *no* one, to believe he had done awful things.

The stew was good: the potatoes were firm, the onions clung together in their crosscut pattern; the bread was toasty and warm. Grand-Pierre drank his red wine and poured some for Marius, since, in our village, you offer wine to any guest who has cycled an hour through the windy night to reach your December home.

"It's dark out," I said, serving coffee. Coffee wasn't my favorite drink, but Grand-Pierre liked it after a meal, and his liking it—with his small glass of brandy—helped me like the idea of it. "Dark out. Cold."

As Marius nodded, the fire, burning low in the woodstove, seemed to chuckle. "Did you hear that?" He leaned forward.

"The fire?"

"He heard an owl," said Grand-Pierre. "Down the canal. Our neighbor."

"Does your forest have many owls?" asked Marius.

"A few," said Grand-Pierre. "That one's the closest—he watches over things all through the winter. You like his call?"

Marius nodded. "A lullaby—except to his neighbors the mice."

When I was a younger girl, such a comment would have made me smile; now I shivered and said nothing.

"This particular owl," Grand-Pierre explained, "nests in a high oak. At least he used to. In what we call the Gnarly Oak Grove. I could show you the tree, but not tonight. You *are* coming back?"

"I certainly hope so. But please—tell me about your owl."

"First, he's fashionable. In the winter, when he tires of his brown coat, he puts on a gray one."

"And does he have tufts above his ears?"

"No. He's, oh, I'd say, about this tall." Grand-Pierre lowered one hand below his knee. "A big head, of course. Big and very round."

"Could it be the sort they call a *fauve?*" asked Marius.

This gave me quite a start, since *fauve* had recently become one of my favorite words. "Fauve?" I echoed faintly.

"Yes." Gazing gently at Grand-Pierre, Marius seemed not to have noticed my reaction. *"Un hibou fauve."*

"Might be." The old man himself, round glasses blinking in the darkness, looked more owlish than ever. "Might very well. You know his Latin name, I suppose?"

"No, Monsieur—ah, Grand-Pierre. Anyway, I prefer it in simple French."

Eyes narrowing, Grand-Pierre peered across the room at Marius. The fire snapped and hissed. "You remind me of someone. Someone long ago."

"Yes, Monsieur?" Marius leaned toward him intently. "Someone who liked watching birds, perhaps?"

"Can't quite remember." But from the popping of his lips, it was obvious he was trying hard.

"Do you remember *when?*" asked Marius with a strange half-smile.

"It may come to me. Sometimes it does. Or it may not. In the old days, with enough patience, it always came. But now . . ." Grand-Pierre shrugged. "The old clock ticks slower."

"Yes." Marius settled back in his seat. "The old clock."

"Perhaps the old clock will remember if it gets some sleep." Grand-Pierre used the arms of his chair to hoist himself upright, then shook hands with Marius, who had risen from his chair as any well-bred boy would. "Good night, young man. Safe cycling to you."

"Thank you, Grand-Pierre. Good night."

As Grand-Pierre trudged away, Marius sat back down. Making no move to pull on his overcoat and leave, he seemed happy to sit and enjoy the fire.

I, meanwhile, grew busy washing the dishes, then arranging the salt and pepper shakers, then arranging them again.

We listened to Grand-Pierre's slippers shuffling from his bedroom to the bathroom. Then the sound of running water; then the flushing toilet; then his slippers plodding back to the bedroom. Finally, we heard the click of his bedroom door as he closed it, which he never did ordinarily.

"Would you like some more wine?" I asked, even though Marius had hardly sipped from the glass Grand-Pierre had poured him.

"No. Thank you."

We heard the creak of the bedsprings behind the closed door, the wind stirring the treetops outside. In the woodstove the fire groaned.

"Where is your room, Zazoo?" asked Marius, as if this were a perfectly natural question.

"Up the stairs," I said weakly. "Up the—the spiral stairs Grand-Pierre built for me." With great effort, I breathed again. "He built the stairs especially for me when I was five and decided it was where I wanted to live. At the top, you know, of the tower."

Rapunzel, Rapunzel, chanted a little girl's voice.

"I'd love to see your room." Unlike me, Marius didn't seem to have any trouble breathing. I assumed he wasn't the slightest bit nervous—until I noticed that his hands were clutched tightly together on the table. "Some afternoon," he went on, keeping his voice calm but his hands locked together. "You know, when it's bright out. You could show me the view from your windows. Does your tower have lots of windows?"

"It's *all* windows," I chattered, flooded with relief and disappointment. "That's what I wanted, so it's how Grand-Pierre built it. A tower that had stood there for centuries. When I asked for windows, he chiseled holes in the stone walls all the way around. I'll show you," I whispered. "Someday."

"Good."

Sixteen years old, I repeated silently. My sixteen-year-old *friend*. "Anyway, at night you can't see out from my room. I mean, if there's a light on, or candles are lit, all you see is your own reflection."

"And we can see that from here." Marius nodded at the kitchen window. "But that's a good idea. A candle *would* be nice—"

I crossed the kitchen and found four candles in the cupboard. We arranged them in a crooked line down the center of the table.

Marius lit the first candle with a stove match. "From your room, can you see both directions on the canal?"

"Yes, and in wintertime, when the leaves are off the trees, you can also see the river. In the summer, sometimes I sit at my window, watching the canal, and wait for the next boat to come along."

"Like me, waiting for birds with my binoculars."

"Yes." This similarity had occurred to me also. "But when I do my homework, I stay down here. It's warmer, and I like to keep an eye on the woodstove, and Grand-Pierre might need help with something. Like tonight, unlacing his skates."

"Oh, he could have untied them."

"I saw you helping—don't think I didn't. Sometimes the simplest thing stops him. It was sweet of you."

"I like your grandfather." Marius cocked his head. "That owl again—did you hear?"

"No." I wondered about the strange look he'd given Grand-Pierre. "Maybe I should be a bird watcher myself. My tower would be an ideal place for it."

"And for other things," said Marius. "Such as writing poems about a cat. Could you recite another verse of your poem for me?"

I watched his eyes in the fluttering candlelight, and his hands, now resting calmly between us on the table. "I'd be happy to recite some of it, but first I need to hear something from you. That business earlier, when Grand-Pierre said you reminded him of someone—?"

"I thought you would ask."

"You seemed to know exactly who he meant. Some bird watcher, you said?"

"Yes, Zazoo. Grand-Pierre may not remember the person I resemble, someone he met long ago. But if he doesn't know her name, I do."

In the flickering light it was hard to read his expression. "You were there when they met? I don't understand."

"No, I wasn't born yet. But she's told me about it, many times." Marius paused as if deciding how much to say. "In fact, she was my other reason for today's visit. I came to tell you about her."

"Some girl, I suppose." I tried keeping my tone light. "Some gorgeous girl—maybe the one you were going to eat those baguettes with, the morning I met you."

Marius laughed so hard the candle shadows danced around us. "Gorgeous girl! In her way, maybe, but hardly a girl. Sixty-two years old—my Grandmother Simone. She's the one Grand-Pierre saw in my face, Zazoo. Other people say the same. They claim our eyes are identical."

"What a crazy coincidence! You come riding along, one morning in October—"

"But Zazoo, none of this is a coincidence. None of it." He passed a finger through the flame of the tallest candle, and was about to pass it through again when I reached out and stopped him. Most boys would have kept repeating the exercise, more and more slowly, just to show that they could. But Marius stopped.

Sixteen, I told myself again. Touching his hand so unexpectedly had given me a shiver, but I couldn't do it again. "I suppose this all goes back to the war?"

He cringed at the word. "In France, everything goes back to the war. Your grandfather met Simone in the Cévennes Mountains, in the same village where I was born many years later."

"The *Cévennes* Mountains?"

"Right. He's mentioned them?"

"Monsieur Klein has. That's where Grand-Pierre took him during the war, to escape the Gestapo."

"Yes." Marius gave me a heartbreaking smile. "You see, it was my grandmother's family who took care of Monsieur Klein during the war."

"Ah?" Suddenly the glow of our candles seemed much brighter. "Monsieur Klein lived with your grandmother?"

"Yes." The room was very still. As we gazed across the flames at each other, I wondered if our hands would touch again, accidentally or not. "Monsieur Klein stayed in their farmhouse for three years. Until the war ended. He worked in their fields, five kilometers from the closest village. It was a safe place for him—their dogs made a racket if any soldiers came nearby."

Rather than ask what I most wanted to know, I sat watching the candles and waiting.

"They fell in love." Marius let out a breath, as if relieved to have said the word. "Two fourteen-year-olds in love, during the grimmest days of the war."

"But you terrible boy, why didn't you *tell* me?" I was so excited by the news, yet so angry with Marius for not sharing it sooner, that I wanted to kiss his lips and punch his shoulder. But before I could decide how to react, I heard the hint of a whimper in the next room. Some ears hear distant owls; others hear baffled old men.

25. His Own Ghost

I was on my feet and moving toward Grand-Pierre's door before I knew I had heard anything. "In the middle of the night," I said over my shoulder, "is when he's fuzziest. I'll just take a look."

"But there was no sound—"

"Oh, I may have imagined it." I swung the bedroom door open.

In the weak light from the hall lamp, Grand-Pierre sat perched at the edge of his bed, feet bare on the floorboards, blinking at the wall.

"Here I am, Old Skate." I tugged him to his feet. Good—he had on pajamas, both a top and a bottom, and just one of each. On any other night it wouldn't have mattered how many tops he wore, or if he had forgotten the bottom part. But in front of company he would be embarrassed if he came to his senses and realized he had dressed oddly. He may have been old, but he did have his pride.

I steered his elbow to the bathroom, then watched to be sure he peed into the toilet and not the corner, as he'd done one night the week before.

Then, tottering back down the hallway, he spotted the apple on our kitchen table. I hadn't seen it myself; during my absence, Marius must have taken it from his coat pocket. Grand-Pierre headed straight for its ruby-bright glow.

"A lovely apple." He examined it as if it were a medieval relic.

"From Normandy," said Marius, keeping his voice low.

"Normandy." The old man cradled the apple in both hands. "These grew in Burgundy, too. You know, during the Awful Time. Before the invasion—"

"The Awful Time?" whispered Marius.

"He means the war." Lifting Grand-Pierre's foot, I slid a bedroom slipper over his bare toes. Then the other foot—softly, so as not to disturb the spell. "Did you eat many apples during the Awful Time, Grand-Pierre?"

"Too many. Winter of forty-four. A hut outside Mâcon." His eyes slid shut as he caressed the apple. "Oil drum for a fireplace. Barrel of apples for food. Apples—more apples. And a few snared rabbits."

"But couldn't you *shoot* rabbits?" I leaned closer. "With your rifle? And weren't there deer you could shoot?"

"Lots of deer. But shooting made noise." His eyes stayed shut while his hands turned and turned the apple. "Too many Germans, too close. Couldn't make noise. Snared a few skinny rabbits. Roasted them, ate like a savage. But mostly apples."

"And you knitted socks?"

He nodded. "Even in the dark, if I had enough needles I could knit a good sock. Sick of apples, though—sick. Miserable diet for a miserable—miserable—" He let out a great sigh. "Don't we have a knife here? A sharp knife?"

I handed him our paring knife and watched to be sure he didn't cut himself, half asleep as he was. Across the table Marius looked on silently.

"Even in the dark," Grand-Pierre repeated. Eyes still shut, he proceeded to trim, in one delicate strip, the red skin off the apple, around and around from stem to base—and while his hands turned the apple, they seemed free of all trembling. He opened his eyes and handed the peel to Marius.

"Grand-Pierre!" Marius dangled the elegant spiral before him. "In a Paris art gallery, you could sell such a shape for ten thousand new francs."

"Huh." The old man chuckled. "Is our stovetop nice and hot?"

"Surely you won't *burn* such a beautiful thing?"

"Watch." Grand-Pierre took his spiral back from Marius and draped it on the woodstove; the peeling sizzled and danced. A sweet aroma filled the kitchen—a wondrous spicy fragrance that reminded me of Christmas cookies being baked. "Well." Grand-Pierre nodded as if such a miracle were nothing. "Smells no different now." He stared through the woodstove to some invisible spot far away. "Cold that winter. *Cold.* Terrible indigestion. But now I'm off to bed, children." He shuffled out of our candlelight glow.

Back in his room I eased him down into bed, made sure his pajamas didn't bind around his armpits, and pulled the covers over his chest.

"We never eat apples," I whispered.

"No," he replied in the dark. "Can't stand them."

"Certainly not. After such a winter as that?" I couldn't help wondering how many other stories had drifted deeper and deeper into the corners of his brain. Backing into the hallway, I closed the door.

26. *The Night of the Nightingales*

We gazed at the creamy apple on the table between us. The fire popped; the last shriveled bits of peeling hissed on the stove. Marius sliced the white fruit into eight neat sections. "You worry about him, Zazoo." He trimmed the core from each slice. "But his memory wasn't so bad just now."

"No, not so bad. And did you watch his hands as they were peeling the apple? They remembered better than his mind did. They were steady. It's the same when he skates. But when he tries putting things into words, he's growing, how shall I say—"

"Shaky?" Marius handed me a slice of the apple. "Lost?"

"Yes." Once I'd seen that Marius might be as nervous as I was, I felt even more tender toward him. "You're very observant. But just a few minutes ago I was so *mad* at you." I felt myself smiling. "I could hardly believe it."

"Mad—why? Because I waited to tell you about the young lovers?"

"More upset than mad, but not only at you. There are so many other things. When Grand-Pierre forces his legs into the arms of a shirt—that upsets me. Or when he wears one pair of trousers over another, or puts them on backward. Or," I went on, "when my best friend decides she hates me, and won't talk to me for a whole week, and then another week, making *me* so mad I won't talk to *her.*" I stopped for breath. "Lots of things." But I couldn't tell Marius that I was not only upset, I was scared as well—about the ache in my chest. Not only was it private, this fear, but it seemed so selfish compared to an innocent girl hanging from a lamppost. "The war," I said at last. "The war upsets me, too. Tonight was unusual. He seldom mentions the war."

"The Awful Time." Marius traced his finger around an apple slice.

"Grand-Pierre finally told me a few things. Both he and Monsieur Klein have told me. Terrible things."

The fire crackled as Marius bit into his apple slice. "Terrible things about a family being executed? A Jewish family who had done nothing wrong?"

"So you already know. Good—I was wondering if I'd be able to tell you, and I didn't want to try."

"Of course not. But Zazoo, you've forgotten to eat your chunk of apple."

"Have I?" Looking down, I saw I'd been turning the soft bit in my fingers until it had gone all smooth and brown. "How odd."

"Here, have another. They're sweet, these apples from Normandy." He handed me a fresh creamy slice. "I'm sorry I didn't tell you sooner about Monsieur Klein and Mémé Simone. And I'm sorry you've been upset."

"The problem isn't you, Marius, it's my *life.* Everything's so . . . complicated. So confusing. Believe me, your cards from Paris have been a joy. Even Monsieur Klein says so. Such lovely paintings you've sent us—"

"Us?" He smiled. "But they're addressed to *you,* Zazoo!"

"Ah, but they arrive at his store. So we admire them together. Such rich colors, such designs. That dreamy Eiffel Tower—"

"Listen to me." He leaned closer across the table. "Those things I didn't tell you? About Monsieur Klein falling in love with my grandmother?"

"Yes—"

"I didn't share them sooner because I had to be sure I could trust you—you know, to keep a secret."

Over the candle flames I leaned toward him, wanting to hold his face in my hands. "And so? Can you trust me now?"

"I can, yes. And not just to keep a secret. I saw you skate with your grandfather, I saw your worried look when he wandered off to bed. But mostly I saw you care for him just now, in the middle of the night. The way you spoke when he fumbled toward the bathroom—" Marius stared at the candle flame.

"You trust me." Just saying the words made me glad.

"I do, yes, and so does Mémé Simone. She asked me to tell you about her."

"*Did* she?" Each new bite from our apple tasted sweeter than the last.

"You see, she's at the heart of this. When Félix arrived at her family's farm—she calls him Félix—she was already fourteen. He turned fourteen three months later. And they both loved birds."

"Monsieur *Klein* did?"

"That's right. But at first he was so shattered from his family being killed, he wouldn't speak. They had to force him to *eat*. Can you imagine? He didn't say a word to Simone until two months after he arrived—the night the nightingales flew north from wintering."

"Wintering," I repeated. "In North Africa?"

"Central Africa, below the desert." Marius crossed the kitchen and lifted the shriveled apple skins from the stovetop. "One night that spring—in April—Mémé found him weeping in the barn. He couldn't stop; she sat with him until he slept. All night she held him. The next morning, when he woke up, finally he spoke to her."

"About his sister? Isabelle?"

"Yes. Mostly about Isabelle's love for birds. You see, Félix had heard the season's first nightingale. Do you know its song, Zazoo?"

"No."

"The nightingale has a lovely sad call." Marius swung the fire door open and tossed the dried peelings inside. "Just at dusk, in early spring, the male sings his heart out to attract a mate. And Isabelle had taught her brother, Félix, to know the nightingale's call. Every spring they competed to see who heard it first. But that year—the year he met Mémé Simone—his sister was gone. 'I heard the nightingale for her,' he told Simone. 'She'll never hear her mate now.'"

"But," I broke in, "her mate was Grand-Pierre. She *had* heard him."

Marius came back from the woodstove and sat down across the table from me. "You and I know that, but Félix couldn't accept it. He felt dead inside, except for hating your grandfather." Marius paused, as if stunned by what he had said. The fire crackled and hissed. "But even as a girl, Simone had wonderful healing qualities. Gradually, she nursed Félix back to life. Which brings me to the saddest part." Marius pulled our two tallest candles together and watched them flickering side by side. "Everyone knew Félix and Simone were in love. At the time, no one objected. There were more important fears. As long as the war dragged on, the biggest concern was for her family to survive—to protect themselves and this Jewish boy they hid on their farm."

"Jewish boy." I groaned. "So *that* was it. Her parents—"

"Try understanding them, Zazoo. Try seeing it from their side." When Marius looked up from the candles, I noticed, for the first time, how piercingly blue his eyes could be. "Mémé's parents were strict mountain people. Simple farmers."

"Simple Catholics." Everyone I knew was Catholic—except Monsieur Klein, who was Jewish, and Grand-Pierre, who had no religion.

"Actually, they were *not* Catholic. Simone's family was Protestant. Huguenots, they were called—Huguenots who, hundreds of years earlier, had taken refuge in the Cévennes Mountains because Catholics were slaughtering *them*. So when the Jews were being slaughtered by Nazis, Mémé's family felt it their duty to take the Jews in. But they didn't feel it their duty, once the war ended, to let a Jew marry their daughter."

"He and your grandmother wanted to marry? Monsieur *Klein?*"

"They did, yes. More than anything. By the time the war ended, they were seventeen." Marius sighed so heavily the candle flames wavered between us. "Her parents said Félix had to leave. The war was over; he was safe from harm."

"But how could they treat him that way? They had lived with him—didn't they care about him?"

"For three years they'd been living together. He was almost a son to them. But you see, religion was the most important thing in their lives. Even more important than their feelings. They said they were very sorry—it made *them* cry, too."

"Sure." I wanted to throw my arms around Marius but hugged myself instead.

"They understood he loved Simone—but she couldn't marry a Jew. Her husband had to be a Huguenot."

"People!" I hugged myself tighter. "How *stupid!* Aren't nightingales probably smarter?"

"Probably." Again, his smile broke my heart.

"Oh, Marius." There was too much to say. Isabelle Klein, Grand-Pierre, my own dead parents. "The world's so *sad.*"

"Yes, Zazoo."

"But if the world is sad, how can I be happy?"

"I don't know." His smile stayed on me. "But I feel the same way. Happy and sad all at once."

We gazed across the table at each other; the fire crackled and moaned.

"Are you sleepy?" His voice was so gentle. "I can leave, if you—"

"Not sleepy at all." I was too happy to sleep! Too miserable! "So your grandmother, Mémé Simone—did she suffer alone, for years and years? Like Monsieur Klein?"

"At first she was wretched. For months she hardly spoke, hardly ate. But time passed, and, after all, her parents weren't vicious, just strict. They tried introducing her to nice Huguenot boys, but she wasn't interested."

"Of course not! She loved Félix Klein!"

"Yes. She did love him. But a year went by, and another, and finally she went away to a nursing school. Which was where she met the doctor. My grandfather. Not young like Félix, and not interested in birds. But he loved Simone and wanted to marry her. And although he wasn't Huguenot, at least he was Protestant, so her parents approved. Their approval was important to her. She married him."

"People are *so stupid!*" My exasperation nearly blew out the candles. "Did she love this—this—doctor?"

"Well, she didn't lie to him about her feelings. Before they married, she told him she didn't love him—not the way she loved Félix—but she did admire him."

"*Admire?* Like a good book or something?"

"Zazoo, Zazoo." The freckles crinkled at the corners of his eyes.

I couldn't help thinking of my parents as they stepped off the path to examine their lily. "I suppose *you* would marry someone you didn't love, as long as you *admired* her?"

"Oh, I'm not interested in marriage. At least not until summertime."

"Birdbrain." As much as I wanted to throw my arms around him, part of me—the scared part—was glad to have the table between us. "Paris is too big a place, is what Grand-Pierre says."

"And he's right." Marius leaned back, beaming at me.

"You should live somewhere smaller, is what I say. Somewhere with your own mailbox, so you don't have to sneak mail from a pharmacy. What's the story with this pharmacy of yours, anyway? Just another non-coincidence?"

"That's right. In our apartment building, one neighbor is a pharmacist. He and his wife live just down the hall. So when you told me Félix Klein was your village pharmacist, I came up with the idea of you writing me at a Paris pharmacy, and asked my neighbor if I could use his business address. At first, I wanted this to be secret from Mémé Simone. He was happy to help."

"And he doesn't have a beautiful daughter?"

"No daughter." Marius chuckled. "Just a wife and baby boy."

"And your Mémé Simone? She's happy, is she, now that she and her doctor are rich, living in Paris? How happy *is* she?"

"To tell the truth," said Marius, "she's lonely. The doctor—my grandfather, don't forget—was a good deal older than Simone. Two years ago, in July, he rolled over one night and didn't roll back. Heart attack."

"He died?" I stared across at Marius.

"He died, yes. They had been comfortable living together, and I'd been comfortable with them. He was a nice old man, my grandfather. A sweet man. I liked him. And yet we were never what you'd call *close.* Not the way I am with Mémé Simone, or you are with Grand-Pierre." He paused, as if uncomfortable with what he had to say next. "The war wasn't easy on Grand-Pierre, either."

"No." I sucked in a quick breath. "Not easy at all."

"That part about eating apples all winter—it must have been rough."

"Very rough." I hoped he would ask no more. "Terrible." Glancing about for some distraction, any topic that could lead us away from Grand-Pierre's war, I spotted the basket of fruit at the end of the table—a basket which, as far as I could recall, had never held an apple. "Do you think an orange would do?"

Marius knew exactly what I meant. "Let's try." He picked up the orange and the paring knife. "How should I peel this? I don't have Grand-Pierre's skill with a knife—but then, he's had more experience."

"Yes, he has." *Please,* I urged silently. *Don't ask more questions.*

"Stuck in that hut by himself, with plenty of game all around, but unable to shoot for fear of being caught. Was he a good hunter, your Grand-Pierre?"

"Yes, he was." It was only when I tried repeating the word that my voice gave out. "Quite a . . . hunter." I grabbed the paring knife from Marius, slashed the orange from top to bottom, and then, with my thumb, yanked the thick skin free of the fruit. It was good to have something to do with my hands. "There." I shuddered. "Finished. We can put the peels on the stove. We can see what they—we can—"

The next thing I knew, Marius was at my side of the table,

rocking me in his arms while I sobbed. He didn't tell me not to cry, didn't claim everything was all right. He waited until I wore myself out, then patted my hair one last time—and then, as if nothing had happened, took our orange peels to the stove.

"I must look like a nightmare."

Marius scattered the peels on the stovetop. "You look like a girl who's been living alone with too many worries."

"We all have our worries. Monsieur Klein says we must take the bitter with the sweet." I breathed deeply, trembled, breathed again. "You've made the kitchen smell wonderful."

"*We* have, Zazoo. A new perfume—prettier than anything sold in any pharmacy." His voice was so tender. "*Eau de Zazoo.* All those Parisian women will be dying for it. We'll be rich and won't have to work—we can just peel apples and oranges. And swim in the canal."

"And watch birds with your Mémé Simone."

"And," he reminded me, "listen to poems? About a sad gray cat?"

"Oh, that. I did promise, didn't I." As exhausted as I felt—empty as a hollowed-out shell—I also felt strangely free, in a way I hadn't since the canal had been warm enough for me to glide beneath its lily pads. "But you haven't told me the rest of Mémé Simone's story."

"Her story isn't over. And neither is Félix Klein's."

"So is that why you cycled along our towpath in October, looking for birds and information? From some hope that his story and hers—"

"—might become the same story again. Yes." On the stovetop, Marius flipped an orange peel with his finger. "That's what brought me here the first time. But now my reasons are more complicated." He watched the darkening scraps of orange skin dance on the stove. His voice had dropped to such a whisper, I wondered if he might be nervous again. "Tell me, Zazoo. Is your poem about love?"

"Oh, not the first verses. They're about loneliness. But who knows? If an old gray cat can be lonely, and a doctor's widow can be lonely, then can't a pharmacist be lonely, too?"

"I guess he'd have to be." Marius sat back down in his chair.

"Well, then, I'll recite the beginning of our poem about the gray cat. Dedicated to young Simone and young Félix, as well as to old Simone and old Félix."

"Tchin-tchin," said Marius, as people say when they raise glasses of wine—or in my case, juice—to each other.

"Tchin-tchin. And when I've finished reciting, you'll have to go?"

"Yes, Zazoo. But I'll be back."

"Soon?" I teased.

"As soon as I can. But recite your verse slowly, so it can take longer. The last part you wrote me, remember, was about the cat's eyes—"

"His restlessly wandering eyes?"

"Right. A cat who yearns to be on the boats floating past, but can't leave his home." Marius spoke so very softly. "His cozy dry home."

"Well, then. Another verse about the old gray cat, recited as slowly as possible. Written by the old keeper of Lock Forty-three, with some help from his assistant.

"The boats came and went;
The old cat stayed and stayed.
He watched, and watched longer,
and waited, afraid
that his chance wouldn't come
his boat not appear—
he'd wait and he'd watch
and he'd live out his years,
never go where he wanted,
never learn *there* from *here,*
never climb, and climb higher,
up the lock ladder—
never find, at its top,
what some possible liar
had claimed was a tunnel
so long and resounding
you could see, from the far end
the world at its founding—
a world of such oddness,
such freedom from fear,
it must have had so much
(he thought with a tear,
with a barely wet hint
of a tiny cat tear)

it must have had so much
he couldn't find—here."

"Cat tear." Marius smiled. "But surely our poem isn't finished?"

"There'll be more—the cat tells me so. He's still sad, but not nearly as sad as before. And neither is a certain funny-looking girl with a button nose and weird eyes."

"Your nose," said Marius, "is perfect." He pulled on his overcoat. "And your eyes? Really, Zazoo. They're so big and dark, but mostly so . . . kind. You truly don't know how beautiful your eyes are?"

"Hold me again like you did before. This time I won't cry."

Marius didn't kiss me. He stood stroking my hair with one hand, his other arm softly around my shoulder. Eyes closed, I leaned my cheek against him until the coarse weave of his coat brushed me awake. We turned to the door.

"You *will* come back soon?"

"As soon as I possibly can. Until then we can write."

"Yes." I watched him pull on his gloves. "Monsieur Klein will be pleased to hear of your visit. But I won't mention Mémé Simone."

"Good." Marius stood very still, as if listening to the wind whistle along the canal. "She'll be pleased, too—by everything. But not surprised." He opened the door. "My regards to Grand-Pierre."

"And mine to Mémé Simone."

Almost formally he kissed my left cheek, then my right one—a friendly double kiss but also much more. He turned his bike on the terrace and, with a wave, pedaled away toward the triple-arched bridge.

27. Magic Cards

There were sides of my new happiness I could share only with my reflection in the tower mirror. Grand-Pierre was often lost in his fog, and knowing about Mémé Simone kept me from sharing the best parts with Monsieur Klein. So I shared my joy with the mirror, not because I liked what it showed me—a flat-chested girl with peculiar eyes—but because Marius said he did.

Still, with Monsieur Klein I could share *some* sides of my happiness. Every few days I stopped at his pharmacy on my way home from school, to study his postcards and to picture him, as a boy my age, in love with a girl named Simone.

"So how is the Klein Collection today? Has our gallery expanded?"

"Let me think, Mademoiselle. Two new Gauguins, one Monet—and *this* acquisition, by the German painter Franz Marc."

"Ooh." I wrinkled my nose. "Nothing by a German, thanks. After what they did during the war—"

Monsieur Klein froze in mid-gesture, holding the card

halfway between us. "But Zazoo, not all Germans were monsters. In fact, this man didn't live to see our war—he died in the previous one. The Nazis hadn't been dreamt of yet. I repeat, his painting would be my next choice for your Paris Marius." He laid the card on the counter.

"A painting by a . . . German." The word left a sour taste. I glanced down at the card, which showed a blue horse standing in front of red and yellow hills. "What's it called?"

"As you see, *The Little Blue Horse.* Isn't it delightful?"

I examined the card again. "Well, yes, I suppose it is." Monsieur Klein was right, yet again. How could anyone *not* like such a painting?

"Franz Marc died twenty years before our war." Monsieur Klein pondered the blue horse. "No, not all Germans were monsters. And not all Frenchmen were saints."

"Even in this village, Monsieur?"

He chose his words carefully. "In this village, as in every French village, there were both monsters and saints."

"That's not so hard to understand—I mean, that a village has both good and bad." This gave me an idea. "But can't a *person* be the same way?"

Monsieur Klein folded his white-sleeved arms over his chest.

"Can't a person," I insisted, "be both good and bad? For example, Grand-Pierre, who was such a skilled hunter—"

Monsieur Klein held up one hand. "A hunter?" His mouth twisted in a grimace. "All right, we'll say for the moment that he was not a killer, your Grand-Pierre, he was a hunter."

"*Our* Grand-Pierre," I said faintly. With one word—a word

I couldn't bring myself to repeat—Monsieur Klein had thrown my mind into a jumble. "Don't say he's just my Grand-Pierre. He belongs to all of us. He's the village's Grand-Pierre."

"You've thought a great deal about this, Zazoo."

"I think of nothing else." Monsieur Klein's sad-smiling eyes stopped me. "Well, that's not true. Of course I think about the boy in Paris, and I think about you—"

"But it all comes back to your Grand-Pierre?" Monsieur Klein paused. "Or as you say, the village's Grand-Pierre? But you're not alone in this, Zazoo—it's precisely the same for me. Ever since you arrived in our village, I've heard how sweetly he treated you, what a gentle man he could be. And such accounts didn't fit what I knew of him."

"No?"

"They didn't fit at all."

"But Monsieur, even if Grand-Pierre *was* to blame for the deaths in your family, and even if he *did* kill German soldiers, didn't he also save your life? By guiding you to the Cévennes Mountains?"

Monsieur Klein's shoulders sagged.

"Isn't it true, Monsieur? Couldn't he be both bad *and* good?"

A truck passed in the street, rattling the pharmacy door with its wheels.

"That," Monsieur Klein nodded, "is exactly the problem—a man being good and bad both. Kind and cruel, cruel and kind. It seems I've waited a long time for someone to correct me on this point. How odd that it should be a young girl from so far away." Frowning down at the little blue horse, he seemed terribly alone.

I had to say something, however stupid. "Let me pay for this one card, Monsieur. You've given me so many beautiful cards, I really should—"

"You really should watch your manners, Mademoiselle, and not insult the rare generosity of an old man. Your feelings for this bird watcher Marius take me back to when I was his age. How old would you guess he might be—?"

"He's sixteen. Far too old, many would say—I mean, for me."

"You're older than you think, Zazoo, anyone can see that. Precocious."

"Thank you, Monsieur." I didn't ask what *precocious* meant.

"But when did you learn his age?" Monsieur Klein seemed relieved to fall back into harmless chatter. "Is there news, Zazoo, that you haven't shared with me?"

"Oh, there might be."

"Withholding secrets is hardly a gracious way to treat your art dealer."

"Not gracious at all. The fact is, he visited."

"Our Marius?" Monsieur Klein picked up the postcard and fanned himself with it as if to cool his astonishment. "All the way from Paris?"

"That's right. Two hours by train and another by bike."

"He spent"—Monsieur Klein glanced behind me as if checking the shop for spies—"he spent the *night?*"

"No, Monsieur, but he did stay late. Ten o'clock, eleven o'clock—"

"Zazoo! This boy *likes* you."

"Yes, I believe he does." *And, Monsieur Klein, he likes you as well.* "But what shall I write him this time? Another poem?"

"Brilliant. A gem of a verse—"

"To go with this blue gem of a horse."

"—from a gem of a girl." He watched me write, then leaned back to listen as I recited the new poem I had spent so many hours composing.

"The sound of a nightingale's silence
is louder than anyone's cry.
The tread of your long-ago footstep
echoes whenever I sigh.
The water gone still and unmoving
can't freeze in my memory's eye—
 it ripples and waves,
 it whispers your name,
 it hears you say 'Soon' one more time."

Turning to the window, Monsieur Klein scowled out at the gray sky. "This poem, Zazoo. It's strange. So . . . *mature,* for a girl your age. To be precocious is one thing, but—"

"Marius is older, Monsieur. I'm *trying* to sound mature. You don't like my poem."

"Oh, I do. I do. But where do you come up with such thoughts?"

"Thoughts?" Seeing the pain in his eyes, I knew I had pushed my experiment too far.

"Your images." He winced. "I thought you said you didn't know many varieties of birds."

"And I don't know many, Monsieur. I'm sorry if I—"

"Then in this poem, what makes you choose a nightingale?" He turned back to face me. "A lovely poem, Zazoo. But why a nightingale?"

It wasn't that I wanted to lie, but I had to keep the secret. "Because of Marius," I said. "He told me, the other evening when he visited, about nightingales. He said that in April the male sings his heart out to attract the female. At twilight."

"But why would he tell you such a thing in December?"

"For me to hope he'll be here when spring comes." The last thing I wanted was to hurt Monsieur Klein, but there seemed no way to undo the distress my poem had caused. "He didn't exactly say it," I went on, "but the idea seemed to be that this spring he and I could listen for the first nightingale. Together. Wouldn't that be sweet?"

"Sweet. Yes, I suppose. Sweet." He turned to rummage in his cash drawer. "Here." He thrust a stamp toward me, then turned again to frown into the street.

With great care I applied the stamp to my card. Monsieur Klein wouldn't look at me. I waited, but he only glared at the sky. "Good afternoon, Monsieur," I whispered, ashamed to have hurt him so deeply.

"Good afternoon," he said. "Zazoo."

I stepped outside, trudged to the yellow postbox, and

dropped my card through the slot. *Kind and cruel.* If mixing kindness and cruelty was the way of the world, I was no different from anyone else. It wasn't enough that Grand-Pierre had not spoken to Monsieur Klein ever since their Awful Time. It wasn't enough that Monsieur Klein's sister had been killed, or that he'd been banished from the girl he loved. Now even I couldn't resist torturing him with clever rhymes about birds. A chunk of roadside ice mocked me in the twilight gloom; I gave it an explosive kick. All at once my chest hurt desperately. I was glad of its pain, glad to suspect I had an early death coming. Filled with pity for myself and the world, I plodded down the darkening street.

28. Old Louie

For several days, not knowing what to say, I avoided Monsieur Klein. Then, as if some part of me felt I deserved it, I came down with the worst cold of my life. My throat turned raw; my head stuffed itself with poison. Through one class after another, I sat blowing my nose and staring out the window and wondering how he felt, standing at the counter in his white jacket, brooding back to his first nightingale. My eyes filled at the thought, but no one noticed, I was so splotchy and leaky anyway.

Soon I stayed home from school altogether, coughing and coughing until it was no longer a suspicion: I *knew* my personal poison was killing me. What was more, I faced death alone, since Grand-Pierre was nearby in body only; his mind seemed a thousand kilometers away. When I told him I was too sick for school, he nodded and went back to his knitting.

Then came the fever. My cough grew deeper and my temperature higher, until one night I trembled so badly I dropped the thermometer while lifting it to my mouth. Its glass tube smashed on the floor; I watched the beads of mercury roll out of sight under the kitchen table.

Grand-Pierre looked up from the book he was pretending to read. "You," he said, "are ill."

"Yes, old man. Do you know the price of a gravestone?"

"Zazeezoo, Zeezoo, Zee. To you, life is so dramatic."

"And it isn't to *you?*" On the floor, the silver globules dribbled into the cracks.

"Not so dramatic, no." He peered at me with such kindness that Monsieur Klein's words *kind and cruel, cruel and kind* returned to haunt me again. Ever since leaving the pharmacy, those words had seesawed in my head. "Time's come," said Grand-Pierre, "to get you to a doctor, even if it has to be Old Louie."

"Old Louie the Leech Doctor?"

One of our childhood games. When I'd been a little girl and had been even mildly sick, Grand-Pierre always announced that I'd have to be cured by Old Louie the Leech Doctor, the cruelest man in our valley, who would smear blood-sucking worms on my legs. As a little girl, I had always laughed, knowing that Grand-Pierre was kind and not cruel and would never send me to such a demon. But in those days I had never truly been sick; the nurse had given us medicine at school, but I'd never had to visit the clinic.

"Old Louie." Grand-Pierre nodded.

Through fevered eyes I watched his face. "And he'll smear me with leeches?"

"It's possible he's learned some new techniques. But I doubt it."

"And how long ago," I asked, "were *you* his patient?"

"In the Dark Ages sometime. I forget."

"Right." I honked at my raw little nose. "So when will we go?"

"Tomorrow, Zazoo. In the morning. You're sure you won't sleep down here tonight? I could make up the sofa for you, near the fireplace—"

"Upstairs," I said thickly. "In my tower. Lots of blankets. You have enough francs saved up to buy me a good gravestone?"

"Certainly." The older he grew, the more Grand-Pierre enjoyed joking about death. "Two, I'll buy—one for you, another for me. Maybe the mortician will give me a discount. But you'll make it through the night, I think. Tomorrow Old Louie can tell you how many liters of blood his leeches will need."

He may have teased me that night, but the next morning at the clinic Grand-Pierre was not so relaxed. As the nurse led me away, he sucked and sucked at the stem of his absent pipe. I could see why: he knew the pain in my chest was about to kill me, leaving him to make his morning oatmeal alone. Who would recite our poems to him when I was gone? I was nearly in tears by the time the nurse handed me a huge blue gown.

"Don't you have a smaller gown, please?" If I had to die, I preferred doing it in something that fit.

"Just the one size, sweetie." Before leaving, she paused. "Is there anything else bothering you? I mean, apart from the gown being too big and your cough being so bad? Anything else?"

"Chest hurts," I said between coughs.

"I know, dear. It feels like you're being torn to bits, but really that's just part of having a cold."

"What I mean is, my chest hurt before the cold started. There's an ache in my chest. Has been for weeks." The thought of breathing my last ragged breath in that green room, draped in such a baggy blue robe, was more than depressing. It was, as Juliette might have pronounced, tragic.

"I'll be sure the doctor takes a good listen to your chest." The nurse picked up my folder and padded away.

I waited. Each tick of the clock brought me closer to death.

Ten minutes later, Old Louie shambled into the room. He wasn't a large man, except in the middle. He looked almost harmless—and when he spoke, his voice was soft and soothing. "Let's hear the piteous state of your lungs." He slid the cup of his stethoscope from spot to spot across my blue-gowned chest. "A pretty girl," he said, as if to prove he was a liar. "With ugly-sounding lungs but a lovely name. Zazoo."

"Thank you, Doctor." I was about to compliment his lovely name Old Louie, but broke into my rasping cough instead.

Not wishing to die, he leaned away from me. "And how is the Big Stone? Does he have a cough, too, and need antibiotics to make him well?"

"No, he never catches cold. But—"

Old Louie slid the stethoscope cup to a new spot. "Yes?"

"His memory isn't so good."

"I'm sorry it's going. Mine's going, too, although perhaps not quite so fast. But I may not have such a memory to lose. A great pity, after all he did for us."

Wanting to hear once again that Grand-Pierre had been a hero and not a killer, I forgot to ask Old Louie if I had three months to live or just one.

"The Big Stone did so much," Old Louie went on, "and finally he brought *you* to us. Our river beauty. They say you swim a great deal, and in the winter you skate?"

I was stunned he knew anything about me. "When I'm not too sick. Will I die soon, Doctor? Before spring?"

Old Louie took a step backward and squinted at me. "Why, no, Zazoo, I don't believe you will. Not before spring, no. Most likely not before your ninety-third birthday. Do you feel like dying?"

"Of course I don't."

"I had heard you were a girl of imagination, and now I believe it. But no, you won't die this time. The nurse tells me your chest hurts?"

I answered with a heart-wrenching series of barks.

"The bronchitis doesn't concern me so much—the pills

will clear up your lungs. But the nurse mentioned some pain you felt before the cough started."

"Well, yes. There was some—some—"

"An *ache,* was it?" Leaning against the wall, Old Louie inspected the ceiling. "A mysterious ache, rather like the feeling of a pulled muscle, right here, across your chest?" He showed me on his own chest, where his stethoscope hung. "Right here where your breasts are starting to develop?"

"My breasts," I repeated in a hoarse sort of prayer.

"Yes, Zazoo. Your breasts. Here, see for yourself." He didn't move closer but spoke from where he stood. "Turn sideways and look in that mirror over the sink." He gazed calmly at the ceiling. "Pull your gown so it's smooth. Now turn a bit more—"

I knew what he was doing but pretended I didn't. I knew because I had done it hundreds of times myself, in front of the mirror in my tower room, turning this way and that in hopes of seeing a shadow of roundness where only flatness had been.

"But I had no *idea.*" Staring at my first hint of shape in the mirror, I decided the blue hospital gown was the most beautiful garment I'd ever worn. Glancing higher, I saw my eyes brimming with pleasure—and was amazed to discover that they, too, were beautiful. How could I ever have called them ugly? Old Louie the Leech Doctor kindly went on examining his ceiling, as if searching for faulty tiles. "No one ever said breasts would *hurt*. No one said anything about—really? *Breasts?*"

"Yes, dear girl. Really. Your Grand-Pierre, I used to think, was a man prepared for anything. Never surprised by any circumstance. But I see now that even he, the Great Stone himself, couldn't prepare you for this one."

"And is it normal? This ache I feel?"

"Most girls don't have such an ache, but some do. And I'm sorry to say it may go on for some time. But I'm pleased to say it's nothing to worry about. Well, then." He patted his stethoscope, or perhaps patted his own chest to thank it for not hurting. "Is there anything else, Zazoo? Of, you know, a private nature? Questions you might not feel comfortable asking in school?"

"Not really," I lied. Was there anything else! He'd need hours! "No, I can't think of anything."

"Well, then, just take the pills the lady out front gives you—three a day, one after each meal—and if you aren't feeling well when the pills run out in ten days, come back and see me. And you'll most likely have a few more feverish nights. When it gets bad, take what we call fever pills for children, even if you don't think of yourself as a child. You have some at home?"

"I think so. Not aspirin?"

"Not at your age. Non-aspirin pain pills. Here. I've got some samples." He fumbled in his desk drawer until he found what he wanted, then handed me a packet. "If those run out, get more at the pharmacy. The antibiotics should fix you up—all but the ache in your chest, which may not go away for a while." He studied me, his eyes half-closed. "Look at it this way, Zazoo. Even having an ache in your chest is preferable to being a boy."

"It is?" *This* was unexpected.

"Of course. Listen to the boys in your class, or better still, the ones a year older. The ones growing like weeds? Listen to how they talk."

"They talk the same way I do."

"Listen again, Zazoo, particularly when they become excited, which, with thirteen-year-olds, is nine-tenths of the time, even if they're trying to act bored. Their voices betray them. Their boy voices growing into man voices don't know which way to turn, so they turn both ways at once and frazzle our nerves. I'm not a young man—some scamps, I know, even call me Old Louie—but I remember when I was thirteen. I used to envy you girls your smooth voices, believe me."

"You're not serious." He wasn't so bad after all. And neither was my face, I admitted. So lovely, my eyes had been, for that one blissful moment.

Everything was lovely, including the kindly nurse who knocked on the door and poked a folder inside. A folder filled with documents, I supposed, that told the doctor which patients were dying and which were not. It was good to know my name had been moved to the safe list.

"Come back," Old Louie told me, "whenever you have questions Grand-Pierre can't answer. Do his thyroid pills seem to be helping?"

"As far as I can tell." Zazoo the Pill Girl. I felt like asking if there was a pill to remind Grand-Pierre to pee in the toilet. "The thyroid pills keep him alive, Monsieur Klein says."

"Well, if Félix says so, it's true. Should have been a doctor himself. Good. Give my regards to your grandfather." Old Louie backed out the door.

Turning to the mirror, I ogled the lovely blue gown. My *breasts,* just think. They surely did ache, though perhaps not as badly as before. I wished I could share the news with Juliette LeMiel. But no, such news could only be shared with Louie the Leech Doctor—and with my old gray cat, wherever he wandered.

Gazing into the mirror at my first suggestion of roundness, I was so pleased with the world that I saw the best thing of all, something no mirror had ever shown me. In that magical mirror in Old Louie's office, I saw my mother's face smiling out at me from deep inside my own face. I was so sure of it that I leaned forward to be closer and smiled back at her through the glass, through the grief, through the years.

29. Dawn Visit

Three nights later we had our first storm of the winter, long veils of snow twisting across the valley. Through my moonlit window, I watched sheets of snow swirl down the river, their shapes making me wonder what was real and what wasn't.

The pills from Old Louie weren't working too well. Late the night of the snowstorm, my fever brought me one tossing river dream after another. In the most exhausting dream, I wasn't even a fish girl but a fish, like the silver salmon trying to swim to her birthplace so she could lay her eggs and die. My body struggled with its fever; my brain made me climb up one waterfall, and then, when I thought I'd reached the top and could rest, up another and another.

Writhing out of my troubled sleep, damp from such hard work, I didn't recognize my tower room in the first light of dawn. I was Zazoo the Gill Girl, gasping in a strange tangled bed, as if yanked from my natural element.

To stop burning up under my sheets, I went to the window and stared down at the snowy river. Such chills shook me that when I tried taking a drink, my hand spilled water from the glass. I pulled off my sticky nightshirt, put on pajamas, and tottered downstairs for two more of Old Louie's fever pills. In the bathroom cupboard there was one tablet left. I drank it down, hoping it would save me from any more waterfall dreams.

Turning for the stairs, I nearly fainted at the sight of Grand-Pierre's ghost. He stood in the dim hallway, eyes glassy. Even when I jumped, his focus didn't budge from some mysterious spot on the wall.

"Grand-Pierre?" I whimpered. I hadn't gone downstairs to help anyone else. *I* was the one who needed help.

"Have to get out," he muttered. "Parachute's ready?"

"No parachute, Grand-Pierre. The war's over." My shivering made it hard for me to speak. "We're home in the mill."

"Home?" Finally his eyes found me. "The—mill?"

"Yes, Grand-Pierre. I'm Zazoo. Your granddaughter."

"Ah." He nodded politely, as if another ghost had introduced us.

"Do you need to go to the bathroom?" I asked, fighting back tears.

"Bathroom?" First the word seemed to please him; then he frowned. "Not now. Have to find my parachute."

"Right." I took his elbow. "It's in here, old man. Come."

Afraid my knees might give way, I guided him to his bed. Outside his window, the first glow of daylight brushed the treetops. "Here we are, Grand-Pierre." I laid him back in his blankets and covered him. "Rest now. Then I'll try to rest, too."

I left his door open and hauled myself, step by dizzy step, up to my tower room. Rapunzel was nowhere in sight; neither was her prince.

I peered out onto the stormy river. My bed wasn't the slightest bit inviting; it might make me a salmon again, thrashing my way up one waterfall after another. I squinted out at the world through the reflection of my face, through the twisting snow beyond, and saw the boat floating toward me on the river. My dark plum punt, without oars, bobbing along in the current. And seated in front, facing downriver—facing me—sat the gray cat himself, unperturbed by the snow whipping around him. He seemed pleased to be in command. Floating toward my window, he never turned his head, never flicked his tail, but stared straight at me. His look seemed to say that if he was out there, unafraid of such weather, why should I be afraid where I stood, inside, all cozy and dry?

Which was when I noticed that my face in the window reflection had started to smile—my face grown up from a faraway child into a French girl with Vietnamese eyes, stunning dark eyes which had first seen their own beauty above a baggy hospital gown.

A curtain of snow blew past, screening the cat from view. I waited and watched for maybe two minutes, maybe ten seconds. Fever, I knew, played tricks with time—played tricks with everything except what I had *seen*. As the dawn brightened, my reflection grew dim in the glass. Still, the gray cat was out there, nearby, whenever I needed him most.

30. *The Sad Dance of Love*

I knew I was too sick to leave the mill, but later that morning I told Grand-Pierre I was going to the pharmacy for fever pills, and went. He didn't seem to mind. It was hard to tell if he had even heard me. He sat by the kitchen window with his silver needles, knitting a sock to cover the longest ankle on earth. I didn't have the heart to point out he had forgotten to stop knitting where a normal ankle ended. Instead, I refilled his cup with tea, poured in the amount of milk he liked, stirred in sugar, and left it steaming beside him.

There was no doubt I needed fever pills, but what I needed most was a good listener. The kids at school wouldn't do. Could they have the slightest idea, any of them, how it felt for me to live with an old man who was fading in front of my eyes?

Or my teachers. Imagine asking Croque Monsieur, so timid he couldn't pronounce *penis* without blushing, to explain how our valley's great hero could be turning into a little boy—and scarier yet, *my* little boy. No. Old Croque might understand the anatomy of a crayfish, but he wouldn't be too helpful if asked about the body of a teenager or the brain of an old man.

Louie the Leech Doctor, with his tired, peaceful eyes, would have listened—but you needed an appointment to see him. Then there were the priests, who were supposed to know about suffering, such as being burnt at the stake like Joan of Arc, poor thing, when the English put the torch to her. But Grand-Pierre had never cared for priests. He said the only good ones had died in the Awful Time—the rest were real estate agents dressed in black. Frantic as I was, if I had known a nice priest, I would have talked to him in spite of anything Grand-Pierre said. But I didn't know one.

So I gave up trying to think of anyone who could comfort me and went to the pharmacy to buy a packet of fever pills to keep those dreams away.

"Zazoo the Snow Girl." Monsieur Klein smiled from behind his counter.

"That's me." I hacked and wheezed and tried appreciating the warmth of the store after the steely cold of the air outside, but I was too miserable to appreciate anything.

"Poor girl, have you been to see Old Louie?"

"Yes, Monsieur. He gave me fever pills—the kind for children, you know. But they're all gone—I took the last one this morning. So I need some more, please."

Monsieur Klein bustled to his shelf of pain remedies. "No mail, I'm afraid, but the pines are gorgeous in their new snow. I suppose you've been watching polar bears along the river?"

"No." I hesitated, then decided he wouldn't make fun of me. "No polar bears. But I did see something else—something just as miraculous."

"Yes?" Monsieur Klein returned with a small packet and placed it on the counter.

"I hope you won't think me crazy, Monsieur, but I actually did see this. My gray cat. You know, the one Grand-Pierre calls my *sad* gray cat?"

"Certainly—from that poem you sent to Paris."

"Yes. Well, Monsieur, this is the truth. Looking out my window this morning, I saw him. He sat in the bow of my boat as it floated down the river toward me."

Monsieur Klein glanced from my face to my fever pills and back, but he didn't smile. "'There once was a cat—'"

"You have a good memory, Monsieur." I was grateful he didn't mock me.

"Ah, Pierre," he murmured. "The poet of Lock Forty-three."

"But Monsieur, he doesn't write poems anymore. *His* memory is *not* good. It's almost gone." I heard the pleading in my voice. "He's turning into his own shadow."

"What are you saying, Zazoo?" Monsieur Klein paused only a second, as if he knew I wouldn't answer. "Are you saying I could talk with Pierre now, as if we were two old friends?"

"But were you *ever* old friends?"

"No. I always hated him." Monsieur Klein said this quite simply, yet he didn't seem filled with hatred, only sadness.

I waited for my fit of shivering to stop. "But you don't hate him now?"

"Of course not, Zazoo, how could I? If he's turned into a shadow, as you say, my hatred for him can only be shadow hatred. To hate someone—I mean properly *hate* someone, with all the attention hatred deserves—takes energy. I'm not as energetic as I was in my youth."

I took up my packet of fever pills and studied its plastic pods, as if each one was a marvel. "So . . . you could talk with him now?" I set the packet back on the counter.

Monsieur Klein gazed at the pills between us. "I believe I could. Yes."

"And what exactly did you say to Grand-Pierre the last time you two dared speak? Forty-eight years ago."

"Let's see." Monsieur Klein sounded as excited as a man recalling his grocery list. "It was on our way to the Cévennes Mountains—he caught his foot between two rocks. I had to help him get free, you see. We spoke only because it was an emergency."

"But why help him get free if you hated him?"

"Soldiers were following us—at least, we thought they were—so we were in a hurry. And only Pierre knew the way across that river."

"If you had known the way, would you have left him there to die?"

"I might have, Zazoo. Yes." Monsieur Klein rubbed his fingertips together. "It's hard to be sure."

"And when you spoke with him that last time, what did you say?"

"I said,'Hold still, Pierre—if you break your leg, we're both dead. Let me find a stick to pry these rocks apart.'"

"And did he answer?"

"He said, 'You're right, I'm being stupid.'" Monsieur Klein let his hands fall to the counter, one to each side of my fever pills.

"And that was *all?*"

"Yes, Zazoo. The last thing I'd told him before that was, if I ever had the chance—ever—I would kill him, and make his death as painful as possible."

The packet contained twenty-four fever tablets for children—four rows, six tablets to a row. I stared at those tablets, each sealed in its own plastic bubble, and remembered an American cruising through our lock who had shown me a bottle filled with hundreds of aspirin pills. In France, aspirin pills didn't come in a bottle, they came sealed individually. It seemed strange to me that different places insisted on doing the same things in such different ways.

"Did you say you would kill him by never speaking again?"

Monsieur Klein chuckled dryly. "Funny—that does seem to have been my technique. But no, I meant to kill him in a more traditional way. A more brutal way. War makes monsters of us all."

"That's what Grand-Pierre says. But you've had many chances to kill him."

"Of course I have. Living nearby all these years—"

"That isn't what I mean, Monsieur, and you know it."

"Do I?" His mouth smiled, but not his eyes.

"All these years, I've come to you for his thyroid pills—and now I see why he sent me instead of coming himself—all these years, you could have done it."

"You're right, Zazoo, of course you are. He's known I could do it, and I've known. But you see, I'm a pharmacist."

"That's my point. You make his pills."

"In this case, someone else does—a company near Toulouse. But I put them in the container, yes."

"It doesn't matter who makes them. You give them to me, in their bottle. How would I know the difference?"

"You wouldn't, and neither would Pierre. And yes, I could easily have ground up his pills and mixed their powder with other powder. He's such an old man, the authorities would never examine him to see how he'd died. . . . But look at the *time,* Zazoo! No wonder we haven't been interrupted—it's been my lunchtime for the last twenty minutes!" Clearly relieved to have changed the subject, he went to the door and clicked its bolt. "Come. There's soup in the kitchen, chicken soup, the best thing for your cold. Much better than any medicine I sell here."

"And do you have cookies?" I, too, was glad to change the subject. The thought of one old man I loved being murdered—by another old man I was starting to love—was not easy to face.

"Not today, no cookies. Can't have them every day—"

"Good, because I brought some, to thank you for the wonderful gingerbread you fed me last time."

"You," he said, opening the door behind the vitamin case, "are a wonder. Did you bake them yourself?"

"No, I'm too sick. And Grand-Pierre doesn't bake anymore; he gets the ingredients mixed up. These are from the bakery. I bought Grand-Pierre his favorite raisin cookies but got plenty for you and me, too."

"A wonder." Monsieur Klein held the little door open for me.

Fever can make you dull in some ways but sharp in others—and this time, leaving the bright lights of the store, I was ready for the dark interior of Monsieur Klein's house. The middle room was as dim as it had been my first visit, but now I paused to take a more careful look.

"Come, Zazoo." He tugged at my hand. "The kitchen's this way."

"I know. But there's something I need to see."

"Nothing of interest," said Monsieur Klein. "Just this tiny storeroom we never used. Not even any windows, just a dark dusty room. Some knicknacks, some tools. Come."

"Don't you have a light in here, Monsieur Klein?"

He sighed. "Well, yes. There's a light."

"But don't you turn it on?"

"When I'm working, I do. Yes."

"But you won't turn it on for me? I want to *see* things."

"I suppose you do, yes." His voice seemed weak in the darkness. "You're a girl of healthy curiosity; naturally, you want to see things." He clicked the wall switch.

When the ceiling lamp went on, the room was not what he had described. Far from being tiny or dark, it was fresh and bright and alive. The walls—at least, what I could see of them—were pale yellow above the floor's polished wood. One wall was all bookshelves; the others were crowded with framed works of art.

"So many paintings, Monsieur! I can barely see the wall! *This* is the Klein Gallery, not your cash drawer out front. So many paintings!"

"They have accumulated, yes, over the years. But as you see, none are originals. All reproductions. Good quality, and yet . . . reproductions. I send away for them."

"And these unbelievable frames? Do you send away for these, as well?"

"I didn't think you'd notice the frames." He spoke in a new voice. A shy voice.

"But how could I *not* notice them, Monsieur? They're as handsome as the paintings! Such dark, glowing wood—surely you didn't buy them in our village?"

"Not in our village," he whispered. "No."

"You shopped for them in the city?"

"Not in the city." He peered across at me. "I make them myself. Over there at my workbench."

Drawing closer, I examined what I'd first taken to be a table: a workbench, set in an alcove, with its own lamp overhead.

Without being asked, Monsieur Klein turned on the switch. A birdhouse was held in the large wood vise at the end of the bench.

"Not finished," he said. "Still needs some filing to smooth

the corners. And a coat or two of varnish. I don't believe I'll paint this one. Just varnish."

"What bird," I said breathlessly, "will be lucky enough to live in *this* palace?"

"Martins, I hope. Probably window martins, as opposed to their cousins the chimney martins. Social types—they prefer an apartment building, like this one, to living in separate homes. *Highly* sociable. I know what you're thinking."

"Then tell me, Monsieur, so we'll both know."

"You're surprised that old bachelor Klein, who lives all alone, would want to sit in his kitchen and admire such sociable birds as window martins."

"As a matter of fact, Monsieur, I was thinking that these will be the luckiest martins in all Europe, to live in such a luxurious home. And have you put paintings in *their* middle room, as you have in yours? Wonderfully framed miniature paintings of green hills and red skies?"

"Only reproductions," said Monsieur Klein, taking part in my joke. "What window martins appreciate *most* is paintings of insects."

I was drifting back toward the largest wall of paintings when he took my hand and gave me a fresh tug toward the kitchen, which made me all the more curious to inspect every last painting and frame.

"Zazoo," he said urgently. "We haven't much time."

"We have all the time we please." I knew he was tugging me away from something. And then, between a still life of three apples and a portrait of a many-times-fractured purple guitar, I found it. "This one, Monsieur, in its slender dark frame—it isn't a painting at all. A photograph, but hardly in focus."

Monsieur Klein waited, hands clasped behind his back.

"Oh, but now I see—there's a little boy standing in the shadows. *He's* in focus. Is he in a café?"

"He is, yes." Monsieur Klein's voice was no longer shy. "A café you may perhaps recognize."

"Old Vernier's café? Here in the village?"

"Yes, Zazoo, though in those days it belonged to Pascin, fuzzy-headed Pascin, a bachelor himself but the most sociable man in the valley and my father's best friend. In fact, it was Pascin who took that photo."

"Is the little boy *you,* Monsieur? But he looks so sad!"

"Wistful, I prefer to think of him, although maybe he *was* sad at that moment. Look again at the foreground. Look where the boy is looking, Zazoo."

"He's looking at the part that isn't in focus. Pascin may have been your father's friend, but he wasn't such a good photographer."

"He was a brilliant photographer," said Monsieur Klein very softly. "Look closer at that moving shape in front. Think about music and sunlight."

One hand at my forehead, I could only stare. "Dancers?" I whispered. "Dancing . . . the tango?"

"The dance they liked best. Yes. Is the photo coming into focus? Do you see them more clearly?"

"Yes, Monsieur. I see that the man isn't tall—not as tall as the woman—and he's bald. The sun glints—here—on his head. He's so very dignified. I can see *that* from the line of his back. He isn't smiling, I don't think. Is *he* wistful, Monsieur?"

"Perhaps. But tell me about her. Tell me about Isabelle."

"From the curve of her neck, I can see she's beautiful. And the curve—there—at the small of her back, is elegant. Did she know how to swim?"

"Swimming was something our parents never taught us. No, she didn't swim."

"A shame, Monsieur. I can see she would have loved swimming. Underwater especially."

"I'm sure you're right."

Something in his tone made me glance across at him. His face had exactly the expression of the little boy staring so tensely from the shadows.

"Chicken soup," he muttered, and darted into the kitchen.

I stood watching his young ghost, eight or nine years old, frozen in a dark wood frame between one painting of a purple guitar and another of a trio of apples. After giving the grown man a moment to recover, I followed him into his kitchen.

When we had finished our soup and had eaten a cookie each, he set his teacup on its saucer. "Zazoo," he said softly, "this is an important day for me. You told me about seeing your gray cat—"

"Some would say I only saw him because I was sick. Feverish."

"Fever or not, it's a lovely image. The gray cat floating down the river—you shared it with me and I'm honored."

"But Monsieur Klein, it is I who am honored. You let me into your house. I mean, *truly* into your house. Into the middle of it, the heart of it."

"I haven't shown anyone else, Zazoo. Not those paintings, and certainly not that photograph."

"You've been waiting for the particular person, as Grand-Pierre used to say. At the particular time."

"Maybe he was right."

"He can't be wrong *all* the time," I said.

"Ah? Not all the time?" Monsieur Klein peered at his hands, then at the tops of his shoes, then back at me. "Zazoo, there's a great favor I must ask of you."

I had a wild hope what it might be. "Anything, Monsieur Klein."

"Simply this: that you no longer call me *Monsieur Klein*. We've shared a great deal in this one day. Secrets between friends. So I'd like you to be my friend and call me Félix."

"Really?" I had hoped he would want something more. But also I was touched that this distinguished man in his spotless white jacket would ask me to call him by his first name. "I'd be pleased to, Monsieur, ah—Félix."

He smiled out the window toward his bird feeders. "I know it won't be easy. And in front of the others—you know, the pill poppers and busybodies—if you feel more comfortable calling me Monsieur, I'll understand."

"But it's so strange you should ask to be called something different."

"Strange? Why?"

"Because not so long ago, Grand-Pierre had a similar idea. The night you told me about Isabelle and your parents and—you know—the lamppost. When I went storming home and made him explain everything, he suggested I call you Uncle Félix."

"He *did?*" Monsieur Klein's eyes bulged behind their glasses. *"Uncle?"*

"Yes. He did."

"Uncle . . . Félix." He moved his mouth slowly, as if experimenting with foreign words. "Uncle Félix."

"Still, I won't call you Uncle if you'd rather I didn't. Meantime, I'll try calling you Félix. But there's a bigger favor I must ask of *you*—"

"I believe I know what it is." Through the kitchen window, he contemplated his snowy backyard. "You want me to make peace with your Grand-Pierre."

"Please tell me this, Félix." Using his first name was *not* easy; I had called him Monsieur Klein all my life. "If Grand-Pierre had been living alone—if he hadn't been taking care of me—would you have killed him?"

Monsieur Klein frowned at his hands. "Gradually, over the years, I came to see that he might as well have been dead already. Killing others, I think, does that to a man. And Pierre had done a lot of killing."

"Yes, Monsieur. I know he killed. But how much was a lot?" Until that moment the kitchen had felt cozy, but all at once I was frozen to the tips of my fingers.

Monsieur Klein himself looked green around the eyes. "I'll try making this quick." His voice came out very low. "Let's see. How shall I put it? You see, Zazoo, when there were no more Germans to fight, Pierre signed up to fight in our colonies."

"So he killed others," I whispered. "Many others?"

Monsieur Klein closed his eyes, then opened them to study me. "How can we know for sure, Zazoo?"

"He was a sharpshooter," I pronounced carefully. "Is that the same as a . . . killer? A . . . murderer?" There. I had said the word aloud, the word I hadn't dared say even to myself, alone, in my tower room.

"Murderer," repeated Monsieur Klein. "Some would agree with that term, yes. Some wouldn't. Of course, the business of a sharpshooter, in a war, is to shoot other soldiers."

"Soldiers who," I went on, "in Grand-Pierre's next war, were Vietnamese. . . . So he killed Vietnamese soldiers. Vietnamese people." This wasn't just the first time I had *said* such words; it was the first time I'd let myself think them. But once the thought started growing, it wouldn't stop. "He killed people. People like my own parents." My mouth was filled with a terrible taste I hadn't noticed before—surely not from my fever? I swallowed, then swallowed again. "Have you ever killed anyone, Monsieur Klein? I mean, Félix?"

"No." He examined his hands as if to to be sure they had never killed anyone. "Most of us haven't."

"Did he kill Vietnamese people because he *liked* killing them?" I scowled outside at the perfectly rounded, perfectly peaceful snowy shapes in the garden. "I mean, as much as he liked killing Germans?"

"Oh, I don't think Pierre liked killing anyone." Monsieur

Klein's voice was so faint I could scarcely hear it. "And as I just said, the more he killed, the more dead he probably felt himself. And the deader he felt, the more he went on killing, in hopes that someone—a German, a Vietnamese—would kill *him*. But he was too unlucky in his good luck. Too invisible."

"Too good at looking like a stone?"

"Yes, sweet girl." Monsieur Klein leaned forward as if intending to reassure me, then sagged back into his chair. "When he came home after our defeat in Vietnam, people said he was more of a stone than ever. His heart had gone cold—all he did was tend his lock in the summer and knit socks in the winter. He was too dead even to fire a rifle, which he had done better than anyone."

"Yes. You told me he had the best eye."

"That's right, and his eye wasn't gone yet when our generals went on their next spree, our glorious disaster in Algeria. But Pierre had turned entirely to stone by then. He couldn't go."

"So was that when people gave him his name—the Old Stone?"

"There was more to it than that," said Monsieur Klein. "His name had started years and years earlier. His *names*. There were many."

"I know. The Silent Stone, the Big Stone—"

"Zazoo." The ice in Monsieur Klein's voice chilled me. "His *other* name. For many, many years, Pierre has been known as the *Tombstone*."

"He—he has?" The back of my neck prickled.

"Yes." Monsieur Klein watched me shiver by the window. "And most commonly, he's called the Cemetery."

"The . . . ?" I couldn't say it.

"Oh, Zazoo." Seeing my reaction, Monsieur Klein looked frozen himself. "I assumed you must *know.* I assumed the village children, cruel as children can be, had repeated it to you. The Tombstone of Lock Forty-three, he was called behind his back, and still *is,* occasionally. The Cemetery. Yes. In honor of all the men he killed, and in honor of the others who died as a result. Men. Women. Children."

"The . . . Cemetery?" My mouth didn't want to form the word. "Little—children? He was *called* that?"

"In honor of his crazy personal war. Yes." Monsieur Klein looked around the kitchen as if to spot some object that might bring us comfort. "For being out of his mind. Or for being, as some claimed, a hero."

"He hates that word. He says only fools use it."

Félix Klein nodded. "On that point, I must agree with him. But there are all sorts of fools. In World War Two, for example—for every soldier Pierre killed, the German command retaliated by killing five villagers. At first. And later, ten."

"The—the—" I tried saying *Cemetery* again but couldn't choke the word out.

"Such reprisals took place more than once. He was, as I said, crazy. Couldn't stop himself. *Sharpshooter.*" Monsieur Klein seemed ready to spit. "Yet many in this valley insist, to this very day, on calling him a great man. Oh, yes."

I could say nothing, could see nothing in my mind but row on row of gravestones.

"So. During all those years, once your Grand-Pierre retired

from sharpshooting, he lived alone at Lock Forty-three with his brandy bottle and his knitting needles."

Staring past the birdhouses mounded under their pure white snow, I clenched and unclenched my hands. "Then why," I whispered, "why *didn't* you poison his pills, if you hated him so much?"

"He never got sick. Didn't need pills. Anyway, he didn't care. He waited for death, seemed to long for death. But death never came. No television, no books. Just his knitting and the canal, the water, the ice."

"Did he go skating?"

"People thought they saw him out on the ice, but at the least likely hours—at three or four in the morning—and in the least likely places, where the ice was too thin to support even such a tiny man."

"Like a dream." I was so tired. The night, the day, had all been too much.

"Exactly like a dream."

This word, when I heard him repeat it, gave me a misty sort of idea. "Do you dream much, Monsieur Klein—I mean, Félix?"

"All the time." He poured fresh tea into our cups. "Every night."

"And has Grand-Pierre, even if you haven't spoken to him or heard his voice all these years, visited you in your sleep?"

"All the time. In my dreams we're all ages, both of us."

"Then he's been in your life, through the years."

"No one else," said Monsieur Klein, smiling bitterly at the teapot, "has been more in my life. That is, until recently. Recently, a particular girl, who sends cards to a lucky boy in Paris, has taken over the center of my life."

"That's nice to hear, Monsieur—Félix. It's wonderful to hear. But as for Grand-Pierre, if he can be in your dreams, maybe he should come back into your real life, during the day. He's old, Félix."

"I know what you're proposing. I'll think about it."

"Don't *say* that! When a grownup says that, it means 'No.' You haven't talked to him in so long, you should come visit and see for yourself."

"See? See—what?"

"That he's not a monster. Not a murderer."

A twitch at the side of Monsieur Klein's mouth stopped me. But stubbornly I went on. "Maybe he *was* a murderer, once. He went out of his mind, yes, killing people, causing other people to die—maybe causing a whole cemetery of people to die. But he isn't a murderer now. He's a sweet old man, and so are you, though a little younger."

"I feel old enough at the moment." Monsieur Klein stared steadily at me. "You think I should see him. You think I should . . . forgive him."

I nodded but said nothing.

"I'll consider it." He let out a deep sigh. "I will. Really."

And I believed he meant it. But as I stepped into the snowy street, I feared he could never bring himself to speak to a man he had hated so long.

I walked slowly home to my mill of a thousand years, a thousand tears, a thousand . . . graves? My grandfather the grave maker? Reeling from so many nightmares, it struck me that I'd forgotten to swallow any of my new fever pills, there in Monsieur Klein's kitchen—had forgotten to swallow even one. And I didn't care.

31. A Special Sailing Sort

Christmas passed unnoticed. I was concerned mostly with my trembles and shakes; Grand-Pierre, who in better times had played his own version of Father Christmas for me, now ignored everything but his needles and yarn. Seated at the kitchen table, he made one sock for a mouse, then another for a giraffe. Outside our windows, the snow sank into the black-flowing river and piled up on the frozen canal. Even if I did get well, skating was over for the season.

Now that Marius had made a second appearance and I trusted him to come back, the other visitor I hoped most to see was not Father Christmas but Félix Klein. A friendly visit from him would have been the most generous present our mill could receive. But I wasn't very hopeful.

My only companion was Grand-Pierre, who was less than perfect company; for hours on end he clicked his needles and gazed out at the falling snow. I would assume I had lost him, but then he might surprise me—such as the night I propped my postcard of Chagall's Eiffel Tower on our living room mantel.

"Where did that come from?" he asked, all the way from the kitchen.

"From the boy in Paris." I seated myself facing his easy chair.

"Boy?" Grand-Pierre buffed his head with one hand.

"Yes." It was hard to know if he had forgotten or if he was teasing, as he might have in better times. "Marius with the freckles, the boy you let stay so late."

"I did? *How* late?"

"A few hours." I had shocked him with this account often enough to know he enjoyed hearing it. "After you went to bed, Marius and I talked and talked. I told him your view that Paris is too big, and mine that he should live with us and watch birds."

"Quite right." Grand-Pierre smiled down at his needles. "This boy knows how to operate a lock?"

"We could teach him." With the paring knife, I peeled an apple I'd bought that morning. "And he could teach us about birds and modern art and I don't know what else. Maybe he'd teach us to sail."

"He knows how to sail, this boy?" *Click-clickety-click*. "Sail a sailboat?"

"If he doesn't, he could learn and then teach us." Laying the strips of peel on the stovetop, I watched Grand-Pierre to see if he reacted. "Marius is a sharp student. He goes to one of the best schools in Paris."

"Sharper than you? Better for *you* to learn sailing and teach *him*."

"But Grand-Pierre, I don't have a sailboat." The peeling's tart sweetness filled the air.

"Ah." He peered at his needles, as if their steady clicking were part of our conversation. "You only have your—your—"

"Only my punt. Yes. My English-Vietnamese row-punt—which, the last I noticed, did not have a sail."

"Then," said Grand-Pierre, "we should give it one." *Click-clickety-click.*

"A sail?"

"Winter project for you. What's that thing called—that post stuck in the hole where we stick your umbrella—you know, that *flagpole*-type thing?"

"The mast." He didn't seem to have noticed the apple-peel perfume, yet he had seen the postcard as soon as I placed it on the mantel. There was no predicting what might connect in his brain.

"And that thingamabob in back, for steering?"

"The rudder."

"Rudder." He nodded, enthusiasm already fading. "Rudder."

"And," I said brightly, "that fin on the bottom, the thing sailboats need to keep from slipping sideways? What is *it* called?"

"Don't know. Tell me again why you need a . . . sail. On your punt."

"But it was *your* idea, Grand-Pierre."

"Was it?" He gaped across the table at me. "Ah. Well, then."

I hoped he might comment that some scent reminded him of the winter he'd spent near Mâcon, but he said nothing. His right hand twiddled its silver needle.

* * *

Once Grande-Pierre had planted the scheme of altering the row-punt, my brain wouldn't let it go. The school library had a few books about sailing; in the shed we had a drill, a chisel, and two saws. I hauled the punt across the snow, skidded it indoors on one side, then turned it upside down on the living-room floor. Now and then Grand-Pierre looked up from his knitting to study my progress; I measured and compared and measured again.

First I made the boat-fin, which my books called the "centerboard"—a board a meter long, which would slide through a slit in the bottom of the punt and jut down into the water to help "stabilize" the boat as it sailed "into the wind," or upwind. Unlike a fish fin, this boat fin had to be removable, for greater speed when the boat sailed downwind. And to support the sideways pressure on the board, I needed to build a "centerboard well," a narrow wooden frame, open at top and bottom, through which the centerboard could slide down into position. The books assured me that because the top of the well would be higher than the water level outside the boat, no water would rise up through the hole and sink my vessel.

It made me nervous, sawing through the bottom of my graceful plum punt; I wondered if it would ever float again. But Grand-Pierre seemed to favor the idea, so I drew lines at the center of the hull, drilled a series of holes, and opened a long narrow slot with the small saw.

Which was when the old man completely lost interest,

leaving me with a punctured boat and a crude wooden box but no idea of how to fasten it in place.

Marius was too far away to help. Old Louie was an expert on leeches, not boats. Of the people I trusted, only Monsieur Klein was skilled with wood. If he could build such perfect picture frames, surely he could anchor a wooden centerboard case to the shell of a wooden boat.

32. Some Sunday Soon

Hope is a funny business. The more you may want something to happen, the harder it can be to mention aloud. And so it was with my hope that two stubborn old men would break their silence—in spite of the fact that I, in *my* stubbornness, couldn't speak to Juliette LeMiel. As much as I brooded about their blockheadedness, I couldn't raise the issue with them. Once Félix Klein said he would "think about" speaking to Grand-Pierre, I had to let him wrestle with his own conscience—or so I told myself. Yet I wondered if I was simply being a coward.

But I wasn't too cowardly to stop at the pharmacy and check for mail—and, when there was none, admire the Postcard Gallery's most recent arrivals. Every week, new cards arrived from museum shops in Amsterdam, Rome, or New York. The painting I chose next showed a girl holding a violin she seemed too lonely to play. This time I couldn't show Félix my message, since it named his own lost love.

Dear Marius—Years ago, Monsieur Klein sent to the Orangerie Museum in Paris for this card of the Henri Matisse painting "Woman with Violin." It matches my mood—just look at the girl's lonely face. Here, winter drags on. A half meter of snow covers the canal; skating is finished for the year. Plus which, I'm sick; chicken soup is all I eat. Do you make chicken soup? Monsieur Klein does. He asked me to call him Félix, which is a story in itself. But on the cheery side I can say this: romance, for the young who are now older, looks promising. Pass the word to Mémé Simone, with my tender regards. Another thing: Grand-Pierre and I decided to turn my punt into a sailboat—I've sawed a ragged hole for a centerboard in the bottom of its once-smooth hull. A scary project which now I alone must finish. Before spring, someone told me, he would revisit. Soon. True? *Zazoo*

Weeks went by, silent in several ways. The deepening snow muffled everything; there was no word from Paris; Grand-Pierre spoke hardly at all. And school, more silent than ever, grew increasingly tense.

It can take effort to talk to a friend. But what I found, when Juliette LeMiel and I perfected our Thundering Silence, was that *not* talking takes far more effort. All through December, all through January, we were terribly busy not talking. The hardest work was to act as if neither of us was aware the other existed. You hear the voice of someone special and you pretend not to hear it, because you know she's working hard at not listening to your voice when you talk to someone else—often someone less interesting than *she* is, but at least someone who's allowed to exist.

I found that the best refuge was to let my mind glide out the classroom window into the open air, free of all worries. The sky was so huge, filled with such mysterious currents and cross-currents. Most of the snow drifted in one downward direction—but closer to the window a few flakes circled upward, just the opposite way. What I couldn't decide was which of my yearnings was greater—to be one flake mingled with many, or to be a solitary marvel, rising freely up and up, but alone.

On a far roofline, my tired mind was caught by swirls of twisting snow, which could only be ghosts—ghosts of a dangling girl, of a German soldier, of my own mother and father. *Especially* of my own mother and father, because of how they had died—flung, like those distant tatters of snow, up into the sky.

As I walked the path away from school, among the drifting shapes I saw my parents as two floating dancers, hand in hand, rising against all laws of gravity. But no, I insisted, I was not Vietnamese. I didn't live in a land too hot for frozen rivers. I was French. I skated on the canal, and when too much snow made that impossible, I waited for spring so I could swim and splash. Surrounded by shrouded shapes, I made my way to the world's smallest art gallery.

* * *

"*Bonjour,* Monsieur Klein—I mean, Félix. Having a good day?"

"Not bad. But Zazoo, you've been crying!"

"Have I? Maybe so. The weather, you know. So lonely, snow."

"Lonely?" He turned to watch the flakes swirl outside his window. "But at the same time, so delicate. Let it comfort you, Zazoo."

"I'll do my best." I tried smiling. "But what would soothe me most, Monsieur, is a postcard. There's been no mail for weeks."

"Stupid me!" Félix Klein tapped his forehead. "You looked so low, trudging in the door, that I forgot to remember to remember."

The card he handed me was luminous—by the same artist, Odilon Redon, who had painted the bouquet of anemones we had sent to Paris. In a meadow-green sea, a blue boat with a gold sail carried two passengers, a man and a woman. Or perhaps a boy and a girl. Their shapes were so faint it was impossible to guess their ages.

I read the card aloud:

"Dear Zazoo, Paris is gray and gloomy, science full of wonders, school dull. Sending you this painting cheers me; receiving a poem would cheer me more. She says Soon, too; I'm not the only one. And Soon means before spring. Yes. But the ice must be gone, the canal navigable, as we say in geography class—such a schoolbook word. I'm anxious to see what holes you've punched in your boat—your plum row-punt with you in it, under the willows. I do remember. Birds and boats are not all I admire.

Marius in faraway Paris"

"Now," said my friend Félix, "are you comforted?"

"How could I not be, Monsieur?" This time I didn't have to work to smile. I read the card's few lines again. Still, my heart felt yanked in so many directions—like a flake tugged by five breezes at once—that I wasn't entirely sure how I felt.

"And now," he went on, "do you believe me when I say you have a life others would envy?"

"Yes."

"A romantic life, Zazoo." He beamed across the counter at me. "Even *I* envy you your life! But one line in this card does mystify me."

"You want to know who 'she' is."

Félix nodded just as the little boy in his photo might have nodded.

"Well, I'm sorry to say I've been sworn to secrecy. But as Marius wrote, we'll know in the spring."

" '*Before* spring,' he wrote." Félix was smiling. "But will you at least explain this part about your boat? He says you've punched holes in it?"

"Yes, Monsieu—Félix. A stupid thing I've done. It was Grand-Pierre's idea, but I went and did it. I gouged a slit, almost forty centimeters long, right down the middle of the boat's hull. With a drill and saw, I did it."

"Pierre's idea, you say?"

"He suggested I turn my rowboat into a sailboat. A book told me I needed to make a hole for that fin-type thing that sticks out the bottom of sailboats."

"The centerboard."

"Correct. But then Grand-Pierre went back to his knitting. So now I have a punt that won't float, which I don't know how to fix. Have you ever made a boat, Félix?"

Monsieur Klein rolled a tube of mascara between the fingers of one hand. When he finally spoke, his tone gave me the distinct sense he was telling me more than he was saying. "Perhaps I could take a look at your wounded punt. This mutilation you inflicted upon it—I suppose you operate inside the mill? Safe from the cold?"

I peered intently at him. "Yes, inside. In the living room, a few meters from where Grand-Pierre sits knitting at the kitchen table."

"A few meters." Félix Klein shrugged toward the ceiling. "And the old knitter sits there, working away on his socks, at all hours?"

"That's right. There can be no avoiding him unless we lug the boat outdoors and give ourselves frostbite."

"I'm too old for frostbite." Félix Klein kept turning the tube in his fingers. "And maybe too old for avoiding Pierre."

"Do you promise," I asked with a smile, "not to poison his tea?"

"Depends on my mood, Zazoo. Perhaps some Sunday would be a good day for boatbuilding. Some Sunday, you know, when my store is closed?"

"Some Sunday would be ideal." I wanted to lean across the counter and kiss his tired eyes. "But it must be some Sunday *soon,* Félix. This boat has to be ready by spring."

"Indeed," said my pharmacist friend. "Some Sunday soon."

33. *Watching the Water*

People seemed to think canal ice just melted, but it wasn't that simple. First, the ice lost its crystal-hard edge, the way a skate blade loses sharpness, and turned all cloudy gray. You could still skate on it; for a good many days there was no danger you'd fall through and drown and be eaten by turtles. But when canal ice softened, you couldn't carve it neatly with your blades—it felt like skating on sand. Mush skating, Grand-Pierre used to call it.

Next, the ice turned soft and heavy and looked as if it wanted to sink into the dark water the same way my wounded row-punt would sink if I tried setting it afloat.

Then the rain began, days and nights of it: an eternity of dull, heavy drops soaking the ground, the soft ice, the weeping tree bark. I switched from winter boots to high rubber boots for splashing through mud instead of crunching through ice. If you're about to turn fourteen, you have to be careful about when to splash through mud, a pleasure left to little girls and bigger boys. You have to be careful, when turning fourteen, not to show frustration if a boy has promised to arrive soon but hasn't said which *soon* he means. You have to be careful about a lot of things.

"Grand-Pierre," I announced one day after school, "let's sit outside and watch the water."

"It's raining," he said. Which was more than he had said in an hour.

"I see that." I wanted to get away from my plum boat, which leaned against the living-room wall. The gash along its hull was depressing. "Let's watch the water anyway."

"We'll get wet," he said, but with a hint of his old smile.

"We can be careful to stay dry." A little rain had never bothered Grand-Pierre before. "We'll take umbrellas, and a towel to dry the bench, and some tea in our thermos, and some sugar—and these little cakes I brought home from the bakery."

"Cakes?" The simpler he grew, the more Grand-Pierre loved sweets. Soon he'd be a baby again.

"One chocolate and one raisin. Let's go watch the water."

"All right." When he pushed himself up from his chair, he stood with his head tilted forward, as if his glasses had fallen somewhere ahead of him and he was searching for them. But his glasses sat on his nose, where they belonged. Only parts of his mind seemed lost.

Once we were out on the blue stone bench, a blanket beneath us and another on top, and our two umbrellas—one black, one gray—double-domed cozily over us, his fear of the weather left and his love of the water returned.

It was like a living thing, Grand-Pierre's love of the water. I recognized it because I felt it myself. Our stretch of the curving canal, in whichever season, at whatever hour, was a far more interesting view than anything in the movies. He knew it and I knew it. Even with the soggy ice sinking like a boat that was barely afloat and might, at any moment, slip down to its watery grave, our stretch of canal was the saddest, loveliest place on earth.

"Home," I whispered,

> "is where the river flows
> humming through the willows.
> Home is milkweed in your hair,
> with hemlock moss your pillows.
> Home, if only you could know,
> is anyplace I see you—
> it's in your heart
> and from the start
> I've known my home would be you."

He sucked gently at the corner of his mouth. "I suppose you're going to say I made that one up?"

"Yes, old man."

He watched the canal and shook his head.

"When I was little, you recited that poem. I couldn't hear it often enough. Ever since, whenever I needed to remember that I had the best friend, the best home in the world, I recited your poem. It always helped."

"You have a friend?" he asked, as simply as a little boy.

"The best friend a girl could have." I took his hand the way he used to take mine. "The old man who brought me around the world and made a home for me."

"That's a long way." He nodded slowly; the rain drummed on our overlapped umbrellas.

"The ice will be gone soon," I told him, as he had told me in the past. "It will turn all black and sink from sight, and then we'll have spring."

"It's raining—spring is here already."

"In the spring, you used to tell me, the river isn't friendly. At least, not for swimming."

"Did I?"

"Yes, Grand-Pierre." I tucked the blanket into his collar like a bib. "You said it one February long ago—an afternoon just like this. I was eight. Snow and soft ice covered everything. You warned me that the winter canal isn't dangerous but the *spring* canal is, with its patches of rotten ice."

"And melted snow. Yes? And—?"

"You said I might be tempted to swim too early, like you'd been tempted when you were young and jumped into water so cold you nearly drowned."

"Ah." He watched the rain hitting a patch of water where a panel of ice had settled into the canal. The drops made shining bubbles as they hit the surface.

"And so we built our boat."

"That sounds sensible." Grand-Pierre glanced at the thermos.

"It was." I unscrewed the lid and poured his mug full, then spooned in some sugar. The older he grew, the sweeter he drank his tea, but sometimes he forgot and put in too much. So now I did it for him. "Very sensible—by far the best thing I learned that year. You showed me how to saw plywood so it wouldn't splinter, and how to use clamps to glue the sections together—"

"We used *marine* plywood?"

"Of course, Grand-Pierre, we were building a boat! You said marine plywood cost three times as much but that didn't matter, we were making a marine item to navigate on a marine canal. Our boat mustn't leak. We had more important things to do than waste our energy bailing it out."

"More important things. Such as what, Zazoo?"

"Such as telling each other how many feet a caterpillar had, and how many feet a poem. And such as making up a poem with the right number of feet for each line."

"What was our poem about, Zazoo?" As he tilted his face toward the canal, his umbrella tilted with it.

Now I was the one who didn't remember. "What—what do you mean?"

"Our poem. Was it about—"

"But how could I remember *that,* Grand-Pierre? We made up so many! Every day, it seemed, we made up a new poem."

"—was it about how much I loved you?" He sat beside me on our blue bench, staring straight ahead and watching the water.

"Oh, Grand-Pierre, of *course* it was. How stupid of me not to remember." I was glad of the rain now, for even though we had umbrellas, the breeze might have blown some of the rain into our faces, which might explain why mine was suddenly wet. But it didn't matter. He wasn't looking at me anyway, he was looking across the water into the trees, or maybe into the past, maybe as far back as Isabelle and some promise he had made to build *her* a sailboat, or a garden, or a cradle for a baby. And it didn't matter because I didn't care if he did see me cry.

"Tears," he said quietly, "are as good as the rain. Yes, Zazoo?"

"Of course. And our poem was about how much I love you, too, you old rock."

"I know, Zazoo." His arm was around me; the blanket fell away from his collar, but we didn't care. We shuffled back to our mill, Grand-Pierre under the black umbrella, I under the gray one. The rain plunked hundreds of drops onto the canal, and each drop made a silver marble on the water and disappeared as soon as I saw it.

34. *Old Men*

It was the third Sunday in February, after lunch, when the knock came at our door and there he stood in his overcoat, a toolbox tugging at one hand.

"Monsieur Klein!" I said. "I mean, Félix. Come in, come *in*."

"The old man is here?" He took a single step inside. "The old . . . stone?"

"In his chair by the window. Asleep. He usually sleeps after lunch, and other times as well. He sleeps a great deal these days."

"Then he dreams a lot, lucky fellow." Félix set his toolbox on the floor. "Or not so lucky. Depends on the dream, I suppose."

"I feel like I'm dreaming myself."

"Yes, I know what you mean." Félix tiptoed three more steps into the kitchen. "Is he . . . grouchy when you wake him from his nap?"

"Not usually." We were both whispering. "He gets irritated with himself when he does stupid things he can't explain, but he isn't often grouchy. Mostly he's sweet-natured."

"That's good, then." We gazed across the kitchen at Grand-Pierre—hands folded over his stomach, eyes defenseless without glasses—where he snoozed in his chair. "And he's sweet to *you?*"

"Very sweet. But I forgot to take your coat! I'm such a bad host—"

"Doesn't matter." Félix managed a tiny smile as he slipped off his overcoat and draped it over a chair. "It's natural for us both to be nervous. Quite natural. I suppose we should wake him."

"Yes." I made no move to wake anyone.

"Pierre . . . ?" Félix called softly across the room.

"That won't work. Let me. Grand-Pierre . . ." I nudged his shoulder. "Grand-Pierre?" I shook him more firmly. "Grand-Pierre, we have company."

"Company." He blew once like a dolphin, then once again. "The Doubtful Duke?" He squinted toward the lock. "The—twit?"

"No, someone from years ago. Someone you haven't seen in ages. Monsieur Klein."

"*Félix* Klein?"

"Yes. Félix Klein." I watched him to see if he realized what was happening. "Here at our kitchen table. He's come to help patch my boat together."

Grand-Pierre hauled himself up from his chair, brushing off his front as if he'd been covered in feathers. Settling his glasses on his nose, he turned toward Félix.

The two men inspected each other: one old, one older; one with a salt-and-pepper mustache, one bald.

"Félix." Grand-Pierre showed no particular surprise apart from the slight sucking at the stem of his invisible pipe. "Félix Klein, bless my stars."

To the slow ticking of the clock, two men who hadn't spoken in forty-eight years peered across the kitchen at each other. For a long moment, neither man moved. Then Grand-Pierre shuffled forward in his slippers and held out his hand. "Welcome to the mill, Félix. The Mill of a Thousand Tears."

But Monsieur Klein didn't take his hand. He seemed to be looking past Grand-Pierre at something else, behavior so rude I was about to comment on the stupidity of old men when I realized he was staring out the kitchen window at the blue stone bench.

"You built that, Pierre?" Monsieur Klein motioned with one hand.

"Yes. Years and years ago."

"And . . . you sit out there?"

"Every day, Félix. Every day."

"Built it with your own hands? Out of river stones?"

"What else could I do? She was gone. They all were."

Félix Klein's good posture went slack; he couldn't speak.

So *that* was it. Stone by heavy stone, hauled by hand from the river, Grand-Pierre had built his bench in that spot because it was where the lamppost had once stood, the lamppost from which Isabelle and her parents had been hanged. Then he had sat there all those years, often with me beside him but more often alone, in all kinds of weather, at all hours, thinking his thoughts.

"Is it . . ." Félix had trouble finishing. "Is it a comfortable place to sit?"

"No," said Grand-Pierre. "Not built for comfort. Built straight and hard. If I wanted comfort, I'd go to the café. Most days, I read out there after lunch—poetry or something. Today I drifted off here in the kitchen. Didn't mean to—"

"There's no need to apologize, Pierre. I can picture you out there, day after day."

"Well." Grand-Pierre fluffed his chest again, as if dusting away the years. "There was nothing to be done. I knew what they called me. The Tombstone? The Cemetery? And they were right. So I built the bench." He spoke under his breath. "My private cemetery. Stones from the river." His chin rose. "You've come to kill me?"

"No, Pierre. No, I haven't. And now that I see you here, now that I see your bench, I'm sorry I ever said such a thing. Ashamed."

"We all do things." Grand-Pierre looked almost disappointed that Félix Klein hadn't come to kill him. "We all say things."

"I came, as Zazoo mentioned, to take a look at her boat. She says you two decided to make it into a sailboat."

"Did we?" Grand-Pierre smiled faintly, then glanced toward the terrace. "So you're not going to kill me."

"Not today, no. Not ever."

"In that case, perhaps we could sit on the bench together sometime. No need for talk. Just sit."

"It would be my privilege, Pierre. I'd like that." Félix smiled ever so sadly. "Which reminds me. Zazoo says you thought she should call me Uncle Félix."

"Did I?"

"Yes, Grand-Pierre," I whispered. "Don't be a tease."

"I don't recall. This was recently?"

"In the fall. After Monsieur Klein told me about—well, about history. Isabelle." When I said the name, both men let out sighs that seemed to have been sealed tight for a century. "You suggested I call him Uncle Félix. When I asked Monsieur Klein if it felt like a good idea, he said he'd think about it. Which, of course, usually means—"

"I *have* thought about it," said Monsieur Klein. "And it's a wonderful idea. If you could bring yourself to call me Uncle Félix, Zazoo, I'd be touched."

"Touched," said Grand-Pierre, who, even when drifting, kept an ear open for the occasional word he might hold onto and polish. "Touched." He settled onto a chair at the kitchen table and regarded the blue stone bench.

"And I thought of something else, Pierre. Something I decided to bring you. It's here in my toolbox somewhere . . ."

"A pistol," said Grand-Pierre amiably. "A small bomb."

"That's right, old anarchist. A little time bomb. I wasn't sure I'd be able to give you this, but now it's clear I must. It's yours and only yours." Monsieur Klein lifted a dark wood frame from between two sheets of tissue paper at the bottom of his toolbox. Very gently, he set the picture on the table before Grand-Pierre, whose face stayed calm but whose knees began to twitch.

This photograph was larger than the one I had seen of eight-year-old Félix Klein. It might have been taken on the same day, and was certainly taken by the same man, Pascin, outside the same café. The late sun threw shadows at an angle across the terrace. Out of focus in the background sat a man playing an accordion; in the foreground, blurred by their motion, two young people danced. At least they *looked* young, holding each other so close. The man's back was toward the camera; he wore a soft hat. Of his face, only the line of his jaw was visible. He didn't seem to be smiling, but everything in his stance showed how pleased he was to be dancing with this woman in front of the world. Only his hat and her face were in focus.

And what a face it was: Isabelle Klein was *radiant.* I had always heard that the tango was Spanish and serious, with neither partner smiling—and true to the rule, she did not smile. Yet she couldn't keep her eyes from glowing. Every curve in her face, her long-skirted legs, her trim-sleeved arms, showed pleasure—and, yes, desire. There was no other word for it. It was a word I had never understood until I saw that grainy photograph on our table. She wanted this man in her arms—this man only—and she had him. Her eyes were in love and so was her body.

Grand-Pierre's knees no longer shook, but his hands pressed the picture frame so hard I feared it might crack. Then his shoulders buckled; wild, wounded moans ripped from his throat. It was so terrifying I turned my face away; Monsieur

Klein gazed helplessly out at the sky. Blindly, Grand-Pierre thrust the picture out to me. I carried it into the living room and placed it on the mantel. After staring for a moment at Isabelle Klein's beaming face, I turned away and found Grand-Pierre a handkerchief.

Gradually he calmed down until only his upper lip shook. He took off his glasses, wiped his face dry, put his glasses back on. "Such a thing." He held his hands out on the table and watched them tremble. "Such a thing, Félix. I'll look at it. I'm sure I'll look at it. But now—"

"I understand, old fellow. We can take only so much punishment, any of us."

"Punishment," said Grand-Pierre. His head rocked slowly from side to side, twice. "Oh, such a thing."

"Yes." Monsieur Klein's eyes were dry, but from the slump of his shoulders it seemed that he, too, had survived a terrible storm. "Such a thing." Gazing around the kitchen, he breathed deeply, breathed again, then rubbed his hands as if bringing them back to life. "Shall we take a look at this boat, Zazoo?"

"In the living room," I whispered. "Right this way, ah, Uncle Félix."

Grand-Pierre watched us go, then pulled on his shoes and made his way out to the blue stone bench.

35. The Time in Between

By late February the centerboard was finished, the rudder was ready to be set in place: my row-punt was turning into a sailboat. When we found the right pole for a mast, Félix said, we would anchor it through the hole in the front seat. Then we could attach the horizontal boom to the mast and be ready to hoist a sail. Over cups of tea we pondered where the guylines should be fixed and where the cleats should be screwed in place. It was a soothing way to pass what Grand-Pierre called "the time in between," those slow weeks waiting for the soggy canal ice to turn dark and sink from view.

But if the canal was only half thawed, the river flowed freely—and the night came, as it did every year, when I had to be out in its current.

Grand-Pierre used to say that a quality he and I shared was our skill at waiting. We could sit and watch, he said, and not grow impatient even when the sun had gone down and we yearned for the moon to rise. But it was one thing for a seventy-eight-year-old man to feel that way, and another for me, now almost fourteen. Marius in Paris had been silent too long; my boat had been out of the water too long. I didn't *feel* like waiting.

I bundled myself in sweaters, wheeled the punt to the riverbank, and slid it in among the reeds. The centerboard casing didn't leak; Félix had sealed it well. But while I rowed, the new rudder would be in my way, so I stored it under the front seat and took up my oars. By the light of broken clouds I pulled upstream through the sleeping town—three, four kilometers, past the skeletons of winter trees as I plowed steadily against the current. The dark homes slipped past, saying nothing, judging no one as I stroked my way to the Haunted Hill Dam.

In the misty shadow of the dam's falling water, I stowed the oars, hooked the new rudder in place, and drifted downstream away from the falls' low rumble. Around the first bend, the river went quiet. Listening to the gurgles and creaks of the night, I steered my little boat by its rudder as the current carried me home to the mill.

And on the terrace, after I hauled the boat ashore, there he stood, eyes dark in the moonlight.

"Marius!" Without thinking I rushed over and kissed his cheeks—first one, then the other. "Have you been here long?"

"Maybe an hour." He was ghostly pale. "The lights were out. Your boat was gone, but I didn't know if you'd rowed up or down the river, so I waited. Can we go inside? I'm frozen."

"Yes, of course. Come." I led him in the door, turned on the light and poked up the woodstove fire with fresh kindling. "Hot chocolate?"

"Lovely." His lips were gray with cold. "And maybe a bite to eat, if you have, you know, a piece of bread or something."

I rummaged for the things to make a toasted cheese-and-ham sandwich. "We have a teacher named Croque," I babbled, keeping my hands busy with the bread, the pan, the butter, when what they wanted most was to hold his face. "Naturally we call him Monsieur Croque Monsieur."

"Naturally." Marius rubbed his arms. "But I have trouble picturing you in anybody's school, Zazoo. You belong out on the water, where you were tonight. Like Mémé Simone. She belongs on the water, too."

"Ah?" I set the frying pan on the stove and let my hands hang uselessly at my sides. "She has a boat?"

"Not yet, but soon. And all because of you, Zazoo. You've become our inspiration."

"Ours?"

"Mémé Simone's and mine. She's seen your postcards—"

"She likes the painting of the lonely girl with her violin?"

"She loves it, and so do I."

"The girl too lonely to play because she hasn't received any mail?" I leaned over the pan so Marius might think the flush in my cheeks came from the stove's heat.

"You're right, I should have written. I wanted to surprise you with a visit, but it took longer than I'd hoped. Forgive me."

"You're here now—that's what matters." Even in the hot kitchen, I was glad to be wearing enough baggy sweaters to give me some extra shape.

"I've told her all about you," Marius said with a smile.

"Ah? I didn't realize you *knew* all about me."

"I mean, all about your swimming and skating." Some color was coming back into his face. "And can you guess, Zazoo, what impresses her most?"

"That I'm so blond and blue-eyed."

He shot me a startled look. "Very funny."

"Sorry." The surprise in his eye let me say what I'd never said before, even to myself. "I guess there's no reason for me to be blond and blue-eyed."

"No, Zazoo."

"I mean, I am French, but I'm Vietnamese, too, at least in a way. There's no denying I *look* Vietnamese. Black hair, black eyes—"

"Lovely black eyes." Very softly he added, "The loveliest."

"Well." A warm silence fell between us. "I don't know about that. But you were telling me what impresses your Mémé Simone."

"Yes." He seemed relieved to get back to his grandmother. "What she likes most is that you cut that hole in your boat."

"Ooh." I winced. "My beautiful little punt."

Marius watched me sprinkle bits of cheese on the ham. "But you sawed a hole in your beautiful punt to make it *more* beautiful."

"Or ruin it. If Félix Klein hadn't helped seal the damage, I'd be at the bottom of the river tonight."

"Simone *loved* your sawing that hole in your boat. She said it showed that you could risk spoiling something to make it better. Which brings me to my main news—Mémé Simone has decided to make *her* life better. She's buying a boat."

"Really?" I flipped his sandwich in the pan. "We used to call this flipping Monsieur Croque Monsieur."

"Who is we?"

"My former friend Juliette and my silly self."

"Then you still aren't speaking?"

"Dumb, aren't we. But what sort of boat will Simone buy? A sailboat?"

"A barge." Marius spread his arms wide. "An eighty-year-old Dutch barge that floats fine and needs some work but should soon be perfect for puttering about on the canals of France."

Finally I began to catch on. "And for puttering through Lock Forty-three of the Water Forgotten by Time?"

"That's right, Zazoo, she's buying it so she can putter all the way here from Paris to visit her sweetheart."

"Visit Monsieur *Klein*?"

"Félix Klein the pharmacist." Marius leaned closer. "We convinced her, Simone says. You and I. If *you* could take a chance by cutting a hole in your punt, and if *I* could say I liked you more than a little, she could take a chance, too. She could hop off her barge at Lock Forty-three and go see if the boy Félix still loves her, as she's certain she loves him."

"She *is* certain?" *More than a little.*

"She's certain." The rosiness was back in his lips; the crinkles were wonderful around his eyes. Suddenly I knew, for the first time in my life, the feeling of wanting to kiss a particular boy and not stop kissing him. "What are you staring at, Zazoo?"

"At you, of course." It was all I could do not to spill the sandwich out of the pan and skip around the table and grab him. "At you and your freckled eyes."

"My eyes," he repeated. "All of a sudden, I feel much better, Mademoiselle. I feel hungry enough to eat a dozen Croque Monsieurs."

"You only get one, Monsieur. But it's huge." I slid the sandwich onto his plate, poured us each a cup of hot chocolate, and sat down not safely across the table but in the chair next to his. "She said we inspired her?"

"Mostly *you* inspired her, Zazoo. You and my . . . my feelings for you." Marius stared at the top of his sandwich; I couldn't blame him. If *I* had been trying to eat a melted cheese sandwich at that moment, I'd have had a serious problem. But Marius worked at his chewing and worked at his swallowing and did fairly well.

"Do you mean that?" I whispered.

"Yes." He nodded fiercely, twice—the first time at his sandwich and the second time at me.

I stirred a spoon around and around in my cup. "It was a strong moon tonight—Marius." I said his name as caressingly as any name had ever been spoken. "Only half full, but bright. I saw it from my punt when the clouds drifted apart."

"I saw it, too, riding my bike here from the train. The same moon you saw."

"Floating downstream, I pictured how the river will look in the morning when the sun's out. When the sun climbs over the treetops, it sends golden minnows up the inside of the bridge."

"Minnows?" He tilted his head sideways like one of his birds.

"Golden minnows. That's what I call the reflections that bounce up under the arches of our bridge."

"And these reflections are pretty?"

"They're hypnotic." At that moment it dawned on me that Marius might actually wish to hold *me*. Kiss *me*. "Very calming, those golden minnows, the way they dart across the underside of the bridge."

"I'd like to see them. Tomorrow morning? Early?"

"Oh, it can't be too early. This is February—the sun won't be up until seven, and then it needs at least an hour to reach a good angle. For the reflections, you know. And your train leaves early." I studied my cup of hot chocolate and repeated to myself how very *calming* golden minnows could be. "At least, your train left early last time."

"And it does again tomorrow. But it won't always."

"No?" Down the canal an owl hooted and went still. "Your Mémé Simone is really buying a barge?"

"She is. Really. In Paris, next week. And then, when my Easter holiday comes, we'll chug down here, she and I. To visit the past."

I raised my cup. "To the past, then. And the future."

"The future." Marius tapped his cup against mine.

Over his sweater, I made him put on my thickest, baggiest sweater to keep him warm on the long ride back. Of course, giving him my sweater meant more than that—he knew and I knew. He said it made him happy to wear it. Then, when his overcoat was on and his cap and gloves were on and I knew it was time for our double-cheek kiss before he rode away, Marius pulled off his gloves and with one hand gently tipped my face up to his. We kissed, and not on the cheek this time. We kissed lips, so softly it was almost a dream. Then again, not quite so softly. For some time we stood that way, our eyes close together.

"Good night, my Zazoo."

"Good night, Marius." I reached up for another kiss. "But not good-bye."

"No. Not at all."

"Your gloves," I whispered.

"Yes." He watched me as if he, too, were amazed that our shyness had melted away. Tugging his gloves on, he stepped outside.

Then he pedaled into the night, leaving behind the last crumbs from his sandwich, and his empty hot chocolate cup, and, under the rim of his plate, a small compass—black metal with a clear glass face. Folded beneath it was a note.

If you should ever be lost in the woods, Zazoo, this can point you the way. Or out on the water, if you need to find true north, or need to know how I feel about you, this can be your reminder.

36. Secrets Told or Kept

My compass was so much better than jewelry, I had to show it to someone. Since Juliette LeMiel wouldn't be interested, I spent my day smiling out one rainy classroom window after another, marveling at how shiny and new the world had grown.

When school ended, rain was still falling. Under my gray umbrella I followed the river path toward the pharmacy. Where the current flowed gently, the water was speckled with silvery stars, promises that yes, he would return, and soon, floating all the way from the Eiffel Tower. *Soon,* twinkled each silver star. Who needed jewelry? It was everywhere I looked.

At the counter, two old ladies fumbled in their purses to pay for various tubes and vials and jars. After showering endless thank-yous and good-byes on Monsieur Klein, they jingled out the door. Their umbrellas, bobbing away on the sidewalk, were the most gorgeous shapes I had ever seen.

"Good afternoon, Zazoo." Monsieur Klein's blue-spotted bow tie was gorgeous, too. "And how was Grand-Pierre this morning?" This was always his first question now, whenever I stopped in to see him.

"He's a bit foggy, Uncle Félix." It was comforting to know there was someone else who worried about Grand-Pierre—and who, by worrying about Grand-Pierre, likewise worried about me. What would I do, Félix Klein may have wondered, when the old man died? I wondered myself. But this was a day for rejoicing. "He said to pass along his best wishes." I propped my umbrella in the stand by the door. Even collapsed and dripping, it, too, was gorgeous.

Monsieur Klein shifted from one foot to the other, as if wishing to avoid our next topic. "No mail today, Zazoo. Sorry."

"That's all right. Soon I may not need mail."

"The boy may visit again? During his Easter vacation?"

"He may. Yes." The compass swung back and forth inside my blouse, in the dip between my happy new breasts. Its tidings—and Mémé Simone's tidings—shouted to get out.

"Young love," murmured Uncle Félix. He nodded toward the rain-slick street. "No customers. Can you believe it—those two beauty queens were my first visitors today? Sometimes it's like that when the rains come. People stay home, wiggle their toes in their slippers, and sip tea. Let's sip some tea ourselves, Zazoo. I baked cookies, hoping you'd stop by. Come and help me eat them."

"But it's not closing time." Bathed in my own happiness, I beamed at this man I could make happy with a few simple words. "Your pill poppers won't like it."

"If they get desperate, let them ring the bell. Just one cookie?"

"Maybe one, if I can stop and admire the Main Gallery on our way through."

"Take your time," he said casually, as he clicked the front lock.

He said it *so* casually that when I passed through the middle room I turned on both ceiling lights so I would miss nothing.

The paintings were the same as before: Vlaminck's *Blue House;* the tilted sailboats of Matisse and Derain; three Cézanne landscapes; Chagall's *Violinist* and *Rooster* and *Cemetery Gates.* But a new portrait hung beside the yearning photo of young Félix Klein: a charcoal sketch of a girl. Even I could tell it hadn't been drawn by a trained artist, yet it managed to catch the girl's kind-hearted smile. A farm girl, perhaps, in the Cévennes Mountains?

"Who is *she,* Monsieur? I mean, Félix?"

"*Uncle* Félix," he corrected with a dreamy half-smile.

"I'm surprised you can tell it's a girl, it's grown so faded, so smudged—"

"But she's beautiful." Clearly, great care had been taken in shaping the girl's face, just as further care had been taken to preserve the sketch for so many years.

"She *was* beautiful," he admitted at last. "I suppose she is still."

"She's alive, then?"

"As far as I know. A poor schoolboy scrawl, Zazoo. There were no cameras, you see, where I lived out the war. No café owner with a passion for photography. But perhaps it's all for the best that I have nothing except this rough drawing."

"But Uncle Félix, surely you don't *need* a photo?" It was so quiet there at the center of his old house; we might have been anywhere. It occurred to me that some photos of Vietnam might be nice to see: my parents, my grandfather, his flat-bottomed boat on the river. I peered at the drawing in its lustrous dark frame. "This is the girl you loved. It must be. When you were—how old? You didn't tell me that part."

"Just a teenager. Puppy love, as they say."

"But surely *you* don't say that! It must have been *real* love, Uncle Félix, or you wouldn't have kept this sketch all this time, and made such an elegant frame for it."

"I suppose it wasn't puppy love, Zazoo. You have a point." He nodded painfully. "Shall we eat those cookies?"

"But why bring this sketch out *now*? If it wasn't on your wall when you first showed me this room, why have you brought it out now?"

"To be fair," he said at last. "To be fair . . . to your poor grandfather. After I tortured him with that photo of Isabelle—"

"But Uncle Félix," I cried, reaching to touch his face as if he were truly my favorite uncle, "he *loves* that photo! For a week after you brought it, it stayed where I had put it, on the mantel. But then I noticed it was gone. He's placed it on the table beside his bed. I believe Isabelle's picture is the first and last thing he sees every day. I believe he *talks* to her, Uncle Félix." There was something almost magical in calling him Uncle Félix. I had never had an uncle before, at least not that I'd known about.

"He does? Pierre talks to a snapshot?"

"It's a beautiful photograph, and you know it. Yes, I've heard him from the hallway. He shares everything with her. I think he always has. But now he can look at her face—her young, happy face—while he talks."

"Ah." Perhaps Félix Klein himself had spoken to a picture once or twice.

"This girl," I said, refusing to leave the sketch. "She was very sweet to you. I can tell. She must have been."

"For a while she was. Yes, for a while. Come, Zazoo. Our tea."

When he had seated me at his table and was telling me that the closest bird was not a martin but a wren, I tried to be good and not break in with questions about young Simone—whom, I reminded myself, I could not, *must* not, refer to by name. But I was too wound up to talk about birds. "Uncle Félix, please tell me this. I know you shop at other stores in our village. Everyone does—that is, everyone except Grand-Pierre. But do you ever shop elsewhere? Do you ever leave our village?"

Félix Klein studied the wren, its feathers fluffed against the chill. "No," he said. "I don't leave the village." And then, when it seemed he would say no more, he answered my next question before I asked it. "I might meet her, you see. Might . . . run into her somewhere." He waved vaguely into the rain. "Somewhere . . . out there. She might pop out of a store, or might come around the corner in some museum—"

"Some museum!" A terrible thought came to me. "Does that mean that you, who love art so much, have never been to a *museum?* In all these years?"

He eyed me sheepishly above the rim of his glasses. "In all these years. Yes, that's what it means. Afraid I'd run into her and her husband. Her children."

"But Uncle Félix, how can you be sure she ever married?" *Don't call her Simone,* I reminded myself.

"She married." He nodded firmly. "She was born to marry. Born to . . . bring comfort to others. Children. Husband."

"Well, if bringing *comfort* was what she wanted, she probably became a *nun.*"

Smiling bitterly, Monsieur Klein shook his head. "Not a nun." He chuckled toward the wren on the feeder platform. "Not a nun, Zazoo. I don't think so."

"This is France, Uncle Félix. Nuns are everywhere. Yes, she must have joined a convent. Nuns don't go to museums, do they? Does the Pope *allow* them to?"

"Oh, he might." Monsieur Klein patted my hand. "You

haven't taken one nibble from your cookie, Zazoo. My feelings are hurt—I baked those for you."

"Not hungry." But I bit off a corner to show some manners. "Please tell me this, Uncle Félix—how can you be sure she won't pop into your store someday? With or without this husband you seem so sure of. Just pop in—today, this afternoon—and ask for some hair dye because her sixteen *children* are nagging her about going gray!"

"Zazoo, Zazoo, the thoughts you do have." After unwrapping the cloth he had placed around the teapot, he poured my cup full.

"But why," I persisted, "couldn't she just pop in here?"

"Because," Félix Klein gently informed me, "she wouldn't. She may have hurt me once, but not from malice. She wasn't cruel, just young and afraid. It was a fearful time, remember. Truly, an Awful Time. I lost my parents—many children lost parents. And she, poor thing, was afraid of losing hers."

The thought of dead parents hushed me into silence; I was embarrassed to have babbled about nuns and museums and hair dye. Monsieur Klein peered across at me as if disappointed that my chattering had ceased. Only when I leaned back in my seat did the compass swing against my chest and remind me of Marius and my wonderful news and the wonderful news for Monsieur Klein that I couldn't share yet.

"Look, Uncle Félix. I've been given a present." In a motion I had already practiced many times—along the towpath, in my tower room, wherever I might be alone—I pulled the cord over my head. Then I slid the smooth-edged compass across the table.

"This didn't come in the mail." Monsier Klein took the sleek black shape in his palm. "At least, not the pharmacy mail."

"No, it came by rail and bicycle—special delivery from Paris. Last night."

"The boy brought it himself? The bird watcher?"

"Marius. Yes."

Monsieur Klein sighted along the quivering black arrow out the kitchen window. "I suppose you've already calculated the precise bearing toward Paris?"

"Northwest, Uncle Félix. Not north by northwest, or west-northwest. Straight northwest. I checked in the atlas at school."

"I'm sure you did." He gazed northwest into the dusk, as if the gauzy rain could tell my future. "Young love. You say he'll be back soon?"

"Yes, Uncle Félix. In just a few weeks."

"And this time, when he visits, will I meet him at last?"

"Yes, you will." It was all I could do not to add, *And you'll meet her at last, too.* The world felt so ripe, and I felt so proud to have kept the secret, that without thinking I said something incredibly stupid. "We can all listen together for the season's first nightingale."

I regretted the words as soon as they left my mouth. But this time the mention of a nightingale didn't turn Monsieur Klein angrily silent. This time he smiled. "Young love," he said again. "It's been quite a while since I've been around young love." He handed my compass back to me and watched as I slipped the cord over my head. "A long while. It might do me some good."

37. The Magic Hat

By the second Sunday in March, we had secured the mast with guylines, installed the swivel holding the boom to the mast, and assembled the ropes, one for raising the sail, one for pulling it toward the skipper. We lacked only the sail itself to make our craft a sailboat, but the local hardware store didn't sell marine canvas. Uncle Félix said he would take care of the problem.

The third Sunday in March, after lunch, he came striding along the towpath with a gold bundle slung over one shoulder and a round box swinging from his other hand. From the blue stone bench Grand-Pierre and I watched him approach.

"The box first." Uncle Félix handed me the wide round package.

I held it out to Grand-Pierre, who ripped off the paper.

"It was perfect for Zazoo," said Uncle Félix. "Perfect for the captain of our ship."

I lifted the lid and gazed at what had to be the most beautiful hat in France.

"A hat," Grand-Pierre informed me.

"Yes." I stared down at it.

"Put it on," urged Grand-Pierre. "Won't sting."

"You put it on me," I said.

"All right." And he placed it—wide, flat-brimmed, shimmering pale yellow—on my head. "Silk," he murmured. "Silk, Félix?"

"It is, yes. Madame Duvier had her estate sale last week; everyone was there but you two. Years and years ago, before her eyes went, she used to make hats. In her attic, I came across *crates* of hats—some she had made, some she had bought. In the old days, she told me, she often took the train up to Paris just to buy silk."

"The old days." Grand-Pierre nodded at the lock, its gate still half open at the up-canal end, as it had been since the Doubtful Duke and Duchess had left us for the Riviera. "This hat comes from . . . the old days?"

"This hat," said Uncle Félix, "has languished for decades in Madame Duvier's attic, waiting for Zazoo to come claim it. I claimed it for her. The instant it caught my eye, I knew it was the ideal sailing hat to keep the sun from her eyes."

"Sailing hat!" I had to laugh. "But it belongs in *Vogue* magazine!"

"Without you beneath it," said Félix Klein, "it's nothing. And look what comes next. In the mail, from a sailmaker in Brittany—colored and cut, trimmed and hemmed to our specifications."

Like its canvas bag, the sail was golden yellow—a darker, deeper yellow than my misty pale hat. We unfurled the sail alongside the plum-colored punt.

"Shall we try?" asked Uncle Félix.

"Now?" I hugged myself at the thought of actually *sailing.*

"It's a lovely afternoon—are your boating clothes handy, Pierre?"

"Wearing 'em."

We all laughed, as his boating clothes were also his clothes for everything else.

"And I'm wearing mine," said Félix. "These old corduroys. And Zazoo, in her lovely smock and captain's hat, is wearing hers. Shall we?"

So we went sailing, we three, for the first time in our lives. Of course, it took some time to arrange the ropes so the boom stayed raised and the sail stayed up. Since Uncle Félix was tallest, he sat in the bottom of the boat and helped me by holding the rope that adjusted the sail. I steered with the rudder; Grand-Pierre sat cross-legged in front of the mast, gazing calmly ahead.

"We won't tip over," he predicted. "No. We won't."

Uncle Félix had suggested that we rig the boom well above its normal height. This, he figured, would make the sail area small, and lessen our chances of capsizing and freezing to death. It should also keep our heads safer from being whacked when the wind shifted or I steered wrong and the boom snapped from side to side just above our heads.

"That was a jibe," he explained, as Grand-Pierre chuckled nervously. "Read about it last night. A jibe, the book says, can be a nasty surprise. You see, the sail changes sides when a wind from *behind* suddenly shifts direction. If the sail switches sides while we're heading *into* the wind, it's called 'coming about.'"

"Jibe," muttered Grand-Pierre, as the boom slammed sideways again just above my delicate hat.

"Good thing we reefed the sail," said Uncle Félix.

"Reefed the sail," echoed Grand-Pierre.

"Your elegant silk hat," Uncle Félix told me, "wouldn't be much protection from a bonk on the conk."

"No. But it goes so well with my plum punt—and so does the sail. You're an excellent judge of colors, Uncle Félix."

"Thank you." He beamed up at the clouds. "Are you happy, sweet girl?"

"Completely. I feel poems popping, as Grand-Pierre used to say."

The old man nodded from his perch in the bow. "Reef the sail."

"He's happy, too," I told Uncle Félix. "So if *you* are, that's everyone. It doesn't matter that we're going kind of backwards. Do you think it would help if we put down the centerboard?"

"The centerboard!" Uncle Félix shoved the fin down into its wooden sheath and slid its crosspin in place to keep it from bobbing back up. "Good thinking, Captain. *Now* we'll move forward."

And we did, zigzagging slowly up the canal, coming about at the end of each zig, then again after each zag. Our converted punt may not have been a racing yacht, but it gave us infinite pleasure.

* * *

And at the bend above the Long Bridge, I spotted Juliette LeMiel walking along the towpath beneath the sycamores. I thought she did nothing those days without her pal Sylvie Tarvan, but she was alone. When we zagged out away from her, she stood and gaped at the sight of us bobbing under our golden sail—Grand-Pierre in the bow, Félix Klein sitting beside the centerboard, and I, seated at the stern, glorious in my yellow-brimmed captain's hat. When we angled nearby, she called out, "Hello, Grand-Pierre. How are you?"

"Fine, Juliette. We've missed you."

As simply as he said it, we all knew it was true.

"I've missed you, too." She paused half a second. "Both of you."

"Come visit," I called from under my magic hat. "I've got loads to tell you."

"Me, too." Juliette stood there like a girl in a movie, one knee slightly bent, the breeze shifting her long hair. Winter was finally over.

38. Golden Minnows

Lolling in the punt, we had the same things to laugh about, the same idiotic Jay-Jay brothers to mock. But mostly, in our relief that we could talk again, we mocked ourselves.

"You have *doudounes* now, Zazoo. Zazoodoons."

"Nothing like yours. Hardly a hint."

"Silly Zazoo." As the day was cool, we hadn't stuck the umbrella through the front seat, but sat moored in full sunlight upstream from the bridge. Tilting her face toward the sun, Juliette closed her eyes. "Any good poems lately?"

"A few. But nothing by Grand-Pierre."

"No, I don't suppose. He's slower now." She stared up at the golden squiggles on the belly of our bridge. "It must worry you, his slowness."

"All the time. But Monsieur Klein—who has asked me to call him Uncle Félix—told me something that helps. You know, whenever Grand-Pierre pees in the closet or something."

"In the *closet?* On your *boots?*"

"During the night, sometimes. It's not such a tragedy—boots can be washed."

"What could possibly help at a time like that?"

"Uncle Félix says friends disappear—people die, even—but then new people come along, unexpected new people. Who'd have thought I might become friends with *him?*"

"Or that he'd want you to call him Uncle. From what you say, he's kind to you."

"And to Grand-Pierre—for hours, they sit and look at things. Out on the blue bench, or here in the punt, they just *sit.* Like fishermen, but without poles. If they were the two of us, I suppose they'd brush each other's hair."

"There's a thought." Juliette lay back and let the sun warm her eyelids; the river flowed around us. "I've missed you, Zazoo. There's no one else I can talk to."

"Not even your mother?"

Juliette frowned up at the bridge. "She's been different lately. Ever since I asked, you know, about being adopted."

"Ah." This was the first time she had brought up the topic. I sat admiring her sunlit hair.

"I *am* adopted, of course. That's the truth." The breeze fanned tiny ripples across the water. "My mother said they adopted me when I was eight weeks old. I've had time to think it over these last few months. *Awful* months."

"I know, Juliette." The sun was warm on my cheeks. "But were they awful only because you had to face being adopted?"

"I thought so at first. But now I see the most awful part was the coldness between you and me. Not talking. Not listening, laughing. That was the worst. And my mother—" Juliette frowned up at the bridge. "She seems to think I don't trust her anymore."

"And do you?"

"Things *are* different, ever since I learned—you know, that she keeps secrets."

"But we all keep secrets. Even Grand-Pierre. I've been learning that during the war he was—well, I don't know how to say this. He was a killer."

Juliette almost laughed. "But that's what men do in a war. Sounds terrible, Zazoo, but that's what they *do.* They kill each other."

"I'm afraid this is worse. Monsieur Klein says that whenever Grand-Pierre killed soldiers, the Nazis killed local men—and women, and children. Innocent people who didn't fight at all. Reprisals. I hadn't heard that word before." Even as relaxed as I felt, I couldn't utter the word *murderer.* Only with Uncle Félix had I been that brave.

"So that's Grand-Pierre's secret?" Juliette shrugged, as though filling a cemetery wasn't too terrible if it had been done in the murky past. She peered closer at me. "But you said 'we.'"

"Did I?"

"Come on, Zazoo. You said, 'We all keep secrets.' What's *your* secret?"

"Oh," I said at last, "there's a boy I met." Once this much was out, the rest tumbled after. "He's sixteen and has freckles and he's—well, he's wonderful. At least, I think so."

For once Juliette was speechless. To her, as far as I could tell, war was mild drama compared to the miracle of meeting a sixteen-year-old boy.

"He isn't from around here, he's from the Cévennes Mountains. He has sort of a lazy southern accent, even though he lives in Paris now with his grandmother. It's complicated."

"You've never *been* to Paris." Juliette peered at me. "Have you?"

"No. But I didn't meet him in Paris. I met him here, one morning last October. I was sitting in this same boat, watching the mist on the canal. He came riding along on his bicycle. His name is Marius and he has freckles."

"You said that."

"Did I? Well, I'll say it again. He has freckles and he's sweet, and this week, unless he lied to me—and he hasn't lied yet—he's coming back for a visit."

39. Canal Lullaby

Easter came early that year, the last weekend in March. The fourth day of vacation, at dawn, I sat at my oars under the drooping willows where I had first seen Marius. But this time, since his grandmother's barge would be arriving from Paris, I sat turned around with my back to the rising sun.

It had been a week since my talk with Juliette. I was thinking of her and of Uncle Félix, of Grand-Pierre and his faltering brain and how it was time to row home and boil up his oatmeal. But as I reached back with the oars, I thought I heard the mutter of a distant engine. Then thought I didn't. Then thought I did. The oar blades waited, poised above the water.

Through the bundling mist of the far willows, a low craft appeared—and there, at its upturned front tip, stood Marius himself. He made a motion to the stern; the beat of the engine slowed as the barge drew near. I pulled toward the canal bank to be out of the way.

He called across, "Good morning, Mademoiselle. Are we far from Lock Forty-three?"

"Around that curve . . . Monsieur."

He smiled the smile of a Parisian boater; the barge slowed some more. "But is the lockkeeper working at such an early hour?"

"I am the lockkeeper, Monsieur."

"Then may we pull you behind us to the lock, you and your row-punt?" By this time the barge was scarcely moving.

"That wouldn't be safe. The rough water from your engine, you know—your wake. Go on by yourselves. I'll wait for the canal to calm down, then row to the lock. I can be there in five minutes."

"All right." He circled his hand forward. The woman in the wheelhouse revved the engine, then waved to me as she passed by—an older woman in baggy pants and a loose sweater. That was all I saw of her before the barge growled away into the mist.

When the choppy water went smooth, I rowed in long easy strokes up the canal. At the first bollard, I tied the punt fast just as Marius and the woman were doing, lashing their barge fore and aft to the canal bank. I ran inside to see if Grand-Pierre was up.

He sat at the table staring gloomily into an empty saucepan. Then he saw me and smiled. "Zazoo. The morning is fine?"

"Yes, Grand-Pierre, the mist is starting to burn off. I should have breakfast ready by now, but I don't, I'm late. We have a special . . . circumstance."

"Circumstance? The gray cat, perhaps?"

"Not today. Today we have company from far away. Come meet them." I led him onto the terrace.

Mémé Simone stood beside Marius, moving only her eyes, which seemed to take in everything. Beautiful eyes, identical to his.

"Simone," said Grand-Pierre instantly. "Young Simone from Le Chambon." As if he had chatted with her the day before.

"Good morning, Pierre." Her voice was slower, softer than most voices I'd heard floating through Lock 43. "You're looking well, as fit as a man half your age—but then you always *did* look a hundred." They double-kissed as if they were long-lost relatives.

"Come inside, Simone. Zazoo will make oatmeal."

She stepped toward me, smiling the same smile as Marius, the same crinkle at the corners of her eyes. "Oh, I may be too nervous to eat. But a cup of tea, perhaps?"

"A cup of tea," I repeated, and then blurted, "I love your eyes, Madame."

"Because they're also his?" She glanced back at Marius, who stood shaking hands with Grand-Pierre. They looked like two gentlemen who would rather stay by the bench and watch the water than follow us in to breakfast. "And he loves *your* eyes, as he's told me himself." She gave me a wonderful low chuckle. "Many times he's told me. But please, Zazoo, don't call me Madame. I'd feel more comfortable if you called me Simone." She nodded firmly, as if answering an unspoken question. "On second thought, I *will* have some oatmeal."

At the stove I salted the boiling water and stirred in oats while Simone prepared our tea. She heated the pot, then measured leaves into the silver tea nut—and all the while she studied Grand-Pierre out the kitchen window. On the terrace beside Marius, he stood slowly polishing the top of his head.

"Ah, me," she sighed. "You've been alone through all this."

"All . . . what?" I pretended not to understand.

"All these years of decline." Simone shrugged toward Grand-Pierre. "All *this.*"

"But it's not so bad. For the most part, he's hardly cranky at all."

"'For the most part.'" She tucked a dish towel around the teapot. "For the most part, you've been alone through all this."

I peered at the teapot she had so snugly wrapped. Where had I seen that done before? But of course—by Uncle Félix, the day of his lesson on gingerbread stars and gruesome history.

"*You* taught him to do that."

"Taught whom?" asked Simone. "To do what?"

"To wrap a teapot that way. You taught Félix Klein. He covers his teapot with just that same . . . tenderness."

"He does?" We stood looking down at the teapot in its turban. "I don't recall teaching him."

"You may not remember, but believe me, he does."

"What don't you remember, Mémé?" This unexpected voice from the doorway belonged to Marius. In our fascination with the teapot, we hadn't heard him approach. He stopped himself from entering the kitchen. "Excuse me, ladies—am I interrupting your get-together?"

"Not at all," said Simone, "we've gotten together quite nicely. And Zazoo just told me the sweetest part. About a teapot." She flashed me the most unbelievable smile, different from any I'd seen on any poster in Félix Klein's pharmacy. Such a warm, trusting smile. I could see in an instant why Marius had pedaled all the way from the Paris train, in October, to try coaxing her lost love back to life.

"It's begun to drizzle," he said from the doorway, "but Grand-Pierre told me I could leave him there on his bench. He wouldn't mind getting a little damp, he said. And he wouldn't mind being alone."

"But," I explained quietly, "he isn't alone. A girl keeps him company out there—a girl he knew many years ago." I unwrapped the teapot, opened the lid and removed the tea nut. "Or I should say the *ghost* of a girl."

Simone's eyes narrowed. "Isabelle? Félix Klein's sister?"

I nodded. "In Grand-Pierre's mind, she sits there with him on the bench. He talks to her; she answers."

Simone and I stared at each other until Marius broke into our reverie, pointing out the door onto the terrace. "Grand-Pierre isn't alone *now,* Zazoo. Someone's joined him on his bench, and I don't mean a ghost."

We looked, and there, facing away from us on the blue stone bench, holding an umbrella over Grand-Pierre, sat the village pharmacist, Monsieur Félix Klein.

40. *The Far Side of the World*

I approached slowly, half afraid he would vanish if I spoke too soon. Marius and Simone watched from the kitchen door.

"Uncle Félix." I sat beside him; on his other side, Grand-Pierre snored gently, hands folded across his stomach.

"The old man's asleep. I mean, the other old man."

"Yes." Choirs were singing inside me.

"I saw him dozing here and feared he'd catch cold from the rain. Thought I'd keep him dry." The mist seemed to have enchanted Uncle Félix. "This is too big an umbrella for one person—it's properly meant for two."

"Meant for two." I beamed out at the trees, the water, the world. "I believe you're right."

"Such a lovely bench," he murmured. "Even in the rain."

"But Uncle Félix." I nudged him with my elbow. "The rain has stopped."

"Ah?" He checked the surface of the canal. "Well, yes. So it has."

"Close your umbrella. Let's wake Grand-Pierre and join the others."

"Others?" He peered north on the canal. "In that barge? Your first sailors of the spring?"

"Our first sailors, yes. But they aren't in the barge. Come." The willows, strung with tiny new streamers, swayed toward us in the breeze. I took his hand. "Wonderful people, Uncle Félix—you'll love them. Did I tell you I finished my poem?"

Dreamily, he brushed one finger along his mustache. "About the cat who couldn't leave his dry home?"

At these words, Grand-Pierre opened his eyes and blinked at us.

"But things can change," I went on. "A poem can change—even a cat can change. Maybe a cat *can* learn to roam."

"Ah?" said Félix Klein, still rearranging the tips of his mustache.

We rose from the bench, turned, and were about to cross the terrace when he saw Simone in the doorway. We stopped where we stood; the morning grew very still.

"Félix," was all she could say. Silence, except the birds along the fence line, calling *wake up, wake up, wake up*. . . . For the longest moment she stayed frozen in the doorway. Then she seemed to shake herself free and ran to him—*ran* like a girl. He dropped the umbrella, opened his arms, and took her in.

"Simone." Her hair was as gray as his; they looked like a couple who had grown old together. Then, suddenly, they were both sobbing, shaking in each other's arms as if they were one big body with a terrible fever.

"Félix Klein." She shuddered, looking up at his face. "It's really you?"

"Yes, Simone." He dried her eyes with his fingertips, then dried his own with the backs of his hands. "Really me, really you. Pierre is our witness."

"Tell me," she said fearfully, pressing her face to his chest. "Do you—do you—like our barge?"

"It's beautiful," said Félix Klein. "Everything is beautiful."

"If you like—" she began, but fell silent. "Oh, I can't say it."

"Don't be scared," he said softly, as if talking to himself. "We were both scared once. Too scared."

She nodded fiercely. "Tell me there's time. There *is* time?"

He stroked her hair. "Yes, my dear. All the time in the world."

"Time?" echoed Grand-Pierre behind them, his voice dim.

They were too deep in their amazement to hear him, but I heard, and peered closer, wondering how much he still held. Time. Memory. Love. Lately, he had seemed almost empty—yet he still spoke, still ate, still thought his thoughts. When he finally did go away from me, for ever and ever, it would leave such a hole in my heart.

"Yes," I told him. "Lots of time. We can cruise up the lock ladder, then through that tunnel you heard about, to a place you used to call the Far Side of the—"

"The Far . . . ?" There was a smile on his face, but it looked lost.

"The Far Side of the World. We're lucky, Grand-Pierre." I knew it was true—but then why was I, like the others, weeping? "We're *lucky.*"

He peered all around, as if searching for our luck.

Marius saved me then, rushing from the kitchen with a tray loaded with steaming cups of tea and bowls of oatmeal. "Breakfast," he announced, setting the tray on the bench. It did my heart good to see him—yet my heart, too, was scared. The only thing I felt sure of was my gray cat, purring somewhere nearby.

We stood in a half circle facing the wooden plank that crossed to the barge. Félix Klein squinted into the early sun, then turned to Grand-Pierre. "How many canal voyages will this make for you, Old Stone?"

"My first." Grand-Pierre struggled to find a word, as if it were a butterfly loose in his head. "My first . . . voyage."

"Your *first?* But—"

"I've run boats through." Grand-Pierre gazed past Lock 43 to the twin rows of sycamores that would guide us into the village and away. "Many boats." He shook his head. "But this is my first . . . voyage. And you, Félix?"

"It's my first time on any boat, except Zazoo's magic punt."

Wake up—wake up—wake up, called the birds. But we were no longer asleep.

Marius smiled at me. "Perhaps the old gray cat isn't so sad anymore?"

"Not nearly." So he sensed the cat, too. Good.

Félix Klein stood close to Simone; Grand-Pierre hummed under his breath at one side of me; at my other side stood Marius. And the gray cat *was* nearby. I was sure of it. He might be grayer than before, and might be older, but he sniffed the wind and knew it was full of wonders.

Grand-Pierre tilted his head to one side. "Give us our poem, Zazoo. Our whole poem."

"All right, old man. Your poem and mine, about the gray cat."

I took a deep breath of the soft morning air. The linden over the blue bench, the willows down the canal toward Paris, the sycamores leading southeast, all leaned closer to listen.

"There once was a cat
down by the canal
who never seemed able to roam.
He considered a swim
but hated the wet—
he thought of a cruise
but couldn't quite settle
for drifting away
from his cozy dry home—
    from his gray-château,
    bridge-below,
    cozy dry home.

"Night after night
day after day
he sat watching the world
float past on its way:
all sorts of canal boats
in all sorts of sizes
in all sorts of colors
did quite hypnotize
    his restlessly wandering eyes, his eyes—
    his restlessly wandering eyes.

"The boats came and went;
he stayed and he stayed.
He watched, and watched longer,
and waited, afraid
that his chance wouldn't come
his boat not appear—
he'd wait and he'd watch
and he'd live out his years,
never go where he wanted,
never learn there from here,
never climb, and climb higher,
up the lock ladder—
never find, at its top,
what some possible liar
had claimed was a tunnel
so long and resounding
you could see, from the far end
the world at its founding—
a world of such oddness,
such freedom from fear,
it must have had so much
    (he thought with a tear,
    with a barely wet hint
    of a tiny cat tear)
    it must have had so much
    he couldn't find—here.

"He knew the sad truth was
he lacked some romancing,
but he wasn't too shy
to practice his dancing
out under the moon-shadowed
clouds so entrancing—
somewhere deep in France,
deep in thought,
deep in cat melancholy
he did his slow dance
in the ferns and the holly:
    a feline fandango,
    a yearning sad tango—
    a lonesome cat dancing alone.

"There once was a cat,
down by the canal,
who found what he never had known:
the world was as wide
as a friendly full heart,
and the girl-cat beside him
would happily chart
their meandering voyage
to its end from its start
    through sad days
    and glad days
    but never apart."

Grand-Pierre made no comment about how the poem ended, but I could tell he approved. We knew each other that well. When he started across the slatted plank to the barge, Marius took his elbow and helped him. Simone and Uncle Félix followed; I went last.

Marius lifted one side, I lifted the other, and we slid the plank onto the deck. As we unlooped the mooring lines from the bollards, Simone turned the key, opened the throttle, and drew a pleased rumble from the engine. We moved smoothly ahead, carving a watery path toward Lock 43 and the future, the past, the Far Side of the World.